Margaret Sutton Briscoe

Jimty

and others

Margaret Sutton Briscoe

Jimty
and others

ISBN/EAN: 9783337398569

Printed in Europe, USA, Canada, Australia, Japan

Cover: Foto ©Andreas Hilbeck / pixelio.de

More available books at **www.hansebooks.com**

JIMTY, AND OTHERS

BY

MARGARET SUTTON BRISCOE

ILLUSTRATED BY

W. T. SMEDLEY AND A. B. FROST

NEW YORK AND LONDON

HARPER & BROTHERS PUBLISHERS

1898

CONTENTS

ILLUSTRATIONS

JIMTY

"But, Major," I whispered, "why is the bridegroom wearing an old coat? That cut is out of date."

The Major's eyes twinkled. "I wondered if you would notice it," he replied. "It's what I brought you here to see. If you will go to luncheon with me wherever I choose to take you directly the wedding is over, I'll tell you the story of that coat."

Half an hour later the Major and I were sitting together at a little table in a small café within the borders of that quarter of our city known as Bohemia. The café was Parisian, unmistakably, from the door-sill, on which a thin layer of white sand was spread in lieu of a mat, to the back of the room, where, perched on a dais fenced off like a proscenium-box, madame the proprietress presided—behind her, a set of narrow shelves holding tier after tier of multi-

A

hued bottles ; before her, a row of neat glass-cases exhibiting different brands of cigars, various cheeses, or tasteful plates of arranged fruits, comfits, and moulded jellies. Monsieur le mari was absorbed in tending the foliage-plants of his show-window as we entered his establishment. He was turning the earth with a hair-pin, evidently borrowed from madame, and looked up to gravely bow to the Major, not removing his little black silk skull-cap. Later, his hands clasped behind his broad back, he wandered with apparent indifference about the room, chirping occasionally to the caged canaries that hung high among the green vines trained to grow upon the walls. Madame bowed to the Major also, with the same grave respect, and the Major called the waiter by his Christian name as he hurried forward to meet us and take our order. Evidently he was at home. "Just glance about you," said the Major, with a certain proprietary pride. "It is easy enough to understand how in a great cosmopolis like this we have only to walk a block and turn a corner to travel from Jerusalem to Bagdad, but I have never known the very aroma of an imported country so perfectly preserved as in this little café. Those art students over there, for instance—aren't they having a good, innocent, Parisian kind of a time?"

I looked across the room through the thin blue mist of cigarette and cigar smoke. The

MONSIEUR LE MARI

ventilation was good, so the air was only clouded, not heavy. From her box madame was smiling her reserved smile upon a party of young men who had just entered and were rather noisily improvising a banquet-board in the centre of the floor by setting a number of the little wooden tables which the café afforded side by side in a row. As loudly greeted additions to the party came dropping in, more tables were drawn up, until the board waxed long and the mirth high.

"Now you and I," said the Major, "old stagers as we are, know just how much or how little all this means. We know those perhaps too loudly called for, dissipated-looking little pint bottles contain pink water and sugar chiefly ; and we know, too, that the young fellow over yonder smoking three cigarettes at once, one in each ear and one in his mouth, is but an innocent party buffoon, and not in the least tipsy. Indeed, I never saw but one tipsy fellow here in all my experiences, and madame pounced down upon him from her perch like a ruffled dove. 'Qu'est ce que c'est ? Qu'est ce que c'est ?' I had thought her a fixture up there, somehow, until that moment. You and I know all this. We even understand this grim little fine for the water-drinker. See it ?" And the Major passed me the carte, set in a wooden frame with a handle like a looking-glass, his finger on these words at the head of the menu :

"*5 c. en plus pour tout dîner sans vin ou bière.*"
"Cheaper to drink than to abstain, you comprehend? Of course we comprehend it all ; but fancy a green country boy, born since the days when his father's cellarette adorned the dining-room, looking in on such a scene for the first time, and you have an idea of what Jimty's expression must have been when one day, about eighteen months ago, sitting at this very table, I looked up to see him standing rooted in that doorway."

The Major cast a reminiscent eye at the café entrance, and paused for a moment to openly overhear and as openly laugh over a story which was being told at the banquet-table by the triple smoker : some nonsense about a farm belonging to the narrator's uncle, where there were three hundred cows at pasture—"all girls."

The Major indicated the noisy banqueters with a wave of his hand. "There was much the same order of party in the centre of the room the day Jimty arrived," he said, "only more noisy if anything ; and, as it happened, one of the number had just told a stale story, so the rest were stoning him to death—with bread-crusts—as the door opened. I think the boy believed he had stumbled into a den of iniquity, until he saw me sitting here laughing."

The Major laughed again at the recollection.

"Are Jimty—if that is the name—and the bridegroom one and the same man?" I asked.

"Oh yes; didn't I tell you so? Jimty! I suppose the name strikes you as odd. It did me when I first heard it. Later I understood that it was but a natural evolution. James Tarleton Stone was the family name, so when it descended to my young friend, every distinguishing abbreviation had been previously engaged. He was therefore given the whole title, James Tarleton, which speedily degenerated into James T., then Jimmy T., lastly boiling down to Jimty. I learned all that over this same table, partly from Jimty, partly from his father; and over this board, too, old Mr. Stone first told his now historic anecdote of the Glass Snakes and Transparent Mocking-Birds. I don't believe I could properly sing you the song of Jimty and his coat outside of this room, for everything here recalls to me some incident connected with him. And yet here comes our luncheon before I have so much as begun. Well, you must let me digress my own way, and I'll sandwich the coat and Jimty in somehow between the courses."

Thus it was that while eating a luncheon, which included snails, and drinking a bottle of the red wine so affectionately jeered at by my host, I heard the Major's story.

"I can't very well even now," said the Major, "touch at once on the coat; for the first time

I ever saw the boy he was not only minus that garment, but every other as well, naked as the day he came into the world, which statement requires as immediate an explanation as possible.

"One spring season about two years ago it happened that I was on a business trip in Virginia, and found that I had to make a stage of my journey by a steamer already overcrowded with a large country excursion party. Luckily for me, as it chanced, I hate a crush above all things, so I stood a little aloof from the press of passengers crowding out on the pier. Suddenly, with no warning whatever, I saw that mass of human beings irresistibly shelved to one side, and I found myself borne back and down in a wild rush for the shore. I suppose my senses were crushed out of me, for I saw and heard nothing more after that until I realized that I was leaning against a pile of lumber on the land, unhurt. Some one—I never knew who—had dragged me out of the *mêlée*. My first conscious thought was that I had surely died, and waked among the sounds of Hades. As I opened my eyes I saw only too clearly what had happened, but—well, I won't dwell on the appearance of the broken pier and disturbed water. The sight matched the hearing enough to unman me. I closed my lids again involuntarily, still faint and sick with the horror. At that moment the confusion of noises seemed to focus into a boyish voice near me. Even then I noticed the peculiar freshness of its quality.

"'Father,' it cried, 'shall I strip before the women and children?'

"An older voice answered like bugle to bugle:

"'Strip, man, strip, and go in as God made you.'

"I looked up to see standing quite near me the most magnificent specimen of young manhood I ever beheld. I believe you thought Jimty as bridegroom handsome as a man need be, but to-day he was a circumstance to the Jimty I first saw as God made him—body and soul; for if ever a man's soul was in his face, it was in that boy's as he leaped by me, stark naked, into the water. It brought me to my feet, and out into the water after him I went —only to my neck, for I can't swim a stroke.

"The boy's father and I worked side by side. We two old fellows had all we could do to drag ashore the bodies, alive and dead—we could not stop to distinguish — that Jimty brought us.

"I thought we were laboring there for hours. It seemed so, though it must have been minutes only. Each time the boy dragged to us a new burden and swam undauntedly back into the horrible confusion of struggling forms I never expected to see him return.

"They say misery makes strange bedfellows, but peril surely makes bed - brothers of strangers. I don't believe the father suffered much more anxiety than I in those moments of waiting. Over and over I heard him murmuring in my ear: 'The boy sha'n't go out again.' 'He has done enough.' 'This is the last.' And I would answer, 'Yes, this time we will stop him.' But whenever Jimty neared us nothing of the kind was ever said. There was something sacred in the remote purpose of his face that no man—even a father—could venture to question. We stood shoulder to shoulder, straining our old eyes to distinguish the one white body weaving its dangerous way among the dark ones. To many of them he must have come as a white-robed angel of deliverance.

"The boy's strength lay in his nakedness. With strong men, as there were, drowning all about him, clutching at straws in the fear of death, the fact that he had his body alone to protect from their grasp was everything.

"At last, after a long space of waiting, in which I fairly gave up hope, we distinguished Jimty, far off on the water's surface, springing high like a tired water - dog, and with each stroke shaking the drops from his eyes. He was panting heavily, with evident difficulty dragging in his load. It was the body of a woman. We waded out to meet him as far as we dared ; but as the boy's feet touched the shallower bottom he shifted his burden into his arms, wading ashore past us as if he had never seen us. We hurried ashore also, to find him already working hard over the body, which he had laid on a tablelike board of the lumber-pile. I touched his bare arm, and he turned sharply, asserting—as a man asserts what he only half believes—that the woman must still be alive, for she had spoken to him twice on the way in.

"'No,' said his father, after a brief examination ; 'she is quite dead now, poor child.'

"As I looked at the face of the young girl laid out there as if for her last rest, I also believed that she had found it. So many all about us were in need of immediate attention that it seemed a waste of precious moments to spend them on this hopeless case ; but Jimty insisting in his belief, we worked over the senseless body, pressing air into the passive lungs—in fact, doing all that our inexperience knew to call back life—until an almost imperceptible quivering of the muscles, proving the boy right, made us redouble our efforts. At last the girl's eyelids began to flutter, and Jimty, in great excitement, caught up his coat from among his little heap of clothing still lying by the lumber-pile. He was wrapping the girl carefully in the coat's folds, when his father grasped his arm.

"'Stand back, boy,' he said; 'she's coming to, and you'll frighten her to death. This isn't the Garden of Eden. You'd better put a coat on yourself, or hide in the bushes, as your betters did before you.'

"Jimty started back with an exclamation, which proved that he had as wholly forgotten his body's nakedness as he had its peril a short while before. He snatched up his clothing, and, just as the girl opened her eyes, vanished so swiftly around the end of the lumber-pile that his father and I burst out laughing—a jangled kind of laughter. Did you ever hear men laughing after a heavy strain? It's not a pretty sound. It seems to jar loosely from the lips somehow, because it has no root in the heart, I suppose."

The Major's story waited while he thrust his hand into his pocket and drew out the coppers necessary for the purchase of a newspaper presented by a tattered, bareheaded, black-eyed little fellow, who had entered the café noiselessly, slipping from table to table. He, too, was evidently an *habitué;* for all those whom he drew near, with his half-sly, half-frightened smile, had a humorous or teasing word to throw him, whether they bought or not.

I, the Major's guest, began to feel myself the only unknown quantity in those four walls. The Major was evidently a regular customer,

MADAME THE PROPRIETRESS

for without question the boy stood waiting, a paper ready in his grimy hand.

"Italian, isn't he?" I asked.

"I don't know," the Major answered. "Ask him."

"Who—I? No, no. My mova she Américaine. My faver? Ho! I don' know."

A shrug, a quick, impish glance of intelligence, conveyed but one meaning, which was to his weird precocity as a neat little jest of life upon himself, and perhaps upon his mother also.

"Here," said the Major, "take your money, gamin, and go. Good Lord, what a travesty on childhood! And yet, do you know, even precocity like that has its uses, as Jimty and I learned. That little fellow's shrewdness once saved us a world of trouble. I don't mean it was worth the price, though. Poor little imp!"

He looked thoughtfully after the child of the pavements.

"Major," I said, recalling him, "is that all? Of course, as an old novel-reader, I know the coat and the rescued girl are the same coat and the same girl I saw with Jimty to-day, but am I also to fill in the time from then to now from my own imagination?"

The Major shook his head and laughed.

"You couldn't do that, for old Mr. Stone occupies a large part of the space, and I defy any imagination less fertile than Madame Nature's to produce him. He was one of her unique masterpieces. I haven't sketched him in for you yet, because I was not particularly interested in him myself, until a little incident occurred which drew my attention to the father almost as warmly as it had been engaged by the son. No, I must begin again where I left off—at the back of the lumber-pile, Jimty's dressing-room, where Mr. Stone and I followed him with the news that our patient had been borne away, board and all, by a physician, who had arrived with his staff of assistants. The girl, though not yet wholly conscious, had been pronounced safe enough. Hers was but an obstinate faint, after all, which we had lacked experience to recognize. Indeed, Mr. Stone and I began to fear that we had devoted attention to the girl at Jimty's direct expense. He had dressed himself, and was sitting limply on the lumber-pile, shaking with the throes of a heavy chill brought on by reaction and exposure. It was rather early in the season for river bathing. Despite his chattering protests, Mr. Stone grasped Jimty by one arm, I by the other, and between us we walked him into a little tavern of the town close by, where we summarily got him into his own bed. It was there, it appeared, that the father and son were temporarily lodging.

"While I poured whiskey down our new patient's throat, Mr. Stone dragged out from a corner what he called his travelling-bag — a curious affair covered with rusty brown woollen laid in stiff plaits that drew in or out at will. Until he opened the clasp and took out a large bottle of powdered quinine and a tooth-brush, I thought he had there his grandfather's old accordion, and wondered what on earth he meant to do with it. After we knew each other better he often urged me to buy such a bag for my own use, but I always told him I never anywhere saw one like it, which was the exact truth.

"To my treatment with whiskey Mr. Stone added a more carefully apportioned dose of quinine from the bottle. At least it was careful from his stand-point, and the measure was evidently his accustomed one — a neat little heap of the powder on the end of his flat-handled tooth-brush twice administered. The amount would have killed me; but Jimty at once fell into a natural sleep, and though the accident had occurred but a short time before sunset, and it was then but a little after, old Mr. Stone and I, quite worn out, followed his example, retiring to our respective beds.

"It was not until deep in the next morning that we all three awoke, but little the worse for our experiences. Jimty, indeed, who had most excuse for consequences, showed no traces of his exertions beyond a few bruises. That's what it means to be young. I might as well mention here that Mr. Stone was plain *Mr. Stone*. He had no title, military or otherwise, which rather surprised me in an old Virginian. He seemed conscious himself that the fact required explanation, and before we parted— which was almost immediately, for I had to hurry on my belated way—he took pains to mention casually his sorrow that he had never been strong enough to give his country active service of any kind. The thinness of his hooked nose, his nervous gestures, and the delicacy of his skin, especially where it was stretched tightly over his temples, verified his statement, even if I had been inclined to question his courage, which I was not. His frail appearance was what made me think of him as an old man, I suppose. In reality he was about my age. Jimty was as unlike his father as two men could well be, except that both had the same pleasant freshness of voice, and that both had blue eyes. The boy was deliberate in all his movements, even to the slow turning of his eyes. His hair had a queer, childish way of standing straight up from his brow, which added to his proper six feet two. Altogether he struck me as a wholesome boy—a beautiful boy. He was then about twenty-one. Before parting with my twelve-hour acquaintances I breakfasted at the same table with them, and we lingered a few moments afterwards in the tavern smoking-room, which faced the street. It was there the little incident occurred which, as I told you, first drew my attention to Mr. Stone. We were all three standing at the large front door, struggling into our light top-coats and fitting on our hats, when Jimty, who was nearest the pavement, paused, and uttered an exclamation which made our eyes follow his out into the street. There a common sand-cart jolted along, driven by a countryman, who was stoutly belaboring his old work-horse in an evident effort to hurry away the unseemly burden. Unseemly was a mild word to apply to his load. The landlord had told us that all the suitable covered vehicles of the village had been called in to carry away the dead and wounded from the broken-wharf to their homes, and still there were not enough. It had been a carnage too terrible to meet with the ordinary decencies which life pays to death. The bodies of two women lay in the sand-cart, with distorted faces and twisted limbs uncovered to the street. As I turned away involuntarily from the spectacle I saw that both of my companions were still facing the street, standing with their hats held at their breasts, and their bared heads bowed over them, as if assisting at the funeral of a dignitary. I uncovered my head quickly, with a sense of shame. Mr. Stone looked up again at the cart.

"'God forgive me—they are women!' he cried.

"In a moment he was out in the street, a white cloth caught from the dining-room table in his hand. By this the bodies were at least hidden during the rest of their last journey.

"Though it was six months or more before I was to meet Jimty or Mr. Stone again, whenever they recalled themselves to me it was as I turned from the smoking-room door that morning to see them standing behind me, father and son, their heads reverently bowed over their hats held high on their breasts. And in after-times, when I felt, as I too often had just cause to feel, that old Mr. Stone was the most exasperating of human beings, I had only to remember this little incident in the smoking-room to soften to him. In some way, too, he had managed to transmit and teach to his boy all that was best in himself of chivalry and reverence. For this alone much had to be forgiven him."

The Major here interrupted his own tale with determination. While not over-garrulous, he loved to talk, and though no gourmand, he duly enjoyed the flesh-pots. I had for some minutes been watching with amusement the struggle between his two appetites. The flesh-pots finally conquered.

"My next meeting with the Stones," said the Major, "brings me back to this café again; but before I go on any further I mean to take a little recess and eat some luncheon. I never

could understand why our physical economy
has not provided us with one mouth for eating
and another for talking. Here am I starving
over a full plate, you politely playing with
your bread to keep me company. What kind
of an arrangement is that?"

While the Major, still grumbling at Provi-
dence, made reparation to himself for his physical limitations, I spent the time in taking an
inventory of the café's guests, and saw with
some surprise that at the little tables there
were a number of refined-looking women, with
and without escorts. When, after a considerate
delay, I pointed out their presence to the Major, he laughed, and explained :

"Oh, that's all right. Art students chiefly ;
but Una could lunch here and leave her lion
outside the door-sill awaiting her in the sand.
Madame chaperons the occasion sufficiently.
She is quite a dragon, is madame. I could tell
you—but no, this is the story of Jimty, and I
won't be led astray. Do you know, it was the
innocent presence of these very women you
speak of that on his first appearance here held
Jimty in check at the door, where I recognized
him, and rose from my table to meet him,
reassure him, and lead him in. I found afterwards that he and his father were in search
of a restaurant where 'only men were admitted.' Old Mr. Stone was just behind Jimty.
I have often wondered how those two ever

lived through their first six months in this great, unwashed city. It was Colonel Newcome and Clive over again. Anything that so much as implied the degradation of women was horrible to them both. This was the father's teaching. If he had not upheld his standard stoutly, Jimty was young enough to have learned in six months to ignore a great deal, as most of us do sojourning in our dear Sodom.

"Asking advice of no one, and moving as they had from cheap cafés to others yet cheaper in search of the minimum of living, they must have stumbled on some odd and to them most painful experiences. They had grown suspicious of everything, even of such a scene as this; yet here was just where they belonged. Cheap, clean, easy-going, eminently respectable, and, above all, really fine French cooking served in steaming hot dishes. When Jimty settled himself in the seat opposite me, which you now have, and his father sank into a chair at the side of the table, I knew they had joined madame's constant following from that moment. I saw Mr. Stone looking at these white table-cloths and the bright, wooden-handled knives with a smile of perplexity at their quality, but great satisfaction in their cleanliness. I could see that the naïve habit our waiters have formed when not too busy—they never neglect any one—of joining, with broken English, in our political discussions rather startled him, but he soon came to like it. We all do. Occasionally, very occasionally, when we talk French, even monsieur himself wanders up to the table, and, his hands behind him, joins in. But he remains a remote individuality.

"As regards Jimty, after the door-sill of the café was once crossed, he had no scruples of any kind to overcome. He settled into his place, almost purring like a lost cat by an adopted hearth, and we met here almost daily. That is, Jimty and I did. Mr. Stone, as a more restless spirit, sometimes wandered.

"It was not at once that I found out all I have told you, or knew how long my two friends had been in the city. This was because I questioned Mr. Stone first, and it was some time before I realized that he always refused me a direct reply. It takes more tact than courage to say no, I think. Mr. Stone had a fine tact that let him deliver the point-blank negative so disguised that the recipient could not possibly recognize it. I have never encountered such command of language as was his, nor a more adroit power of choosing a word which would *not* express his real meaning. While he seemed to be baring his very heart to you, you might be sure—after you grew to know his ways—that the information you were seeking and he meant to keep was wrapped away somewhere in the flow of speech. So soon as I made this discovery I waited for my chance, and one night when Jimty was dining here alone with me I put the direct question to him, 'How long have you been in this city?' 'We've been here over six months,' said Jimty. Though a man, and so large a one at that, Jimty had still a country lad's habit of standing as it were 'at gaze' when a question was suddenly asked him. He would not only turn his eyes, but his whole body, to his questioner. Bucolic as this was, it always attracted me. As he answered my abrupt and evidently embarrassing question he faced me fully, as usual, flushing, as he had reason to ; for, when we parted after the wharf accident, I had given my card with my address to Mr. Stone, urging him to seek me out if ever in my city. I had noticed at the time that he only answered by telling me that he had just the week before sold his old home in Virginia, but that he would be glad to have me accept the hospitality of his relations' homes if ever in his county, where the taverns were poor. I must mention that later on, in a second business visit to Virginia, I did use the card of introduction Mr. Stone then gave me, and was passed from house to house, from hand to hand, as a precious parcel. I came back having covered miles of my journey without a hotel bill in my pocket ; and then, and not until then, did I reach an adequate understanding of the loneliness my two Virginia friends must have suffered when first lost in the toils of my home city, which is not a city of homes.

"'Why haven't you looked me up?' I asked Jimty. 'Did you know any one here?' Jimty had not his father's squirrel-like gift of secretion. The nuts he would fain have hidden in his jaws were easy to draw out. I discovered that they had purposely stayed behind at the tavern where I left them after the wharf accident, and followed on my very track by the next train. To a mind not drilled by old Mr. Stone this avoidance of me was inexplicable and fairly offensive. I implied as much to Jimty.

"'But we had been through something together,' he explained, 'and father felt it would have been presuming on that to have told you we were going to your city. You see we had not a single friend here. You might have felt us on your mind. We meant to hunt you up as soon as we were on our feet.'

"Only then did I know that they were not 'on their feet,' though I had before suspected it. By degrees I won the whole story from Jimty, told with no sense of humor; he was as deficient in that as are most country-bred boys. The returns from the sale of their home had been nominal, owing to old mortgages; and the father, or rather the son, had been trying every plan to husband this small stock of money which they had brought with them to the city, where both hoped to find employment.

" 'We took one room at first, and while I was out looking for work, father cooked our meals over our open fire,' said Jimty. 'We found that much less expensive; but we had only one frying-pan, and father would throw the grease from it into the fire. Once he burned his hand badly, and once he set fire to the mantel-piece. I was always afraid I'd find him seriously hurt when I came home.'

" 'Why did he keep on doing it?' I asked.

" 'Oh, I don't know,' said Jimty. 'Father's very apt to keep on doing anything he does once. Finally our landlady stopped our "light house-keeping," as she called it, and I was glad of it.'

" 'Jimty,' I said, 'you asked her to stop it. You know you did.' You see, I had not been studying the boy's methods of dealing with his father for nothing.

" 'Yes,' he answered, quietly; 'I had to. It was the best way. Then we went from place to place for our meals, each worse than the last. Then'—his eyes lit up—'then we came here.'

" By his honest, good-looking face, apparently, for he had no other introductions, Jimty had won for himself a fairly good business position, with better prospects ahead, but he was now worrying over his father. The money they

"'THUS IT WAS THAT I HEARD THE MAJOR'S STORY'"

had brought with them was dwindling rapidly. Mr. Stone was living upon it exclusively ; he would not touch a penny of Jimty's earnings.

"'When that little is gone, and he has to call on me, I don't know how he will stand it,' said Jimty, in distress. 'If only father were a little less proud !'

"'Is he too proud to work ?' I asked.

"Jimty eagerly assured me he was not ; that he would do anything but live on charity, even his son's—which seemed to me laudable enough, and not just what I had expected.

"Mr. Stone was a man of curious contradictions.

"'What work has your father done before this ?' I inquired, and the query seemed to render Jimty desperate.

"'That's the first question every one asks,' he said. 'Of *course* father has never done any work at all. He had no reason to before the war, and since—' He paused, with an embarrassed look at me, which I did not then understand.

"'Since then,' I said, 'I suppose you have been living on your land alone.'

"'You can't eat land,' said Jimty, gloomily. 'Nobody can eat land. We had to eat. No ; the truth is, father made a terrible mistake a few years after the war. He married again, a rich New England woman. They lived together wretchedly for about fifteen years, but now they are separated entirely. Father only married her for my sake. He didn't know how I should hate it as I grew older.'

" 'Was she a step-dame to you?' I asked, cautiously. Jimty was blurting out his facts with a freedom I did not wish to disturb.

" 'Oh no,' he replied, quickly. 'She was very good to me—too good. Her money smothered me. She would give me anything before I knew I wanted it, and seemed to grudge everything to father. They were so different. She kept account of every penny, while father never kept a book in his life. I know it was hard on her sometimes, but if father had owned anything it would have been entirely hers, and he never could understand her feeling differently.'

"This was one of the cases where Jimty's sense of humor failed him. I managed to reply sympathetically, but my heart was on the side of the second Mrs. Stone, married for the boy's sake alone. I had already learned something of Mr. Stone's business methods, and a strain of thrifty blood in me responded to her trials in dealing with a husband whose keeping of personal accounts was (as he had once jovially confessed to me) confined to 'knowing to a cent how much he spent, as he always spent every cent he had.'

" 'What finally separated them?' I asked.

" 'I did,' said Jimty, shortly, 'Just as soon as I was old enough I remonstrated with her.

She told me then to my face that it was for my sake alone she had stood my father so long as she had, and "an old Virginia gentleman was a luxury she could not afford." ' "

The Major set down his lifted wine-glass and laughed aloud at his own narrative. "Poor lady!" he said, shaking his head—"poor lady! I never met her, and probably never shall, but if ever woman had my respectful sympathy, she did. Think how she must have loved that boy to have endured for his sake the kind of life I know she led for fifteen years or more! Her New England soul must have died daily, and yet at her one and only recorded outburst to Jimty the boy whirled away insulted, with his father on his back, to seek their fortunes. Their fortunes, forsooth! I failed to see how Jimty was to afford the luxury Mrs. Stone had groaned under.

" 'Is there no possibility of reconciling them?' I asked Jimty, but he crushed the hope.

" 'None. Of course not. They parted three years ago. Mrs. Stone went back to her own people, and father and I tried to keep up the old place with what we had left. She did offer to leave us an allowance ; indeed, she begged us to take it—and it was a liberal sum too. We parted kindly enough, but of course father refused her money. When we found the old home could not be kept up we sold it out and came up here.'

" So far as I could discover from all this, Mr. Stone had, in the term of life granted him, made but two serious attempts to earn his bread — first by matrimony, next by cooking —both efforts ending with the fat deliberately thrown in the fire by his own obstinate hand. Neither experiment exactly yielded a record with which to approach a business man ; yet, when it became evident that without influence Mr. Stone could never gain a position, I ventured—with some misgivings, I confess—to use a little present power which I happened to possess with a business acquaintance by persuading him to try Mr. Stone in a vacant clerical position in his office. The salary was a very small one, but it was something, and the duties were light. They did not include accounts.

"Now I don't know that you have noticed it," went on the Major, glancing about the room, "but it is our custom in this café to openly overhear any good story that is being told at one of the other tables. As it is the custom, there is nothing rude in it. So soon as he had settled into his business position, Mr. Stone, to my surprise, shot at once into the place of *raconteur* of the café. We had never possessed before, and never shall again, any one else who is capable of improvising such irresistibly comic stories with so little point, or such rippling fancy interlarded with as inimitable negro dialect. Mr. Stone had only to lift his far-reaching voice, wonderfully clear and youthful for a man of his age, with 'Now I'll tell you a true story; you mayn't believe it, but'—and the whole room was attentive.

"There was one delightfully idiotic tale of Glass Snakes and Transparent Mocking-Birds for which he became quietly famous. Some day I will tell it to you, or Mr. Stone shall. This was the first story he ever gave us, and it immediately assured his position. His talents in this line had been so unsuspected by me, and their expression was so evidently the outcome of the man's happiness, that I felt reproached in not having realized before how his failure to gain work had preyed on his spirits.

"'Ah!' he said to me, 'I tell you, Major, it's not the dinner he eats that fattens a man; it's knowing where to-morrow's dinner is to come from.'

"But through Jimty I learned that his father's satisfaction had yet deeper roots. He had confessed to his boy a passionate pride in the fact that he—an old and ruined Southern gentleman—was yet proved capable of taking up his life where it had broken off and beginning over again in the world. This was another of the odd, half-veiled nobilities of the man's character disclosing itself. To me, watching these two grown men made blissfully happy with a bare living income between them was painful. It gave too significant a hint of their past.

"Contented as they were, it was not entirely plain sailing for my two friends. Jimty could not always control his father's eccentric economies, as expensive in the end as his occasional bursts of extravagance, but he met such emergencies with a dogged kind of courage, taking them apparently as but a part of his day's work. He reminded me in those times of a sturdy little horse uncomplainingly digging its way up a steep hill. Mr. Stone must have been a heavy burden to carry, and close as was the relation between the two, as father and son, it was also anomalous. As for Mr. Stone himself, he seemed to harbor no further misgivings regarding anything in life. His oyster was opened wide. When he was not telling his stories, which he seemed able to draw in limitless stores from a bosom as eternal as Abraham's, he would relieve his feelings by leaning back in his chair and humming to himself over and over two lines of an old-fashioned hymn tune which ran,

> 'But when I am happy in Him,
> December's as pleasant as May.'

This was all, and the air never varied.

"I am afraid 'him' meant Jimty, for he always looked at the boy as he sang. Under these circumstances you may imagine my feelings when, one morning, among the letters on my desk I found a rather curt note from Mr. Herrick—my acquaintance and Mr. Stone's employer—informing me that, much as he had desired to serve me, it was impossible for him to continue with Mr. Stone's services. It was not difficult to read between these lines that Herrick, along with the second Mrs. Stone— poor lady!—had found an old Virginia gentleman a luxury too expensive. I confess I was a coward. I could not face Jimty with the news. I sealed up the letter, with a line from myself, and sent it to him by a messenger. I thought I should see him and his father at the café that night, but at the last moment I was called away from town for several days, and when I returned I was still reluctant enough to be a little late for dinner. When I did arrive here I lingered at the door, rubbing my feet in the sand on the threshold and peering over at our table. There was Mr. Stone leaning back in his chair, looking at Jimty, as usual, and the first thing I heard as I drew nearer was his contented, bumblebee-like droning:

> ‘ But when I am happy in Him,
> December's as pleasant as May.’

Jimty was sitting at his side of the table with a couple of little books laid by his plate.

“ Mr. Stone hailed me jovially at once. Unlike his boy, he rarely moved his head except to throw it back in talking, but his roving blue eyes saw everything.

"'Welcome, stranger ; you've come back just in time. Jimty is about to draw the first check he ever made out in his life, in the first check-book he ever owned. It's a great moment, I assure you—isn't it, James T. ?'

"I looked from Mr. Stone to Jimty's smiling face, and sat down, wondering, while Mr. Stone went on to tell me how he had always hated check-books himself, as he liked 'to feel the money slip through his fingers.'

"'Jimty here,' he went on, 'hates so to see good money go out he means to charge everything and pay in checks, only to spare his feelings.'

"I suggested gently that check-books had some value also as a kind of record, but Mr. Stone gave vent to his usual contempt for anything like the keeping of accounts.

"'I never felt any need of records,' he said. 'When I went travelling, for instance, I used to take the sum I had to spend and put half in my right-hand pocket and half in my left. When I had used up all my right-hand pocket, I turned around and came home on my left-hand pocket. I call that sensible and careful enough.'

"Far from the depression I had feared to find, it seemed that Mr. Stone was in highest spirits. When, late in the evening, a café acquaintance joined us at our table, and Jimty made his father tell that idiotic story of the Transparent Mocking-Birds and Glass Snakes for the hundredth time, I listened, and, in spite of myself, laughed out of all proportion to the story's point. I had never heard Mr. Stone handle the tale better. Nor could I detect any underlying anxiety in Jimty's manner.

"Indeed, the new bank-book lying by his plate lent such an air of prosperity, I began to think my letter of ill tidings must have miscarried. But, as we were leaving the café, Jimty managed to fall behind for a moment with me.

"'It's all right, Major, thank you,' he whispered; 'don't let father suspect anything. I was lucky enough to have a rise of salary the day I got your letter. I saw Mr. Herrick about it, and was able to arrange to pay him very nearly what he pays father. It was the best way. I think it would have killed father to lose his position.'"

The Major sat silent, as if recalling something he liked to dwell on.

"Did you ever hear anything to equal that?" he asked. "*Paid* Herrick to retain his father's useless services; and you would have thought he was telling me of the simplest business arrangement! Ah, my dear friend, I won my spurs fighting against the South in the sixties, but it was brother against brother, if ever war was. I am, in fact, Southern on one side of the house, but I never—no, not when I recognized my own first cousin across the battle-line— felt the tug of my Southern blood and sinew claiming me as when I stood by that café door and heard Jimty explain why he stinted himself to feed his father's child-like pride. Do you know, the South and its people have always seemed to me somehow as a deep river that, in contradiction to every law, still persists in murmuring and flinging up spray and foam like a shallow brook. The best stuff of the South flows deep down in a common undercurrent. Their Lees and their Stonewall Jacksons and, yes, their Jimtys, rise only as occasion calls. Meantime those who are nothing but the foam on the top of the waves pass for the general type of the South. They are, of course, one type, but only one—the most conspicuous, the least valuable. Oh yes, delightful enough, except to live with. I could not have lived a week with old Mr. Stone."

I ventured to draw the Major from generalization back to narrative. The café was beginning to empty slowly. I wished to have the thread of the tale I was hearing unreeled to the shuttle on the spot where it had been wound.

"But old Mr. Stone," I asked, "was he so easily deceived?"

"Of course. But not for long, though Jimty took every precaution. He had opened his private bank account chiefly in order to pay Herrick by a monthly check, which he sent through the mail. You know it is impossible to keep a secret like that. One night Jimty came into the café, looking white and scared, to tell me that his father had disappeared. He walked up to my side and stood there in his usual direct way, as a child comes in trouble. There was nothing childish about him but his surface ways. He brought a short note from his father to show me. He had found it a few moments before, awaiting him in their room. As I remember, it ran, in substance—

" ' You should have known me better, dear boy. I must earn my own bread. If I am in sickness or need I will send for you. I forbid you to look for me. God bless you!
" ' Your devoted   FATHER.'

"Mr. Stone had taken away with him just half—to a penny—of their small remaining capital, the accordion-bag, and his own clothing; nothing more. At first Jimty, and I too, believed that Mr. Herrick must in a moment of impatience have betrayed the secret. Yet it was unlike him. I had reason to believe that his word, once given, became a law unto himself. On the other hand, knowing him as a practical business man to the backbone, his retaining Mr. Stone so long in his office, even at no expense to himself, had all along been rather a matter of surprise to me, though I recalled how Mrs. Stone, at considerable expense, had borne with the father during fifteen weary years for the sake of the same advocate. Under all the circumstances I thought our first and wisest move was for me to see Herrick alone, and gain from him what further information I could; so I left Jimty at his desolated room, and went on up town to Herrick's house.

"Herrick received me in his private library. He is a large, heavily built, strong-featured man, with a hard voice and a good-natured laugh. He was laughing when I came in, and seemed to know at once what I was there for.

"'Old Stone, I suppose?' he said. 'Major, I don't think I deserved that Old Man of the Sea of you. Socially, I don't doubt, he's delightful, but he certainly has the business equipment of a jackass. That's a fine boy of his, though; nothing of the jackass there. I was glad to accommodate you, of course, by keeping the old man (on the boy's terms), yet I tell you now frankly, I wouldn't have kept him on any terms for you or anybody else if I hadn't been really touched by his son's extraordinary offer. It's not often you run on anything like that in business life. You know how he came to leave me, of course? No? Well, my book-keeper carelessly left young Stone's check open on his desk, and old Mr. Stone's magpie-like eyes saw it in passing. His mind is every bit as quick as his eyes. It works like a back stitch in a matter like that. He went on his way past the desk straight to my private room, and taxed me with deductions I could not deny. He resigned his position on the spot.'

"'And has since disappeared,' I added. Then I told Herrick of the letter and its contents.

"'No!' he said, easily ; 'you don't say so ! Well, so much the better for the boy ; that is, if the old man doesn't bring his debts back with him when he comes. Mark my words, as soon as his money runs out he will run in. Oh, you needn't bother to look for him. Sometimes I think vice is easier to deal with than worthlessness. At least it can be depended on to take care of itself.'

"Herrick's manner vexed me, but as I wanted his help in the matter, I answered moderately that I thought he missed seeing certain qualities in Mr. Stone which made me fear he would starve before bending his pride and returning unsought. 'In the mean time,' I urged, 'the man was wholly unfitted to care for himself.'

"I had never before met Herrick on anything but business terms. I knew of him only as a self-made man, but of his family and home life nothing whatever. I was entirely unprepared for it when he flung out towards me an arm as strong as a horse's leg, with—

"'Major, any man who has his two arms *free* can put bread in his mouth and a roof over his head if he chooses to. If not, let him go. Suppose he does have to sleep in a field once in a while—why not? He has all fate promises him. If you were to come to me telling the story of a man with a child clinging to his hand and the wife he loves hampering his arms, then I should know what you meant. It's when he has given hostages to Fortune—hostages to Fortune—there were never stronger words—that he learns how to suffer. You can starve your own tough flesh and let your own bones go cold, but when the flesh of your flesh and bone of your bone are suffering for what you would kill yourself to give them—God knows, sometimes I hate the sight of the luxuries about me! If I could have commanded them earlier, my wife would be with me.'

"He got up and walked across the room, leaving me overwhelmed. This was the man behind the hard voice.

"I had nothing to say. What could I say? Bodies were not made to talk with naked souls. At least mine was not.

"Herrick came back to his chair frowning.

"'I beg your pardon,' he said. 'I don't know what has upset me this evening. My wife has been gone only a year, and left us about this time. She lived to enjoy some years of luxury, so I ought not to resent things as I do, I suppose; but I have always been confident that her early hardships were what really caused her death. One little plunge in cold water would not have killed a strong woman—it did her.'

"'Herrick,' I said, 'do you mean she was drowned?'

"'Yes,' he answered, 'I suppose you might say so. *Shock*, the doctors called it. She was only in the water a moment before I dragged her out. A wharf we were standing on settled and sank. There was terrible loss of life. My only child was saved as by a miracle, poor little girl!'

"While he was speaking I was as sure as you are at this moment that the accident had taken place in Virginia, that I had been a witness of it, and that Herrick's daughter was the girl Jimty had saved. In his expansive mood it was not difficult to lead Herrick on. When I left him that night it was too late to see Jimty again, but the first question I asked the boy as he entered the café for breakfast was not concerning his father, but, 'Jimty, what kind of coat did you wrap about the girl you pulled out of the water at the Virginia wharf?'

"'A new corded black,' he answered, looking at his rubbed coat sleeves; 'and I wish I had it now. She can't want it, and I do, badly.'

"'There were plenty of corded black coats there, and plenty of women wrapped in them,

I suppose,' I said.   'What had you in the pockets?'

"'I don't remember anything but a green
housewife and a little old corn-cob pipe. I have
missed that pipe more than the coat.   Why do
you ask?'

"'Because,' I answered, 'if your coat was a
new corded black, and had a housewife and a
corn-cob pipe in the pockets, the girl you saved
was Herrick's only child. He has advertised
for you and been looking for you ever since.
He showed me your coat last night. He keeps
it carefully folded away among his own, and
says he means to until he finds the man to
whom it belongs. You have only to walk up
town to slip into it and your fortune.'

"'Well, I certainly sha'n't,' said Jimty. And
from this position I was not able to move him
an inch. In vain I argued that I had not intended he himself should claim the laurels
Herrick had plaited and waiting. As soon as
he understood me Jimty sternly exacted a
promise of silence, and, indeed, I had now no
right to speak to Herrick without his permission, though I devoutly wished I had been less
reticent when the coat was first shown me.
Unfortunately I had waited to verify my sus-
picions. For days I wrestled with Jimty on
this question. It was our sauce with each
meal. He knew as well as I what Herrick's
mere interest would mean for him in the busi-

ness world, but he was, as it seemed to me, unreasonably, foolishly obstinate. Finally I had a chance to bring the girl herself forward as argument.

"'Jimty,' I said, 'I do think you are a fool. You don't know a woman in this city excepting madame, and there's as sweet a child as any man could ask for'—she was quite Jimty's age, but they were both children to me—'simply waiting to receive you. Her father called me across the street to-day to meet her. He has a right to be proud of her. She's as pretty and pink as a bonnet rose. You would never have known her for the dead-looking girl we laid out on the board by the water.'

"Then my young man blushed—blushed until I saw I had somehow hit near the real cause of his obstinacy.

"'I did recognize her,' he said. 'Mr. Herrick sent for me the other day to explain to me himself how Father came to leave him. She stopped in at the office for a moment while I was there. But if you think I am ever going to be led up to any woman as the man who saved her life stark naked you are mistaken. I have been mortally ashamed of that ever since it happened. The amount of it was, I lost my head; but why in the world Father didn't make me keep on *something* I can't see yet. It was perfectly ridiculous—unnecessary—theatrical.'

" He tramped out of the café, hot and angry, leaving his dinner half eaten. After that I let Master Jimty alone. While I reserved to myself the right to believe that Miss Herrick would have indubitably followed her mother but for the thorough measures which Jimty now characterized as unnecessary and ridiculous, I am quite old enough to avoid argument with a young man whose self-consciousness is wounded, and also to hold my laughter in check until the door closes between him and me.

"During this time a search for Mr. Stone was being quietly made in every direction by Jimty and myself. To my satisfaction, it also developed that Herrick seemed to feel a certain responsibility in the matter. He sent for Jimty at his office several times to ask what news he had, and finally, as the days went by with no news whatever, went so far as to offer to engage a private detective at his own expense. This Jimty refused decidedly.

" ' Father would never forgive it,' he said.

" ' You needn't tell him,' Herrick suggested.

" But Jimty shook his head, remarking, in his serious way, that he had ' tried not telling father once too often.'

" Herrick laid his big hands down on the table and laughed. He had followed us here to the café to make this offer, and was dining with us. Jimty's seriousness always seemed to amuse him.

"'Your father's general habits of life ought to give us a hint to begin with,' he said, looking at the son with a question in his eye.

"'Father never sprees,' said Jimty, in his own vernacular, and Herrick laughed again.

"'Well,' he said, 'if that's the case, and it's to be a still-hunt, you can count me in. I'll find him for you. I never made up my mind to get anything on this earth that I didn't gain it sooner or later—sometimes too late.'

"I knew he was thinking of his dead wife. Herrick was in his way as curious a mixture of feeling and harshness as Mr. Stone of worthlessness and nobility.

"From that time on Herrick's spirit of combativeness seemed roused, and it was his indomitable will and plotting mind that converted the search for Mr. Stone into an organized effort, such as Jimty and I could never have made it. I saw then how the man had forced his way up through the world. His powers were only strengthened by failures, and we kept failing all along the line. Every trail we followed ended in a lost scent. Finally, after all our labors, it was left to that miserable little newsboy to give us the clew. He knows his city as a rat its holes. One night, when the three of us were dining here together (Herrick had formed the habit of dropping in occasionally on his way home), I saw madame glance over at us from her perch. Now madame, as a fixed rule, keeps her expressive eyes to herself. They are generally behind her lowered white lids. She was talking to the newsboy — had drawn him into her proscenium-box, in fact— and was standing with her hand on his shoulder, evidently questioning him, for he was squirming uneasily. The gamin hates questions, as does any other man of the world. Madame raised her lids again, and with her eyes beckoned monsieur, who came to her at once. They whispered together, still holding the child. Then monsieur's hand replaced madame's on the boy's shoulder, and he was steered unwillingly towards our table. They are the most discreet couple I ever met, monsieur and madame. I had not known that madame realized Mr. Stone's disappearance. She had never shown any consciousness of his presence as an established guest, barring the grave bow she gives to all regular comers. Monsieur, I knew, was more or less interested in our search, for he had singled out Jimty as the one being on whom to bestow more than an impersonal and business-like attention. The boy had a wonderfully unconscious power of attracting his fellow-beings of all classes and kinds, witness Mrs. Stone, Herrick, monsieur, and myself. Every day, as monsieur passed our table, he would pause an instant at Jimty's side, and with his hand behind his back, ask, in a low voice, if he had any news; then, at Jimty's answer, he would cluck sympathetically in his throat and pass on. I don't know how he divined our anxiety over Mr. Stone, for we had cooked up a fable concerning his absence with which to meet inquirers at the café. I think now that madame was monsieur's informant. I have gained faith in her sphinx-like omniscience since the night she sent the little newsboy travelling down the room to us under monsieur's hand.

" 'This child has seen him,' whispered monsieur, and with Gallic breeding instantly retired. The boy stood blinking at us, and Herrick fell on him at once with brusque questions, to which he got sulky, half-scared replies. Yet the child insisted, with funny little noddings of his head, that he had seen Mr. Stone the night before.

" 'Ze gentleman like zis,' he said, and set his crooked little forefinger over his stubby nose, which immediately became Mr. Stone's beak. Herrick roared with laughter. Jimty reached past him, and drawing the boy to himself, whispered to him, and gave him some coins, at which the child looked full in his face with his black eyes and said :

" 'Yes, I seen him at ze zeatre-house when I sells ze papers. He was'—he darted a glance across at Herrick and went on glibly—'he was selling ze tickets at ze door.'

" While Jimty was trying to arrive at the

location of 'ze zeatre,' I leaned towards Herrick.

"'That child is lying,' I whispered.

"'Of course,' he answered ; 'but we may as well look there as anywhere. I know the place he means, or know of it. It's a kind of beer-garden.'

"To the kind of beer-garden we went, Jimty walking between Herrick and me, an impatient half-step ahead. The strain of his father's disappearance had changed him in some ways for the better. His face was thinner, and had in a measure lost its boyish look, and he was more alert in body and mind. As we neared the building he left us and ran forward, pushing open the big double door of the beer-garden entrance, and walking up to the ticket-window, where I think he was as confident of looking through the opening into his father's face as if he had already seen him. When we came near, it was to discover an individual as wholly unlike Mr. Stone as was Jimty himself, raking in the admissions with soiled, fat hands. He rapped on the window-ledge crossly at the boy, who stood gaping. Herrick laid a note on the ledge, and held up three fingers over Jimty's back.

"'The little boy lied,' he said, gathering in his change. 'I thought so. But we might as well go in.'

"Inside we found a large, gaudily tricked-out room, with small round tables scattered about holding beer-glasses and lounging elbows. Men, women, and children were present, but the greater number of the last two were crowded on rows of benches set before a green-curtained platform. Some performance was evidently about to begin. We chose a remote table, gave an order for beer, and waited, Herrick and I looking about us carefully. Jimty dully followed our lead. His disappointment at the ticket-window seemed to have deeply depressed him.

"'I still think that child was telling half the truth,' said Herrick. 'I frightened the other half away from him. We'll get some clew here, if nothing else.'

"But Jimty glanced about the room, shaking his head; and while I agreed with Herrick in thinking the newsboy was concealing something he was afraid to tell, I also agreed with Jimty in thinking that Mr. Stone could have no part or lot in such an assemblage, composed chiefly of German-Americans, respectable, bourgeois, and just escaping vulgarity. The entertainment provided, while harmless in its way, was in touch with the audience. There was a great deal of cheap music and shifting colored lights and general buffoonery. The first rising of the curtain revealed a skirt-dancer, a Mademoiselle La Rée, 'creatress of all she does,' as the programme assured us. The girl danced well and gracefully, changing herself at will from a misty butterfly to a writhing serpent or a kaleidoscopic figure by a twirl of her voluminous skirts. I knew Jimty had never seen a skirt-dancer before, but it failed to rouse him. Herrick, it appeared, had never seen one either. His daily life of business excitement, he said, made domesticity his chosen relaxation. He watched Mademoiselle La Rée with contemptuous interest. She was followed by the dullest and dreariest kind of songs and dances, of varying nationalities; but we sat through it all, and were rewarded at last by what brought a smile even to Jimty's gloom. Six negro minstrels stepped out on the stage. The deception of the blacking and general make-up was so clever I thought them all Africans, until Jimty, more experienced in the race look, pointed out to me that the two end men were white. After the usual passing of songs and jokes, one of the end men told a foolish story, challenging the other to cap it, so the second man stepped forward and began to speak in a droning, irresistibly comic singsong. Herrick and I looked across the table at each other. Jimty rose to his feet. It was the story of the Transparent Mocking-Birds and Glass Snakes.

"'That's my father's story,' said Jimty. 'He is here somewhere.'

"On either side we caught Jimty's arms and forced him back in his chair.

" ' Where are you going ?' said Herrick.

" ' To ask where my father is, of course. There's the back door ; let me go.'

" I could not find words or heart to tell him. Herrick blurted it out.

" ' Be still, boy,' he whispered ; 'that *is* your father.'

" I felt Jimty start and quiver under my hands.

" ' It is not !' he exclaimed ; but he sat quiet, staring at the platform.

" The story was rising from absurdity to absurdity, the audience applauding with wild cat-calls and shrieking with laughter. There was but one being in the world who could tell that particular story in that particular way. Disguised as he was by paint and wig and blackened face, this delight of a third-rate audience, the evident drawing-card of the management, the end man of a negro-minstrel troupe, was old Mr. Stone.

" Jimty's head bent lower and lower. An expression of pitiful humiliation was creeping like a blush over his face.

" ' Well,' said Herrick, finally, 'the old man is doing the only thing on earth he knows how to, and, by George ! I respect him for it.'

" Jimty turned away, dropping his arms on the table and hiding his face in them. For a while we sat silent. I signed to Herrick to let him be, but he would not, and bent forward.

"'This is all nonsense,' he said; 'don't take it so hard. There is no shame in it, my boy; and if there were'—for the first time I heard his hard voice soften; he laid his great arm across Jimty's shoulders—'if there were, I have a cloak waiting for you at home that would cover everything.'

"That's all," said the Major. "You have heard the whole story now, and you saw the finale at the church this morning. *Addition!*" This last to his waiter, who hurried off, calling "*Addition!*" in his turn to madame, who made out the account at her stand.

"But I objected. "Major," I said, "you have not told me all. How did Mr. Herrick know the coat was Jimty's unless you betrayed him?"

"I? Oh no. The girl recognized him at a glance as she passed him in the office, and told her father. I believe women see more with their eyes half shut than we with ours wide open. Jimty was such an innocent it was easy for a man like Herrick to get enough corroborating testimony from him without his realizing it. That was the cause of Herrick's sudden interest in the search for old Mr. Stone. He waited for his own time to speak. That was like Herrick. What of the old man?" The Major laughed. "Well, do you know, 't was a month before we could persuade him to leave

"'{ MR. STONE IS NOW A SEMI-PROFESSIONAL
RACONTEUR'"

his minstrel company. He insisted that from
never having a dime in his pocket he now had
dollars, and that he liked his new-found inde-
pendence. The truth is, backbone was a heri-
tage in that family. Mr. Stone had only mis-
laid his for threescore years or so. I couldn't
help respecting his resolution from his point of
view. Herrick would only laugh and cheer the
old man on, but Jimty was so distressed we
finally hit on a compromise. Jimty persuaded
his father to meet us half-way, while Herrick
and I arranged the sordid details. Mr. Stone
is now a semi-professional *raconteur*, rather the
fashion for select half-literary entertainments.
You may stumble on him some night. If you
do, make him tell the tale of the Glass Snakes
and Transparent Mocking-Birds. It was that
story, by-the-way, which gained him the place
in the minstrel troupe. The manager over-
heard him telling it at the café, and made over-
tures. Do you know, my friend, that we are the
only guests left in this room, and that madame
is growing restless?"

It was true. I saw madame's eyes. They
were expressive. We rose and wound our
way among the little tables towards the
door.

"My hat, Jean," said the Major. "Good-day,
madame, monsieur."

Our feet grated on the sand at the door-sill.
I looked back from the pavement to see

madame following monsieur to the open vestibule. Together they set in place the little wire grating that proclaimed the luncheon hour over.

THE PRICE OF PEACE

In a corner near my fireplace stands an old spinning-wheel, on the body of which two large letters are carved—" D. W.," the mark of the maker. The wheel is silent and decrepit, its useful days long past. Spin it never will again; yet whenever I look at it standing there in its corner, the foot-worn treadle rises, the wheel hums, and for me spins this:

" Oh, Reuben," said Mrs. Grey, " ef that sight don't make my very blood boil. No, don't you look. Keep yer eyes on the mare, and I will, too; then maybe Sarah will think we didn't see her. Drive fast, Reuben, and *don't* look."

Reuben Grey fixed his eyes on his mare's ears, and gingerly beat her lazy back with his worn-out whip.

" Say somethin' to me as we pass, Reuben," whispered Mrs. Grey; " it 'll look more nacheral."

Reuben's mouth worked foolishly, but no words came.

"Now we have passed her," said his wife, with a breath of relief as the buggy jogged on; "but yer didn't say a word, Reuben."

"To save my life, I couldn't think o' anything ter say. I never can when folks come on me sudden."

"Then you might ha' said that. What I didn't want yer to look at was pore Sarah. Dan'l Whip has got her settin' up beside him on the roof of Mr. Buzzard's house while he's mendin' the chimbleys. It's a shame, it is."

Reuben turned around in his seat to look back.

"Now, Reuben," cried Mrs. Grey, "yer've done it after all, and o' course she saw yer!"

Reuben was shaking the buggy with his laughter.

"Ef that don't beat all!" he cried. "I heard Dan'l Whip was doin' that to Sarah, but I didn't ha'f b'lieve it. Got her h'isted up there on the roof, sittin' in a chair at her knittin'! Oh, my!"

He beat his knee gently with his huge, doubled-up fist, which was no larger than his big heart. "Pore Sarah," he said; "pore Sarah! An' 'tain't as ef he did it for fondness."

"Fondness! He jes does it to be hateful, Reuben. I al'ays feel 'bout him jes like I do of a bat, that ain't bird nor beast, but a kinder crawlin' vermin. Dan'l Whip certainly ain't a man."

"That ain't any fault o' his. He was born like that, Mary, honey—all humped together. I've been thinkin' these years here lately that he's been gettin' shorter, an' it ain't onreasonable that his temper should shorten, too. I don't hold Dan'l Whip full respons'ble."

Mrs. Grey shook her head. "I ain't so sure, Reuben. He's cute enough 'bout thinkin' up new ways to be hateful. This haulin' pore Sarah up onter roofs when he's chimbleys to mend, now, who'd 'a' thought o' that but Dan'l Whip? The only holiday she had was when he was up on roofs; while he's makin' spinnin'-wheels at home he has her under hack all the time. What in the world made her marry him I don't know."

Reuben stretched out his hand to catch a wisp of sweet hay that hung on a low branch. The road was narrow, and ran between intruding bushes. The fingerlike twigs had snatched part of its load from a passing hay-wagon, which could be heard rumbling on ahead. Selecting a juicy-looking straw, Reuben took it between his teeth, chewing its sweetness as meditatively as a cow might. He leaned back in the buggy, bracing his feet against the worn dash - board, which showed marks of having thus braced them for years. The reins fell in loops from the horse's neck.

"When Dan'l Whip married," said Reuben, "folks talked the other way. His body warn't much, to be shore, an' his head was 'bout as big as the biggest watermillon you ever saw, like it is now, an' his eyes was just as squeeched up. But talk! He could talk like a book. We all thought he'd be a somebody, and Sarah warn't nothin' but a field-hand. She was reapin' in my father's field when Dan'l first saw her. 'Dan'l Whip,' says my father, 'what on airth are you goin' to marry a girl out the field fur?' You see how folks felt about it. 'I'm sick o' boardin',' says Dan'l. 'I want a home - table. She re'p' like a man, an' I'm goin' to marry her.'"

Mrs. Grey's soft brows knit. "She's as strong as a man now, Reuben; that's what gets to me. Dan'l don't more 'n come up to her waist; she could pick him up under her arm an' walk right off with him."

"Well, she don't do it, nor nothin' like it," said Reuben. He lowered his voice: "Mary, did you ever hear that story 'bout Dan'l Whip an' Sarah an' a table? I jes pooh-poohed it at the store when I heard it, but it do seem kinder cur'ous, the way Sarah jumps an' runs an' tumbles over herself whenever Dan'l Whip says 'Come.'"

Mrs. Grey pursed up her lips. "Reuben, you know I ain't one to gossip. That I knew this thing for weeks, and said nothin' 'bout it

to yer, shows that. My cousin Lyddy ain't one
to gossip either. She oughtn't to ha' told her
husband, an' then it wouldn't 'a' leaked out at
the store."

Reuben looked up, his blue eyes full of interest. "That come from Lyddy, did it? Then
it's got to be true."

"It's as true as sin, an' more disgraceful.
Lyddy says she saw Sarah walkin' roun' an'
roun' that table, cryin' kinder sof' and wringin'
her hands, while Dan'l Whip stood in the middle beatin' her with a leather strap."

Reuben's jaw dropped. "My goodness, Mary!
that's a' awful thing. Somebody ought to stop
it. But what I don't see is why Sarah don't stop
it herse'f. What made her walk?"

"That's what I ast Lyddy. She says at first
she believed he must 'a' had her held by a halter; but there warn't nothin' at all holdin'
Sarah but Dan'l Whip's will. Ain't that awful,
Reuben?"

"Ha-a," said Reuben, moving his feet uneasily, "it makes me crawl. But, Mary, honey,
I'm 'fraid yer 'll think I'm sorter heartless, for
I do think I'm goin' to laf in a minit. Sarah
she's so everlastin' big, and Dan'l he's little
enough to have ter crawl on a table ter reach her.
Don't you see yerse'f it's sorter funny, Mary?"

His clean-shaven lip twitched as his laughter came and possessed him. Mrs. Grey looked
at her husband unsmilingly.

"I don't see nothin' to laugh at, Reuben Grey. Lyddy wasn't laughin' any; she said it was a sight to cry over."

"What I'm studyin' over is how Lyddy saw it," ruminated Reuben.

"Lyddy," said Mrs. Grey, with a slight embarrassment, "was on her way to see Sarah; but when she got to Dan'l Whip's, an' heard this kinder cryin' sound, she didn't like to knock. There's a slat out o' one o' Dan'l Whip's shutters on the left side the house, an' when Lyddy once looked through that crack she didn't want to do any knockin'. Don't you reckon it's water that mare's wantin', Reuben?"

The mare was turning her head longingly towards the road-side, where a weak little stream, trickling down the hill and under the matted underwood, was led by a split log into a half-sunk barrel. There was no check-rein to the rope-pieced harness. Reuben had only to sit still in the buggy and give the mare her way. As it was a warm day, she drew in the water gratefully with deep, whistling sounds.

"Mary," said Reuben, turning to his wife, his face working with laughter, "I've been kinder keepin' somethin' 'bout Dan'l Whip to myself, but I can't keep it no longer. You remember the mornin', a week back, when he came out from town in sech a hurry to see me? Well, what yer s'pose he wanted? 'Mr.

Grey,' says he, whisperin', 'will you kindly lend me twenty dollars?'"

"La, Reuben," Mrs. Grey interrupted, "what did he want it fer?"

"That was what I ast him, an' you could ha' knocked me down with a feather when he tol' me he wanted to buy a divorce from Sarah."

"Sarah!" repeated Mrs. Grey. "Why, she's the only thing keeps folks anyways decent to him. Dan'l Whip must be losin' his mind."

"Egzactly what I says to him. 'Dan'l,' I says, 'Sarah's shorely been a good wife to you.' 'I know,' says he, still whisperin'; 'but there's a lawyer parsin' thro' town, an' he tells me he can make a divorce for twenty dollars. Ain't that the cheapest thing, Mr. Grey? I'll never get a bargain like that agin,' says he; 'an' I want you to lend me the money for it. I'll pay you back.'"

"'No, Dan'l Whip,' says I, 'you certainly won't, fer I ain't goin' to lend it to you first. You ought to be 'shamed o' yerse'f,' I says; but I laffed so he went off ragin'. There must be somethin' kinder ridic'lous to me in ev'ry-thing Dan'l Whip does, Mary. I laffed to my-self all the week at that, an' it makes me laf now to think o' it. Buyin' a divorce jes 'cause it's cheap! Like that stovepipe hat you got fer me some ten years back 'cause it was sech a bargain. It's been in the garret ever sence, 'ain't it?" Reuben pulled the flapping felt hat he always wore deeper over his brows, beneath which his eyes twinkled.

"I don't see nothin' alike between 'em," said Mrs. Grey, stiffly.

Her husband tightened the reins and "clucked" to his mare. "Maybe there ain't, honey," he said, as they wound down the river-side road again.

Between the little town of Riverton, which the pair were leaving, and their farm ran the South Branch of the Potomac, brawling, noisy, and rapid, ever quarrelling with its banks, too often rising in wrath to sweep over them, carrying destruction for lines of high corn and low-lying wheat-fields. If the South Branch, with its rich alluvial banks and wealth of fishes, were more his friend or his enemy, Reuben Grey had yet to decide. He was thinking of this as he looked down at the waters rushing by on the right side of the road. On the left bank the great gray "hanging rocks" arched high above them, holding in every crevice where earth could gather the hanging plant of the region, its gay pink head drooping and swinging against the gray wall with every wind. A hundred feet beyond the hanging rocks lay the ford, good or bad as the South Branch willed. On this day the ford happened to be kind, but Mrs. Grey breathed more freely as the mare emerged dripping on the other side.

"It seems like I never can get used to that gratin' sound of the wheels on the pebbles when the current gets to pullin' so hard midstream, Reuben," she said. "The mare's real frisky to-day, ain't she? Why, whatever ails her now?"

"She's scared of that thing comin' down the road," answered Reuben. "W'o', Molly! It ain't nothin', you foolish woman. I'm blessed ef I know what it is myself though, Mary."

Straight down the road a feather-bed, topped by some pillows and colored comforts, seemed to be speeding directly towards them, and with no perceptible means of locomotion; but as it drew nearer a pair of unsteady, bandy legs could be distinguished sticking out from the bottom of the pile.

"Oh, my!" said Mrs. Grey, wofully; "I know what it is. It's Uncle Sam moving into his cabin again."

As she spoke the object turned, and, wavering as one of those tormented beetles over whose backs children delight to clasp pea-pods, moved from the road to a tiny log cabin set in the bushes. Through the open door of the cabin, after much backing and pushing, the feather-bed vanished. When the buggy passed the door was closed.

"There," sighed Mrs. Grey; "he's shut in again for days, I s'pose, an' all his work lyin'. I wisht to mercy your mother was alive, Reuben ; or else I wisht she'd taken off all the old negroes with her. To this day I ain't anythin' but the 'young mistis' to them, an' they don't heed a word I say. I'm gettin' perfictly sick of it. You ought never to have let Sam build that cabin, Reuben."

"Oh, it don't matter any. You take the ole niggers too hard, Mary, honey. Sam he likes to have a kinder hole o' his own to crawl inter when he gets mad."

"I don't see how that cabin's his any more 'n his room at the house is, Reuben. He's made it outer your timber, an' set it on your land."

"What's started him now ?"

"There hasn't anythin' happened but jes what he deserved. He's taken to lyin' in bed here lately deep inter the mornin', an' when he chooses to get up, Ozalla she *will* cook a red-hot breakfast for him. To-day I jes stopped her, an' put by some cold victuals for Sam. He was as impident when he saw the plate ! He went r'arin' 'roun' the kitchen, tellin' me he warn't goin' to make a gobbige-box of his stom-mick for nobody."

"I jes hope you ran him out with nothin'," said Reuben, indignantly.

"I had ter ; but I always feel as if your mother was lookin' down at me when I scold Sam. I can't bear to interfere with the old negroes, they was here so long before me."

"Makes n' odds," said Reuben, easily ; "I've

known Sam to keep mad for a week after he'd clean fergot what started him. He'll come home ter - morrow, maybe. The reapin'-machine's lef' more or less grass over there in that field, Mary, 'ain't it? I reckon I'll take that scythe there in the fence corner and trim off the stray locks. I never did think much o' machines anyhow. You can drive the buggy on to the house. Holler for one of the little niggers to take it when yer get there."

The horse taken to the stable by a "little nigger," the locks of grass shorn, and supper in the farm-house eaten, Reuben Grey and his wife sat together happily on the vine-covered porch in the twilight. Down on the river-bank the frogs sang loudly, following their shrill leader. The farm-yard creatures were almost silenced for the night, and Reuben Grey himself was wrapped in content. His feet, clad only in their stockings, were resting on the rungs of his chair, which was tilted back against the side of the house, his pipe was in his mouth, his wife was by his side. What more could man desire?

"Reuben," said Mrs. Grey, looking up from the knitting which she did not need to see, "I do think I hear somebody hollering at the ford."

"Reckon not," Reuben answered, drowsily; but as he raised his head to listen his chair dropped forward with a jerk; he reached quickly for his boots.

"It sounds to me kinder like a lady," he said, drawing his boots half-way on, then rising to stamp his feet deeper in before he hurried to the ford. To keep a lady waiting was not in Reuben's code. Mrs. Grey could hear the sound of the pole scraping on the boat, and knew later by the voices on the road that Reuben must be bringing some one back with him. As the two figures advanced through the dusk she could not at once recognize the face of the new-comer, who seemed to hesitate at the steps, as if doubtful of her welcome.

"Here's Sarah Whip, wife," said Reuben ; and Mrs. Grey rose at once.

"Well, Sarah Whip, I didn't know yer for a minit, I was so surprised ! I'm real glad. You haven't been on this porch sence—I do' know when. Have yer had yer supper ?"

"No," answered Reuben ; " she 'ain't had any. Jes get her some, Mary. Set down and wait out here in the cool, Sarah — Mary won't be a minit. Do you take tea or coffee ?"

"Coffee in general," answered Sarah, dully ; "but I ain't particklar, Mrs. Grey."

"Mary's got both," said Reuben.

He followed his wife, whose hospitality had already sent her to the kitchen. "Mary, honey," he whispered, "don't you hurry with that supper. Somethin's happened, and Sarah Whip's got it on her min' to tell. Jes let her get through oncet, and make her some strong coffee, pore thing."

He rambled out to the porch again with a step always purposeless, however direct his aim.

"Well, Sarah, chile," he said, as he seated himself.

Sarah looked up. She was a tall, fair woman, with high cheek-bones, gentle blue eyes, and a deprecating expression. Her face began to work suddenly, and she flung her blue apron over her head.

"I knowed there was trouble as soon as I saw you," said Reuben. "Jes set there and let it bile over, honey. What's he bin doin' to yer 'sides settin' yer up on roofs?"

Sarah rocked her body to and fro, talking through her apron. "I tol' him you saw me on that roof—I tol' him so. I can't stan' it no longer. When I runned out here to the river jes now I didn't know ef it was to th'o' myself in or to holler to you. Then I seemed to hear him runnin' after me, an' I hollered."

"You oughter 'a' hollered long days before this, Sarah. Now you take that thing offer yer head an' listen to me. I ain't goin' to do any talkin' round to yer, but straight at yer. You tell me ef this thing I hear 'bout you and Dan'l Whip and a table an' a strop 's true?"

Sarah dropped the apron as one trained in obedience, but she wrung her hands and rocked as she poured out her story.

"Yes ; it's true whenever he gets mad at me. I'm 'mos' crazy with it all. Ef I didn't know jes when he was goin' to do it, it wouldn't come so hard. But no matter how early in the day he gets mad at me, ef it's right after breakfast, he don't say not one word till night. He jes waits till after supper, when I've took the cloth off the table an' folded it an' put it in the dresser drawer. Ef I hear a scramblin' behind me, then I know it's him gettin' up on the table; nor he don't say a word then, but jes waits for me to turn round from the dresser. Sometimes it's as much as five minutes, it seems to me, before I kin turn. I jes keep prayin' there, 'Lord, help me ; help me to bear it, Lord'; but nothin' don't help me." Her voice rose to a wail. "Ef I don't walk right around that table like I know he wants me to, he 'most kills me when I do come. Oh, I don't see how I can stan' it any more! I had ter run away ter-night, an' I reckon he will kill me ter-morrow night for doin' it."

Reuben Grey was moving restlessly in his chair. "Sarah," he cried out, "you ain't called on to stan' it ! Now you look here. I ain't one to run ag'in Scripture; I'm believin' the wife should be subjec' to her husband ; but, honey, I've bin livin' in this world some time, an' one thing I've come to see. I've come to see it so true that I've done what I reckon yer 'll call awful audacious. I've made a kinder proverb of it, and in my Bible I've added it to the proverbs of Solomon—in pencil. It's jes this: 'An' the price o' peace may be wa-ar—may be wa-ar,'" he accented with his earnest forefinger. "I ain' tellin' you to do anythin' that's wrong when I tell you this: the nex' time you know Dan'l Whip's mad, an' you hear him scramblin' on to the table behin' you, Sarah, don't you pray like yer've been a-prayin'— 'Lord, help me to bear it'; you pray like this: 'Lord help me not to bear this ondecent thing; for the price of peace may be wa-ar, O Lord, wa-ar!' You pray that way, Sarah, an' then you turn roun' an' carry out the will o' the Lord as He puts it inter yer heart ter act. Now the best thing you kin do is to eat yer supper. I hear Mary carryin' it in."

Mrs. Grey was a good woman. She set the supper on the table, and busied herself about Sarah, watching without a question the poor soul eat and choke and wipe her eyes. With the good food, the warm coffee, and the warmer kindness, Sarah gradually took heart to relish what she ate. A contagious peacefulness pervaded all of Reuben Grey's surroundings.

"Eat, honey, eat," he urged. "Mary an' me love to see people eat. Eat till you bu'st—I wisht yer would."

He laughed himself so heartily that Sarah had begun to join timidly in his mirth when, with a nice morsel half lifted to her mouth, she dropped her fork on her plate.

"What was that?" she asked, trembling.

As the others listened the sound which she had heard was repeated—a cry too shrill for a man's voice, too deep for a woman's.

"It's Dan'l at the ford," said Sarah, desperately, rising with a moan, as beaten children turn at call to run screaming towards the fate they dare not escape.

"Sit still there, Sarah," said Reuben, sternly; "it's me Dan'l Whip's callin', an' it's me he'll get."

He stretched out his hand for the flapping hat, and strode from the room. The two women followed him to the porch. Standing there, they could hear through the darkness the beat of Reuben Grey's heavy footsteps on the road, then his powerful voice: "Who's callin'?"

Every word he spoke came to them clearly. From his replies they could guess at the meaning of the rabbit-like cries from the other side of the river. Sarah grasped Mrs. Grey's arm, a liberty she would not have dared to take at a less crucial moment.

"Yes, she's here!" shouted Reuben.

The inarticulate cries answered. Then Reuben's voice rose again :

"No, Dan'l Whip ; I can't pole over fer you to-night ; the boat's up."

"I tell yer she is pulled up."

"Well, I ain't goin' to, then."

"I'll drive Sarah in fust thing ter-morrow mornin'."

"I don't care ef yer do swim; yer won't drown anybody but Dan'l Whip. There ain't no use bleatin' at me like that, Dan'l. I said I won't, and I ain't."

"Ef yer do, yer 'll grow to the stone yer settin' on, that's all. Good-night to yer."

When Reuben returned, Sarah was waiting for him, tremulously standing in the wedge of light which the open house-door let out into the dark porch. Reuben came into the light also, his eyes smiling, his head turning from side to side as in some keen enjoyment. He was holding his closed hand close to his nose.

"Hol' out yer han', Sarah," he said. As Sarah stretched out her shaking arm, he laid a brown, velvety blossom on her palm.

"There warn't but five shrubs lef' on the bush. I'm goin' to give you two, Sarah, an' keep three fer myself. Shrubs jes suit my smell. I don't know nothin' that substitutes a shrub after it gets all hot and smelly in yer han'. Come along, Sarah; you finish yer supper, then ye 're goin' right to bed fer a good night's rest."

Sweet, homespun, chivalric soul! Reuben Grey on his mountain-side, hoeing his fields, knew a fine code that only nature had taught him.

The following morning, after the early farm breakfast, the buggy, which was to take Sarah into Riverton was brought to the gate before the porch. Reuben Grey's eyes dwelt with full satisfaction on the dilapidated vehicle, the half-groomed horse, and the makeshift harness, but not upon Ozalla's boy, who stood at the horse's head in the place which Sam should have occupied.

"You, Henery? Where's yer grandad?" asked Reuben.

Henry's already large upper lip swelled with the smile it dared not express. He ducked his head into his breast.

"Gran'fa's down in hes cabin," he answered.

That Sam was in his cabin, and why, was known to the smallest darky on the farm. Mrs. Grey, who was just within the door, packing a basket of fresh eggs for Sarah, stepped out to the porch. Her soft brow was puckered and her kind face troubled.

"Reuben," she said, "Sam didn't come to the house fer his dinner nor supper yestiddy, nor his breakfast to-day. I declare, it do worry me so. I can't bear to think of anything on this place bein' hungry."

Reuben laughed at her. "Mary, honey, you *air* so sof' 'bout them ol' negroes. Don't you bother 'bout Sam. Ain't there potatoes in the field, an' 'ain't he only got to dig 'em? Ain't the chickens walkin' round as tame, an' 'ain't he only got to knock 'em in the haid? Sam's a-takin' keer o' himse'f, don't you fret. Air you ready, Sarah?"

Sarah was waiting to bid Mrs. Grey a farewell piteous in its tearful resignation. Mrs. Grey patted her reassuringly on the shoulder with her motherly hand.

"Pick up heart, Sarah," she said; "an' come again some time when there ain't no reason at all fer it, jes to talk a bit."

This was her only reference to Sarah's trouble. The mountain folk can show a reserve fine and delicate as their cliff flowers.

Sarah climbed into the buggy, and, Reuben following her, they jogged down the road towards the unbroken line of green trees that wound through the farms, marking the river-course.

"When Sam and I was boys," said Reuben Grey, thoughtfully, talking half to himself and half to Sarah, "I kin jes remember worryin' for a whippin', an' my mother warn't one to spare the rod neither. Many's the hot switch Sam and me stood up to together. She generally licked us in pa'rs; fur ef one was bad, she could be pretty nigh shore the other put him up to it, ef he didn't do more. But there war times when I'd get kinder tired, an' didn't want ter go on bein' bad; but havin' got

started, I warn't goin' to stop short o' a lickin',
an' then I jes wearied fer it before it come to
halt me up. I use' t' think, Why on airth don't
they hurry up an' lick me an' make me stop? I
kin remember thinkin' that as well! It's helped me a lot in dealin' with folks sence, Sarah.
It's kinder made me tol'rant when they're too
outrageous. I jes think 'bout them ol' days,
an' my blessed ol' mother, an' that dear ol'
peach-orchard back the house, full o' switches,
an' then I says to myself, 'Don't you be too
ha'sh, Reuben; all that pore soul wants is a
good lickin';' an' then, ef I kin, I up an' give it
to him, sometimes one way, sometimes another. Now, Sarah, you come along here with
me; I got somethin' to show yer before yer go
home."

They had entered the green belt edging the
river. The trees, arching over the road, framed
in the ford and the farther bank, where the
broken road rose again out of the water. Near
the ford, set in the dingle, stood Sam's cabin
with its sulkily closed door. Reuben Grey
flung the reins over the back of his mare, and
drew from its socket the stubby whip.

"W'o', Molly," he said.

Molly stood quiet while her master descended, followed by Sarah, wonderingly. Reuben
walked straight to Sam's cabin. He lifted the
butt of his whip as if to beat upon the door,
then changed his mind.

"Sam," he called, in a quick monosyllable; "Sam!"

As if drawn by an invisible string, an unwilling, shuffling step approached the door, which opened a crack. A white, rolling eyeball peered out. Reuben made an impatient side motion with his head, and the door swung wide, exposing a figure that might have come off the end of a haymaker's fork. Sam's clothing, never neat, was that of a scarecrow; his gray locks were a tousle. He stood with his dark lips swelled out, his head thrust forward, his shifty eyes opening and shutting sulkily. The little white goatee that stuck out from the side of his chin was as crooked as his temper. Reuben scanned him over.

"Well, Sam," he said, "you do look—"

Sam swallowed resentfully, drawing his features closer together after the manner of a terrapin retiring into its shell.

"You see this, Sam," said Reuben, raising the whip he held. Sam drew back a step, blinking. Reuben went on sternly: "What I'm standin' here considerin' is ef I ain't called on right now to haul yer out o' there an' give yer the worst lickin' yer ever had sence yer was a boy. 'Tain't as ef I was hankerin' to do it; it's kinder hot to be whippin' to-day. But I don't seem able to decide ef I ain't neglectin' a dooty in parsin' it by. There's jes one thing yer kin be shore of, though: ef, when I come out from town, I stop here an' *do* fin' yer in this cabin, hot nor nothin' else won't help yer. Min', I ain't sayin' I ain't goin' to lick yer anyhow; but ef yer are here when I come out, why, it 'll be right then an' there, an' with this very whip, yer 'll get your lickin'." He cut the stock through the air in emphasis. "I'm goin' to hev peace, an' nothin' else, on this yere farm."

Reuben's whip punctuated forcibly for him once more as he stalked away. He did not deign to turn his head as he moved to his buggy; but Sarah, following with less dignity, saw Sam's exit from the cabin. At a right angle to his master's footsteps, with the swift, loping run of his race, which even in his age he retained, Sam was making for the shelter of the house.

"Look, Mr. Grey," said Sarah. Reuben looked, and a smile in which there was no surprise and no unkind triumph spread over his features.

"Sarah," he said, stopping short to speak, "what did I tell yer? Don't you see how the price o' peace may be wa-ar, honey, may be wa-ar?"

Peace had indeed returned to the farm when Reuben came back from his journey to Riverton. The river was sparkling in the sun, his own fields lay smiling before him, Sam was crooning over his work, and Mrs. Grey wore her most placid face. But Reuben himself was disturbed. All through the day this disturbance grew upon him, and late in the afternoon it found utterance.

"Mary," he said, "I'm jes thinkin' I'm goin' to ask yer to make supper a' hour earlier this afternoon. I'm considerin' goin' back to Riverton. I feel kinder worried 'bout Sarah an' Dan'l Whip."

Mrs. Grey laid down her knitting to look up. "Why, Reuben, it ain't like you to be interferin' with man an' wife. What kin you do ef Dan'l chooses to beat Sarah, and Sarah lets him?"

"It don't seem like I could do nothin'," answered Reuben; "but I reckon I'd like supper early, Mary."

"Didn't you say Dan'l Whip warn't onpleasant this mornin'?"

"He was pleasant enough, all but his eyes. He was settin' there, workin' away on his spinnin'-wheels. He didn't say nothin' at all 'bout Sarah runnin' off last night. I'd 'a' liked it better ef he had. I reckon I'll have supper early, Mary."

There was a mild obstinacy about Reuben which his wife rarely opposed. Before dusk he was on his way to Riverton, and he reached the village by the time the lamps began to shine through the windows into the streets. Checking his mare before the town store, Reuben tied her at the horse-rack in company with half a dozen other nags and buggies of similar dilapidation. As he entered the store, ever more or less crowded, answering to the club of a higher civilization, his advent was loudly welcomed; but on this occasion Reuben confessed himself hurried. He ordered a list of groceries, to be packed in his buggy against his return, thus giving explanation for his visit to the populace waiting to receive this statement as their due. His account rendered, he was more free for his mission, which led him at once to Daniel Whip's home. The Whip cottage stood a little apart from the village, on a side road.

"Here 't is," said Reuben to himself, as he reached the house and paused before it thoughtfully. All the shutters were closed, but a bright light from within came streaming through the cracks.

"Was it the lef' side Mary said?" murmured Reuben, hesitating on the road. "Yes, 'twas the lef'."

He walked softly to the left side of Daniel Whip's house. There, towards the bottom of one of the windows, a broader band of light burst through the shutter, from which a slat was missing.

"Lyddy must ha' seen real well. There warn't no reason she shouldn't," thought Reuben, as he bent his head and looked into the house.

The one lamp, which was in the centre of the supper-table, lighted the small room brilliantly. The china on the shelves, Daniel Whip's half-finished wheels in the corner, his tools near by—everything, in fact, except Whip himself—Reuben could see plainly. Directly opposite the window, at the head of the supper-table, sat Sarah.

"White and scared as a rabbit," sighed Reuben to himself. He looked at the supper, and thought that the poor soul must have made an effort to have it especially good. A high-backed arm-chair was placed opposite Sarah, with its back to the window where Reuben stood. There, he judged, the master of the house must be; for dish after dish was deprecatingly pushed by Sarah towards this chair, and they seemed to disappear in its recesses. Sarah's own plate lay face down before her; she had not so much as turned it over.

No word was being spoken. To the genial soul at the window this was the darkest feature. Finally, the dishes which had been disappearing full into the chair began to come back empty, and Sarah rose to clear the table. She went to her work slowly, with faltering footsteps. When all the dishes had been taken away, she seemed to hesitate, and stood with the centre crease of the cloth held in her fingers for a full minute before she jerked it off.

There was still no sign of life from Daniel

that Reuben could see. Close by the window stood the dresser. As Sarah approached it to open the drawer and lay the cloth away, Reuben was looking through the broken slat full into her despairing face. She was standing quite still, listening, and he held his breath lest she should hear him. At that moment came a sound that blanched the woman's cheeks and made the watcher's back crawl. It was Daniel Whip scrambling up on the table. Reuben could not see him, for Sarah blocked his view ; but he could imagine him standing there, with his " watermelon head," his " squeeched - up eyes," his "humped-together body," the cruel strap ready in his hand. He knew Sarah was mentally seeing the same sight ; for her figure was bent despairingly, and it seemed to Reuben that she was looking out through the broken shutter straight into his eyes, while her eyes were growing fixed and strange. Her lips were moving.

"Lord help her !" thought Reuben ; "she's prayin' !"

Suddenly Sarah's eyes lighted up ; a dash of bright red came over her cheek - bones. She wheeled so abruptly that Reuben Grey started back. He heard a scuffle, one rabbit-like cry, and when he regained his post of observation Daniel Whip was not on the table.

Sarah was standing by the arm-chair, looking down into its recesses. She held a heavy leather strap in her hand, and spoke in a high, excited voice, mechanically as a parrot.

"Well, Dan'l Whip, you do look!" She went on rapidly, yet as one feeling for words. The thong was raised waveringly.

"You see this, Dan'l? What I'm standin' here considerin' is ef I ain't called on right now to haul yer outer there an' give yer the worst lickin' yer 've had sence—sence—I mean a worse lickin' than you ever give me with this strop. 'Tain't as ef I was hankerin' to do it; it's kinder hot to be whippin' ter-day; but I don't seem able to decide ef I ain't neglectin' my dooty in parsin' it by. Min', I don' say I ain't goin' to lick yer anyhow; but there's jes one thing you kin be shore of: ef I ketch yer again on this table, hot nor nothin' else won't help yer. It 'll be right then and there, an' with this very thong yer 'll get yer lickin'."

She made the strap whistle through the air as she spoke, and jumped herself at the sound, but went on doggedly:

"I'm goin' to have peace, an' nothin' else, on this here farm—house, I mean."

The thong whistled again in her hand; but this time Sarah seemed to find a certain pleasure in the sound, for she repeated it, looking from the stinging lash to the chair.

"Dan'l Whip," she cried, suddenly, "don't you dare to speak or move! Yes, yer may squeeze back in your chair, and stare yer eyes outer your head. This thong's better to hear than to feel, as I can tell yer. I said I warn't hankerin' to use it on yer, but 'deed I don't know. Now I'm at the right end o' it fer once, I do seem to feel as ef five or six good licks— now 'tain't no use your sayin' a word, Dan'l Whip; sure 's yer do, I'll light right in, an' ef I get started, I ain't sayin' I *could* stop."

Reuben Grey, at the window, was clinging to the sill in dismay. Sarah had been like some dumb brute unconscious of its strength. Now that she had learned her power, it was sweet. The weight of an awful responsibility settled on Reuben's shoulders. Sarah was slapping the strap across her palm thoughtfully.

"When I grabbed you off the table jes now, and chucked you back in that chair, an' yanked this thong outer yer han', Dan'l Whip, what I meant to say by it was this: I ain't never goin' to walk roun' that table to be licked no more, not one time; but I can't be shore 'bout lickin' you now with this thong—I'm kinder 'fraid of breakin' yer. You ain't big, like I am. I'm just wonderin' how yer ma ever done it 'thout killin' yer."

A sudden thought seemed to strike Sarah. Her face cleared; she turned away, and laid the strap on the high mantel-shelf. "Dan'l," she said, returning to stand and look down from her height into the chair, "I've made up my min' clean. I ain't ever goin' ter lick yer with that thong. It's too crool, an' you so little." Her tone grew almost affectionate. "I know jes how crool it is. Ef leather didn't smell so etarnal bad burnin', I'd th'o' the thing in the fire once fer all. What I'm studyin' over now is, ef I oughtn't to do yer jes as your ma mus' ha' done yer many a time when you got yer ugly tempers on—jes like I'd do my own chile ef I had one. I'm considerin' turning you right over my knee an' spankin' yer good ; that couldn't do yer no harm, and it might—ach ! Don't you speak a word, Dan'l Whip !"

Reuben Grey withdrew from the window as softly as he had come. He stepped from the house to the road, and with the same unnecessarily cautious step he crossed the town, seeking his mare and buggy at the horse - rack. Then he carefully counted over the packages of groceries, to find the number correct. As he drove down the road from Riverton, Reuben Grey was whistling softly and happily to himself.

Whether Sarah decided to spank or to spare Daniel Whip, he had no curiosity to learn. "Anyhow," he ruminated, "he knows now she kin and may, an' that's the whole p'int."

AN ECHO

"WHY *doubt* my soul, why *doubt* Je-ho-vah's a-aid?"

trolled out a rich voice.

"That's not a drinking song, Ewey," said the young foreman.

The mocking notes rolled out again:

"Thy God, the God of bat-tles, still sha-all *prove!*"

The foreman struck his hand on the man's shoulder.

"Hold your tongue, Ewey! Aren't those negroes enough? Hear them howl. Powers! what a night!"

"I was preaching to them, sir," answered Ewey.

"It sounded more like blasphemy. Nothing will quiet them until this storm passes over. Hello, that was a close call! There go the electric lights. The current's cut off."

A piercing flash of white light had split the heavens, followed by a crash, beneath which the earth seemed to crouch. The furnace and furnace-shed, brilliantly lit by artificial light a moment before, were left in total darkness, from the depths of which came the trampling of hurried feet, howls of mingled fear and excitement from negro throats, answered by shouts of derision from the white laborers.

"We shall have a stampede here if this keeps up," said the foreman.

The rain, driven by the wind, slapped as a flat hand on the roof and the sides of the shed. The lightning and thunder seemed to know no before or after. Within the shed, torches carried on high by their bearers wandered aimlessly about here and there, dropping a trail of sputtering fire behind them. Each vivid electric flash was greeted by another howl from the negroes, drowned the next moment by the thundering cloud-bursts. In the intermittent light the young foreman could see the dim outline of the huddled figures in the shed, the movements of those who held torches, and, above him, looming up in the gloom like a mountain-side, the huge bulk of the furnace.

"This might be the scene of the Crucifixion," he said, half aloud. "'There was a darkness over all the earth — and the earth did quake, and the rocks rent.'"

Ewey glanced about him. With a coarse oath he assented easily. The foreman turned and looked at him.

"Are you all ready for the midnight cast?" he said, shortly.

"All up, sir."

"Then find a torch and light it. We may as well sit here in this corner until the storm passes."

The oil-torch which Ewey found and possessed himself of by right of might was already lit and in the hand of a passing workman. He stuck the flambeau in a crevice of the wall, where it guttered and gasped in the wind, smelling horribly. The storm was a trifle farther off. The electric lights were reviving, but the corner where the two men settled down was remote and lighted only by the torch.

The foreman sat on the edge of a wheelbarrow, his knees crossed and nursed in his hands. As Ewey flung himself on the ground at his feet he looked down at him carelessly, observing the brawny figure, the knotted hands and over-developed shoulders of the day-laborer.

"Here comes Zanny as if fire were after her," said Ewey.

A large white and yellow cat came bounding out of the darkness into the circle of torch-light. She sprang to the knee of the young foreman, nestling close against him and purring loudly.

"Poor Zanthippe is as scared as the negroes," he said, stroking her. "Did the last litter of kittens go the way of the others, Ewey?"

"Bones and all, sir. The rats eat the kittens,

and she eats the rats. She's a cannibal, is Zanny."

He stretched out his hand coaxingly as he spoke, and the furnace cat descending, curled into his arms, rubbing her head against him. The young foreman, forgetting both man and beast, was looking out at the storm through an open panel in the opposite wall of the shed.

"When I was a child," he said, simply, "I used to think that God had a gold carpet on His floor, and when the heavens cracked open, as now, the gold showed through."

Ewey, resting his head against a block of wood, softening his pillow with his interlocked fingers and the palms of his hands, was looking out at the storm also.

"Why doubt, my soul, why doubt Jehovah's a-aid?"

he hummed softly.

"Where did you learn that?" said the foreman.

"At home," answered the workman, still gazing out into the storm abstractedly, and lifting one hand to stroke the cat's long back. "At home. My father made his choir sing that every Sunday until his congregation kicked."

The foreman started. "His choir—his congregation?"

Ewey looked up quickly from under his contracted brows.

"Humph!" he said, half-humorously. "I

thought I had gone beyond a storm's loosing my tongue, but it seems not. That's all true enough, as it's said; but my father and his choir and his congregation are facts that don't seem to dovetail exactly with his son, do they?"

"Your father was a clergyman?"

"Yes."

They were both silent. For the first time the foreman noted his workman's clean, closely cut hair, his crisply curling beard and mustache, the whiteness of the muscular chest exposed by the carelessly loosened red shirt, the rough beauty of his features, and wondered why all this had never struck him before.

"You are an Englishman, are you not?" said the foreman.

"Yes, I am English."

"Was your father a Dissenter, or of the Established Church?"

Ten minutes before, he would not have believed Ewey could have understood the wording of this sentence.

"The Established Church? Oh yes. Dissenters are rarely men of position in England."

"Then your father—" began the foreman. He checked himself.

Ewey rolled over on his side and looked up at his superior.

"What do you want to know?" He held up three fingers as he spoke. "There is my story

—a rule-of-three. Given, a younger son of a younger son of an impoverished younger son. Result—a poor devil worth thirteen and a half cents an hour, working eleven hours a day one week and thirteen hours by night the next, and twenty-four hours at a stretch in the long turn every other week. This on three meals a day, composed of tin - pail for breakfast, ditto for dinner, ditto for supper. If you want to make money invent a cheap metal that doesn't taint the honest laborer's food."

The grossness of speech and accent usual to him had partially fallen off. He spoke with those careful inflections and the trained voice that belong to an Englishman of refinement. His companion, looking with the eyes of an imaginative man into the mocking face before him, saw it as the blurred photograph of a finely cut original. He recognized that the defiant blue eyes might once have been only dare-devil and merry, the figure, now over-developed by toil, once that of the trained athlete, the too serpentine poise of the head, spirited and aristocratic.

"Having known a life utterly different," said the foreman, "how do you stand the laborer's world? I won my present position by a six-months' novitiate as a workman; but if I had not known that the theoretical knowledge in my head was there as a ladder by which to climb out, I could never have stood it. You have no such hope ahead. How can you stand it ?"

The workman stretched himself out on his back again and laughed.

"Why not? It's exciting work. Battle, murder, and sudden death are all here. Besides, at a moment I can quit and go away from this as I came ; or at any time I can crook my elbow with the boys and forget it all."

He raised his hand to his mouth and flung his head back suggestively.

"I suspended you for that last month," said the foreman. "If I had known all this I should perhaps have been more lenient."

Ewey raised his hand quickly.

"I want no favor. You think me unhappy, don't you? I am not. I was never unhappy but once in my life. Then every night for three weeks I decided to cut my throat, and every morning I woke up laughing."

He stopped and laughed again, winking his face as in keen enjoyment of some memory.

"I was *held* for twenty-one days," he said.

"In prison ?"

"No—in the 'tangles of Neæra's hair.' Do you happen to know 'Lycidas'?"

"I know that it is by Milton," said the foreman, wondering.

"I have the advantage of you. I know 'Lycidas' by heart. It was my father's favorite poem, and he made me learn it as a punishment for pinning a towel to his surplice at the back. I have enjoyed many advantages. I suppose you never had the advantage of finding yourself in the streets of London—without a penny in your pocket either?"

"No," said the young foreman, gently. "I have never been abroad."

He was choosing his words carefully lest he should jar an atmosphere in which the man before him had for a time returned to first conditions, and flowed into his proper level as naturally as water obeying its law.

This foreman had only known Ewey previously as a workman who looked him straight in the eye, on whom he could ever depend in a crisis, and to whom he spoke rarely, save to issue an order, then with shortness and decision. He knew now that this last had been an unconscious recognition of inability to obtain obedience, except of Ewey's choice.

"London is not a nice place to find yourself in at night when you haven't a penny," said Ewey. "I suppose I lost my head a little or Neæra wouldn't have caught me; still, I was pretty green. I think I was the oldest and the youngest and the greenest and the wickedest of the honored sons of my college when I ran away from Alma Mater."

"You are a college graduate?"

"Not much! I ran away, anticipating a less voluntary exit. But I took my humble degree in college opinion as a *tumbler*. I was the best there. A travelling circus accepted me greedily as such. This thunder to-night is a murmur to the applause I caught at the performances. The manager doubled my salary in the first month."

"And did no one recognize you ?"

"Oh no ; besides, I got tired of the life as I shall of this, and ran away again before long."

" To what ?"

"Everything. A tumbler knows how to fall on his feet. I had no particular trouble—until I met Neæra."

He laughed again, burying his hand in the cat's soft fur, drawing it between his fingers as he rambled on easily through his story.

"I met Neæra in London. I had about come to the end of things then. I thought I might as well go home for a time and take breath. But I came in on one side of London at ten o'clock at night ; home lay miles out on the other side. My money gave out with my supper. I suppose you have camped out under hedges ?"

"Oh yes," said the young foreman ; "many times when a boy."

" I had been on the tramp for days, but if I didn't long for a hedge to roll under that night ! I thought the population of London must be policemen. I never sat down but one came along. My feet were so sore I could hardly move. I felt as though I had scrubbed them off tramping and was walking on the raw stumps. I have thought I was tired here on the twenty - four hour turn sometimes, but when I remember that night I feel as fresh as paint."

The young foreman's mind went harking back to some "long turns" he had himself known. He shook his head.

"I have never known greater weariness than the long turn myself," he said. "In the last six hours of one I have sometimes ceased to care if I lived or died. Where did you go finally?"

"Straight to Neæra's tangles. I was crawling along at a limp when I saw an old church near me with stone buttresses. I decided that it might do to creep behind one of them, where I could sit with my head on my knees, and sleep. I squeezed in behind the stones, and was just about to crouch down in the corner, when I struck against something soft that said, 'O—ouch!' It was Neæra."

"A woman?"

"A woman, and a clever one, I tell you. Just as she screeched I heard the patrolman's steps outside, so I clapped my hand over her mouth and held her. When he had gone I said, 'My dear, I am very sorry to disturb you, but you will have to share your quarters, such as they are, and I hope I haven't hurt you—I didn't

mean to ; I only wanted the officer to get by.'
Then I took my hand from her mouth and let
her go. I thought she would yell again, but
she didn't. She only said, quite coolly, that I
was welcome and no offence taken. I thought
she seemed like a good-natured, sensible girl,
so I told her as we were both in the same hole,
and that not a very big one, two heads being
better than one, perhaps we might find a way
out of it. 'I'm not a London man,' I said,
'so I know none of the tricks of the trade. Is
there any place here where people can sleep
for nothing?' I knew one trick by heart before
she got through with me !

" 'Yes,' she said, after a minute, 'there is a
place, but they wouldn't let you or me in.'

" 'Why not?' I asked.

" 'Well, it's only for married people.'

" 'Come right along,' I said; 'who'll know
whether we are married or not?'

" 'Oh yes, they will know, too,' said she.
'They always ask, and you wouldn't lie about
it, would you?'

" 'I'd do more than that for a spot to lie down
on,' I said. 'Where is the place?'

" 'Round the corner from here ; but you'd
have to do more than lie and more than I'll
do. They'd make us both *swear* to it before
they'd let us in.'

" I was so worn out, my knees were like water
and my head swam. 'Come on,' I said, 'I'm

game for that, too. Come on, like a good girl now.' And, if you believe me, I thought I had a hard time persuading her to it.

"When we got to the house, she leading the way, we were taken to a kind of office, and there I swore, by all I held, or didn't hold, holy, that Neæra was my wife, and that I, Hugh ——, never mind the rest, was named Joseph Daw."

"Then your Christian name is Hugh ——, not Ewey?" said the foreman.

"Hugh, Hughie—'Ugh, Ewey. It depends entirely on your station in life. The circus people over there called me ''Ughy.' It stuck, somehow, and crossed the water with me in another spelling.

"Well, to go on, the matron of the place took Neæra off with her down a long corridor, and a janitor carried me off down another long corridor into a room full of beds with sleeping men in them. He pointed out an empty bed to me and I tumbled in, thinking it the easiest-earned bunk I ever slept in. It didn't seem to me that I had been asleep for ten minutes before somebody shook my shoulder and woke me. Then I saw that it was early morning, and the men around me were dragging themselves out of their beds. A tall man, with round spectacles and a big nose, had his hand on me.

"'Joseph Daw,' he said —'Joseph Daw.

That's your name, isn't it?'   I was about to say it wasn't, when he added, 'You came in last night late, didn't you?'

"Then I remembered, and thanked the Lord I hadn't spoken, and that he had told me my name, which I couldn't have told him then for my neck.

"'Yes, sir,' I said.

"'Then your wife is doing very well, and you have a fine boy.'"

"What!" exclaimed the foreman.

Ewey beat his hand upon the ground in an ecstasy of enjoyment.   The tears started from his eyes, which were screwed up with laughter.

"That's what I said," he cried, between his gasps.   "And the doctor ('twas he who came to tell me) laughed in my face and went out."

"Ewey," said the foreman, "you don't mean—"

"Yes, I do," answered Ewey.   "Did you ever hear of anything as clever as that woman?   I sat up on the side of my bed and thought it was a nightmare.   I suppose I must have looked queer, for the man from the next bed asked me if I were sick.

"'Yes,' I answered, 'powerful sick.   Look here—don't tell I asked you—but what sort of a place is this, anyway?'

"'How did you get here if you don't know?' he said.   'It's a Maternity Hospital.'

"'A Maternity Hospital!   Then what are

you and I doing here?' He looked at me with his head on one side.

"'Say, you must have been mighty drunk when you came in last night,' said he. 'We're here to work out the doctor's bill and the medicines and the board for the missus and the kid.'"

The foreman burst into irrepressible laughter.

"Ewey," he cried, "I don't believe one word of it. You are making up this story as you tell it."

"So help me! I'm not. That morning I saw the name in big gold letters over the door in the sunlight, and I saw the iron gate and the iron railings around the grounds, too. I can see them now. There I was, and there I had to stay, breaking stones for that hussy and her baby's board for twenty-one days. Afraid to say a word, I was. She fixed that the first thing. They let me go in to see her 'for just a minute,' they said, and showed me the baby. O Lord, it was awful! She lay there watching me like a crab. I just said one word to her through my teeth when I bent my head down over her to fool the nurse. 'You little fiend!' said I.

"'You perjurer!' says she. 'It's ten years for perjury, you know. You swore you were my husband!'

"I was scared out of saying another word. I

didn't know what the law was. There I stayed, sir, all those twenty-one days, mad enough to kill her and myself one minute, and my insides all tickled with laughter the next. If it had only been breaking stones, that wouldn't have been so bad, but they let me, *let* me, as a favor, clean myself up to sit by the bed and see her and the baby ! That was what took the man out of me."

"And you both played it out to the end ?"

"To the end, sir."

Ewey had been gradually dropping back more and more into the manner and the vernacular of the workman.

The storm was now farther off, the lightning less vivid, the thunder more muttering than threatening. The cat, stretching her legs and arching her back, disengaged herself from her human comrades, walking off with stiff tail. The tenseness of the atmosphere was relaxing, the vague echo of a past which had waked momentarily in the workman was dying also.

"When that twenty-one days ended," he said, "we walked out of the door side by side as man and wife down the long plank - walk to the iron gate of the grounds, she carrying the baby. I saw her watching and watching me, and putting her fingers to her eyes. When we got to the gate, says she, ' Jo,' with a sniffle, ' hold the baby a minute. I want to get my handkerchief out of my pocket.'

"'All right,' I said, real sweetly. I was watching the man at the gate. I began to hold out my arms slowly like, but just as the gate opened I made one dash. I never stopped running for miles. I could hear her calling after me. She may be standing there calling yet—"

An impatient voice from the other side of the furnace broke in:

" Here you, Ewey," it growled, " I want you to quit your lying round, sharp, and give a hand on this sledge."

It was the furnace-keeper, known as Rocky Mountain, from his birthplace and his nature. The cinder was ready to be tapped from the furnace. The other helpers were at work at the cinder-notch. Ewey moved leisurely, slouching to his feet with a carelessness which did not conceal the enormous power of his muscular and nervous force. Rocky Mountain was not apt to "fool" with Ewey. Once, in a fit of rage, the latter had chased the keeper from the "pig-bed" with a red-hot crow-bar, and the circumstance was not forgotten by either.

"Comin'," answered Ewey, easily. "Good-night, sir."

He stepped to the other side of the furnace, where a volley of abuse greeted him, which he answered in kind—and more. The foreman listened, still sitting thoughtfully in his corner. The busy life of the furnace was again resumed in preparation for the midnight cast. He could hear Rocky Mountain growling and swearing at his helpers as usual. Under his directions the drill, which was to pick open the tapping-hole and let loose the molten iron, now ready and white-hot inside the great crater, was being rammed backward and forward in regular strokes by a number of men.

They began to sing in a rude melody, keeping time. Most of the singers were negroes, but a white man's mocking voice, which the foreman recognized, was leading them. He improvised, singing a line alone, which the rest caught up in chorus:

" Rocky Mountain *grumbling !*"

sang Ewey, clearly; and the negroes followed, gutturally:

" Rocky Mountain *grum*-mer-lin !
Yes, Lord !
Rocky Mountain *grum*-mer-lin !
Yes, Lord ! *Drive* her in !"

Again the solo:

" Better quit your grumbling !"

Chorus:

"Yes, Lord ! Better quit your *grum*-mer-lin !
Drive her in !"

Solo (high and derisive):

" Ewey, he's a-coming !"

AN ECHO

Chorus again :

> " Yes, Lord !"

Solo :

> " His *crow - bar* in his hand !"

This sally died away amid roars of laughter. The foreman rose and walked to the tapping-hole.

Ewey, his arms and chest bared, was working at the drill, his great muscles moving with power and regularity.

"One muck of a hole, boss. She's clean through to the other side," he said, coarsely, and with an oath added.

He was the workman only. His fellows laughed again. The young foreman looked long at him, and did not reply.

"God only knows whether Hugh or Ewey is the real man," he thought, as he turned away; but in his heart he believed that it was and had ever been *Ewey*.

G

"THROW up the left—jump with the right. Throw up the right — jump with the left," chanted Madame Jeanne in time with the music; and herself suiting the action to the word, she sprang high and twirled low before her pupils with the most surprising agility; for Madame Jeanne was no longer young.

"Oh no, no !" cried she, still with the music and looking back over her shoulder at her imitators, who paused in confusion. "It is Mrs. Schuyler who is all wrong again."

The music stopped as madame hurried to seize one of the breathless dancers by the waist, drawing her into proper position.

"Here is the trouble," said Madame Jeanne, reproachfully. "You have left your corsets on again."

Mrs. Schuyler reddened and released herself with a petulant little wriggle of vexation.

"I can't help it, madame. I can't, indeed. I feel too disconnected without them."

"As you will," said madame, with a shrug.

"Come on, ladies — music again. Throw up the left — jump with the right."

After all, it mattered very little if that class never learned its skirt-dance. It was to them but a new amusement, a freak, an excuse to buy a gaudy costume with queer, blunt-toed slippers and round, fluttering skirts. The only good that could ever come of these lessons might be a little added grace and a little healthy exercise.

"The rich have queer fancies," thought madame, as she wove out the figures before her class; but then, their money was as good as that of the professional dancers she taught, and if they liked spending it so, why, throw up the left — jump with the right. It was all one to madame.

So madame thought, and Mrs. Schuyler was perhaps the only one of the class who understood and half resented the retired artiste's unconscious contempt of these amateurs. In her day Madame Jeanne had been a celebrity; but now, with her own gray hair uncovered and her once *beaux yeux* hid behind round spectacles, she leaped and bounded in her incongruous gauze and spangles before large classes of both professionals and amateurs.

"The old thing actually dignifies her profession," thought Mrs. Schuyler, with a smile. "Well, I suppose it is a good thing. I almost wish I had a profession. How glad she is to be rid of us."

The clock had struck, and madame moved with waving arms and tripping feet to the head of the room, where she stood kissing her hand and courtesying low to each pupil as she filed out.

"Ah, my dear little Fairy !" cried madame, in a new voice, springing forward. "Come, come ; I am ready for you."

Mrs. Schuyler, who had been the last to move, looked back to see a little girl enter the room and run to madame, flinging her arms about the old dancer's neck. Madame Jeanne embraced her pupil with equal effusion. She was a pretty little thing about seven years old, with a vain, foolish little face, as much in keeping with her spangles and tulle as madame's appearance was out of harmony with hers. Mrs. Schuyler was moved to look, in the dressing-room glass, at her own black and pink voluminous gauzes, comparing them with her face.

"It suits, and it does not," she decided. "I am not so frivolous as I look."

In her heart there was anything but frivolity. She was, in fact, waiting for the pain which clutched her weak back to subside before she began to dress for the street. Not for worlds would she have confessed that the strong corset she obstinately wore was clung to as a support. The relief its clasp gave her might be temporary, injurious in the end, but the pain without that artificial strength was more than she could bring herself to endure. Perhaps, after all, this exercise was bad for her; still she would try it a little longer, as she had tried everything else.

She was in no hurry. The rest of the class, laughing and chatting, were in process of change from butterfly raiment to more or less severe street costumes. Some had already gone, but Mrs. Schuyler was still idling.

"Over again—over again—over; fine, fine, my Fairy!" came from behind the curtained door which led to the dancing-hall, and Mrs. Schuyler peeped in through the folds.

The little pupil was turning like a wheel about the room on hands and feet. Madame's eyes gleamed behind her glasses; she was clapping her hands.

"Poor little dot!" murmured Mrs. Schuyler.

"I'm tired," said the child, bounding to her feet at last. She walked to the side of the room and there leaned into the arms of another child who had sat watching her—a small boy not very much older than herself, but with an elderly little face. The protecting air with which he received the younger child was positively maternal.

"They should both be in their beds by now," thought Mrs. Schuyler.

The boy's face troubled her somehow. It was as a familiar sight to her, or reminded her of well-known features. Yet she could not place him. He was oddly dressed in a fantastic plaid suit, ill-made and ill-fitting, which added to the uneasiness of his unchildlike look. The private class, passing out in groups, paused at the hall door outside to watch the little professional. Madame was proud to show off her pupil.

"You will hear from Fairy," she said, complacently. "She has great talent—jump higher, little one—higher. An audience helps her, you see—higher." Mrs. Schuyler could hear the applause and the thoughtlessly open flattery of the child.

"Poor little dot!" she thought again. "I wonder if she has a mother."

She glanced into the room once more and then turned resolutely away. She had never liked to watch children since the hour she learned that the delicate little blossom she had held in the hollow of her arm for one short day was the only bloom she might ever expect. She was herself too delicate a plant to flower and live. Whenever she was reminded of that one brief day the pain at her heart was so great as to make her vow forgetfulness, and so, as she had taught herself to do, she turned from the sight of the children in the dancing-hall and went back to her toilet. She was alone in the dressing-room when she was finally ready to leave, and as she passed out she paused involuntarily to watch the lesson, which was still in progress.

"You are careless," madame was saying, severely. "Now do all that over again."

"The music's wrong," fretted the child.

"The music is right. Drop that handkerchief behind you and pick it up again."

Madame stamped her foot and the child whimpered, but, as she was bidden, dropped the handkerchief behind her close to her heels, and bent backward to reach it with her hand thrust over her head until it seemed to Mrs. Schuyler the little spine must break.

"Oh, but that must hurt her," she cried, advancing; "and she's such a baby."

Madame laughed.

"That—that's nothing. I could pick up the handkerchief in a flash before I grew old. You like it, don't you, my pet? and you did it beautifully this time."

The child sprang into madame's arms and was caressed.

"Where is the boy?" asked Mrs. Schuyler.

"There," said madame, pointing to the window.

A boy of the same size as the one Mrs. Schuyler had seen was standing at the window, peering with childish interest into the street where the carriages were passing.

"That's not the same child," said Mrs. Schuyler; "he has on a tweed suit, and the little boy I saw was dressed in plaid.   Where is he?"

"Here," cried madame, laughing, "show the lady the front of your trousers."

The little boy obediently came forward at her call, his head hanging, his face scarlet. Madame laughed loudly with unthinking cruelty.

"His mamma," she explained, "is very poor. She had those remnants, each only enough for half a suit, so she asked him if he would rather have one leg of plaid and one of tweed, or have the back and the front of the trousers different; and he said he'd have it as it is, because then people might think he was two boys."

Mrs. Schuyler could not help smiling, but she looked at the abashed lashes lying on the boy's red cheeks, and sat down in a chair, drawing the child kindly into her arm.

"That's just what I did think.   I believed you were two boys.   You were a clever little fellow to choose so."

"His mother made the suit herself," said madame, in a laughing aside. "She doesn't sew well."

"The little girl is dressed very differently," answered Mrs. Schuyler, looking at the gorgeous spangles and expensive gauze decking the small creature.

Madame shrugged her shoulders.   "That's

another matter. The girl is a genius. She will support the whole family in time. She has danced in a few private houses and at a club dinner already. Between ourselves, the mother is a lazy piece. Any one may support her who will. She would never work."

"I would have scrubbed before I dressed the poor boy in that clown costume," murmured Mrs. Schuyler, indignantly. "It's cruelty to the child."

"Oh, he," said madame, lightly; "he is not the favorite. When the little girl is bad mamma whips him."

The aside was not with carefully lowered voice. Mrs. Schuyler saw the boy dart an ashamed look at her, saw his unchildlike gray eyes fall and his mouth twitch. Suddenly she recognized the likeness which had before caught her attention.

"What is your name?" she asked him.

"George," answered the child.

Mrs. Schuyler started. She turned quickly to the little girl, who hung back, but not with real shyness; that she had lost, if she had ever possessed it.

"My name's Fairy," she volunteered.

Mrs. Schuyler scanned the bold, foolish little face with keen eyes, and apparently did not find there what she sought, but her eyes fastened on a pair of gold armlets which held the short gauze sleeves in place.

"And who gave you these?" she asked, rising and touching the armlets.

The boy replied.

"They were father's once. He wore them put together as a watch-chain."

The color flew to Mrs. Schuyler's face.

"Where do these children come from? Who are they?" she asked Madame Jeanne, abruptly.

Madame walked to the side of the room, and from among the numberless pictures of posturing professionals and framed testimonials from managers and patrons, she selected one of the writings, which she brought to Mrs. Schuyler.

"Blood will tell," said madame. "This is from the manager of that child's grandmother. Ah, she could dance! I taught her all the last year before her début."

The testimonial was a half-jesting tribute to Madame Jeanne as a teacher, and was signed by a well-known manager. "Madame La Coste shows that she has been trained by a master-hand—or foot," the writing ended.

"That," said madame, with pride, pointing to the dancer's name—"that is my Fairy's grandmamma, Madame La Coste. You may have heard of her."

"And the child's mother?"

"She also is named La Coste—Sara La Coste."

"La Coste!" repeated Mrs. Schuyler.

Madame raised her eyebrows and turned to hang the testimonial on its nail.

"I never gossip, I never question. Sara is known to me by her mother's name only, and I teach the little one for the sake of her dead grandmamma. The children live not far from here. They come alone. The boy brings the girl."

Mrs. Schuyler hesitated for a moment, looking from one child to the other.

"I will take them home in my carriage," she said, suddenly, "if you will give me the address and if the lesson is over."

"As you will," said madame—thinking again "the rich have queer fancies."

Mr. Schuyler was standing before his dressing-room mirror, trying to fit an old-fashioned white peruke upon his head. His costume led up to the wig, which was the finishing-touch. A painted sketch of George III. in full court dress stood on the toilet-table as a model for frequent consultation. The masquerader, absorbed in his toilet, missed hearing a rap at his door, and started when it was more loudly repeated. The door opened before he could reply, and Mrs. Schuyler entered, starting back in turn as her husband faced her. He laughed and came forward, a man seemingly of rather serious mould for a masquerade. In his ordinary garb he was what might have been termed unimportant-looking, but he had a kindly, sympathetic face.

"Don't you remember it's 'Old Christmas'?" he said, pleasantly. "This is our night of misrule at the club. Do I look like a fool?"

He turned to the glass, and, receiving no answer, went on: "If I do, I suit the character of my namesake. I suppose George III. was a fool, wasn't he? '*What—what—what*'—that's my catch-word, isn't it?"

"Those are the very words I have come to say," replied Mrs. Schuyler. "Yes, I had forgotten 'Old Christmas.' George, I want to ask you a question. Did you ever see these before?"

Mr. Schuyler turned from the glass quickly.

"Dear, has anything happened?" he asked. "You look faint. I am afraid this dancing is bad for you. Sit here."

He rolled an easy-chair near her, and, as if accustomed to thus caring for her, drew his wife into it and arranged the cushions; only then would he turn to the armlets she still held out impatiently.

"These?" he said, taking the armlets from her. He lowered his voice and hesitated. "I gave these to you, dear, not long ago. You used them for a day."

"No—no," she cried, shrinking. "I have those laid away with the—the other things."

Mr. Schuyler turned the links over in his hand.

"Why, these belonged to James," he said. "We each had a pair exactly alike. They belonged to my mother and her twin - sister. James wore his as a watch - chain. See, here are the marks where they were riveted together."

"I thought I remembered your telling me so," said Mrs. Schuyler.

"How did you get them?" her husband asked.

She only replied, "Tell me something of James's life abroad."

Mr. Schuyler frowned slightly. "I think you know as much about it as I do. It is not a pleasant subject. He was too young to have lived abroad alone, but as the younger brother I could do nothing to prevent.it."

"Did he really marry the woman?"

"Yes, that was all regular, fortunately—or unfortunately."

"And her name?"

"Was Sara La Coste. She was the daughter of a French opera-dancer connected with an English company. James met her in London."

"Yes," said Mrs. Schuyler. "I thought that was the name. Go on."

"I can only tell you further that they went to Paris to live and were unhappy together.

They parted after a very few years. I am under the impression that James settled a small fortune upon her and left her. But I only know that he came home alone, and has been —I can't say delicate, but very reticent on the subject. And now tell me why you ask all this."

"First, had they children?"

"I don't know. I imagine so. James was, as I say, reticent over the whole matter. I asked him once if there were children, but as he chose to answer, foolishly, 'Oh, about a dozen or so,' I really don't know what is the truth."

"I know," said Mrs. Schuyler. "The woman still calls herself Sara La Coste. She is now in this city and very poor. There are two children, and I have them in the library downstairs. No, I am not raving," she laughed, in reply to her husband's anxious look. "I found the two children at Madame Jeanne's, and as soon as I learned their names and saw these armlets I believed I knew who they were, and so I have brought them straight home to you —a boy and a girl—our own nephew and niece. James can't know all that is happening. The girl is taking charity lessons from madame with a view to the stage and supporting her wretched mother. She has already danced in semipublic; and the boy—oh, I don't mind about the girl so much, she is like her mother, I know she is—but the boy is one of us ; so like you he might have been ours, and he has your name. James must have named him for you. The mother dresses the girl like a princess and the boy like a clown. He is pitiably neglected, and looks so cowed and wretched and ill-treated that he made my heart sick."

She broke down with an excited sob, and rising with a nervous movement looked into the dressing-table mirror. "Oh, why do women who don't deserve them or care for them have children? If I were only strong, George! Look at me now. With just a little excitement, a nervous wreck." She looked contemptuously at the reflection of her delicate face—"a piece of faded pink calico ; that is what I look like."

Her husband drew her back into her chair, his arm about her.

" Pink calico fits my needs better than brocade," he said, soothingly. " James tried the brocade."

" But I am so worthless. What do I make of my life or yours ?"

" You only make me perfectly happy," he answered. " Stop grieving, dearest ; am not I more to you than ten sons? Come, tell me more of the children. Do I understand you have stolen them ?"

" Yes, for the time I have. I wanted you to see them. James must be told at once. Something must be done. Come with me to the library and see the children yourself."

They went down the stairs together, and Mrs. Schuyler opened the door. Her husband paused at the threshold, looking in at the two children, who stared at him in turn.

" Do they look like the children of your brother, or like those of a circus-rider?" asked Mrs. Schuyler.

The little ones had thrown aside their outer wraps, and Mr. Schuyler uttered an exclamation as he looked at the two variegated costumes.

" The girl is as badly dealt with as the boy, if in another way," whispered Mrs. Schuyler.

" They are both a disgrace. If I can force him here, James shall see them just as we see them now—indecent little parroquets."

" But I am sure he cannot know."

Mr. Schuyler shook his head.

" You have more faith in James than I have. It is his place to know."

" Where shall you find him at this hour?"

Mr. Schuyler looked at his watch. " I'll find him at the club by now. He is their chosen king of misrule to-night—and his own every other night, I think. This is disgraceful!" He looked again at the children, whom he had not approached.

" I can't feel that they are of our blood," he said. " They look like little mountebanks."

"Not the boy," said Mrs. Schuyler, quickly.

"No," admitted Mr. Schuyler. "Not the boy, in spite of his clothing." He turned to the door, but his wife intercepted him.

"You must not leave them alone with me," she cried, tremulously. "The mother might be looking for them. Madame Jeanne would give her my address. I am not able to face a scene. Take the children with you. You can leave them in the carriage outside the club and bring James out to them."

"Will they go with me?" asked Mr. Schuyler.

"Oh yes," she replied, sorrowfully. "They came with me unquestioningly. They obey any one who orders them, just as little poor children do. Do take them with you."

Mr. Schuyler still hesitated.

"There is just the chance that they are not James's children, after all. It seems a risk to run off yet farther with them. I am not as adventurous a spirit as you are," he added, smiling. "I shall never die with my boots on, as you probably will."

"They must belong to James," insisted Mrs. Schuyler. "Don't you see how like you the boy is? It makes my heart ache to look at him."

"Yes, he is like me. I suppose I must follow your plan. If the mother should pursue us tell her I am taking the children back to her. Give

me her address, by the way, for if James dis-
owns them or will not take them, they must
go back to their mother, I suppose."

"How hardly you judge James," Mrs. Schuyler interrupted. "If they are 'his he will of
course take them. James likes me better than
he does you. Tell him it was I who found the
children, and I who sent them to him. Tell
him they are an Old Christmas gift from me
to him."

Mr. Schuyler did not understand children ;
he was always shy with them, and having none
of his own he was ignorant of their needs. It
was, therefore, a somewhat serious matter to
him to look across the carriage at his two
strange charges, sitting obediently on the narrow seat opposite. He could think of nothing
to say to them, and needed to consider how best
to approach his brother concerning them ; but
when he opened the carriage door and stepped
out to the street before his club-house the light
from the entrance lanterns streamed in and he
began to regret his long silence.

"Fairy's scared," whispered the boy, pointing to his sister. He himself was very white
of face, and his eyes were round and inquiring.

Mr. Schuyler could see, in the corner of the
seat, a tossed mass of gauze and spangles half
covered by the coarse wrap the child wore.
She was sobbing with terror, and yet, as Mrs.
Schuyler had noted, was painfully submissive,

for, supposing she was to be lifted from the carriage, she scrambled down backward from the seat, and, shaken with sobs, turned her wet face to the door, holding out her arms to be taken.

Mr. Schuyler was a kind-hearted man, and the sight vanquished him. It was impossible to leave the little ones outside and alone in the carriage, nor could he bring himself to give up his mission and return to his wife unsuccessful. In the end he compromised by ordering that the carriage should be driven about the block until the children were reassured by him, and until he believed the most tardy revellers must have arrived for their night of misrule. Then he made a hasty dash up the club steps with a child clinging to each hand. As an old member every corner of the building was familiar to him, and he hurried to a small cloakroom, too small for use, he knew, on this crowded night. As he dragged the staring children through the halls lined with Christmas-trees and gay with gilded wreaths, a passing glance in a mirror made Mr. Schuyler hasten his steps. He realized for the first time what a curious group they made, he in his royal dress and the children as fantastically arrayed as if they, too, were part of the Old Christmas revels. They met no one on the way, however, except a smiling servant, who evidently accepted the trio as a part of the evening's pageant. Mr. Schuyler breathed a sigh of relief as he closed the cloak-room door behind him. There was an angry protest in his heart that a man might not sin alone and alone suffer his own consequences, but as these were not the first harvests that the younger brother had reaped for the elder, he smothered his resentment, and, as usual, did what he could.

After some coaxing, aided by the boy, who seemed to have regained his wonted self-control, Mr. Schuyler persuaded the little girl that she was not afraid to wait for him in the brightly lighted apartment. As soon as he might he left the children together, hurrying to the large hall where he knew his brother would be found. The boyishness which had moved him to plan and dress with genuine pleasure for this night had all been wiped away by the late occurrences of the evening. He now looked down on his costume with disgust, and wondered how he had ever seen amusement in such buffoonery. The feeling of disgust grew on him as he neared the hall, from which he began to hear loud bursts of laughter and applause. A crowd of masqueraders gathered about the door met him with genial greetings which he forced himself to return, but it was almost more than his patience could stand to hear on all sides congratulations that he was brother to the man he had come to arraign with the story of two sadly neglected children and a deserted wife. It was evident that James Schuyler was at that moment distinguishing himself in some way most pleasing to his subjects — his name was on every lip. Looking up at a stage which had been built at one end of the hall, Mr. Schuyler saw his brother and could have groaned aloud with impatience. There, the life of the evening, the chief actor in a Christmas play written by himself, paraded the king of misrule, witty, brilliant in his improvisations, and glowing with the pleasure of success.

Mr. Schuyler made his way behind the scenes, and met the triumphant king as he made his exit and the curtain fell.

"Hello!" said James, genially, as he saw his brother's grave face. ".How are you to-night? I'm just a boy again. Old Christmas comes but once a year. What makes you look so serious, George?"

"Because I've something serious to say to you," began George, in a lowered voice.

James laughed.

"Did I ever see you when you had not? Worrying over me is what makes your hair grow gray."

He flicked back a grizzled lock on George's forehead.

Troubled and hurried as he was, the younger brother could not resist looking up at the black-haired man by him with a half smile.

"We all as a family grow gray early," he said, dryly. "You are peculiarly lucky."

"None of your sarcasm. I know as well as you do that I dye my hair, but I swear it's not for vanity. It discourages me too much to see the marks of old age creeping on every time I look in the glass. What do you think of the play?"

"I have been too troubled to think of it. I must see you alone and at once on a matter of importance."

"But, my dear fellow," pleaded the king of misrule, "it's utterly impossible for me to talk business now. You must see that yourself. There goes the curtain up again. My cue comes in a moment. Stand here by me," he added, good-humoredly, "and listen a bit. I wrote all the lines for the mummers myself."

He was as excited as a playwright whose all hangs on the public verdict. In the doubtful passages he gnawed his lip, and where the hits told he rose on tiptoe, his face glowing, his brow triumphant.

"I can't attend to you now, George. You must see I can't," he repeated, and then brushing gently past his brother with a courtesy which never failed him, he rushed on the stage as his cue sounded.

Mr. Schuyler walked back to the body of the hall. It was useless for him to linger there, as he saw, and after the curtain fell for the last time he had yet to wait patiently and even to make one of the uproarious procession which swept round and round the hall, kept in step by a heavy brass band playing in a balcony overhead. However reluctant, he was forced to the honor of carrying aloft the dish with the old-time boar's-head, while others followed in his train bearing grotesquely inscribed banners and high-held dishes containing other emblematic absurdities. Not the least ridiculous sight in Mr. Schuyler's eyes was that of his own brother being carried in mimic reverence on a chair at the procession's head. As the procession at last broke rank Mr. Schuyler seized his chance.

"I must speak with you," he said, resolutely, drawing the king from his throne. "It is imperative. Come away with me quickly."

"Why not speak here?" asked James, indolently. He was vexed at this persistence. "Have you bad news for me?"

"I don't know what you may call it."

James Schuyler glanced at his brother with a kind of tolerant affection. "It can't be very bad. Your wife's all right or you wouldn't be here. You show for yourself, so every one I care for is excluded; and if it's money, it would rather amuse me than otherwise to find myself a pauper. It would give me something to do."

"Only to ask 'God bless me and my wife,

and my brother George and his wife,' would include more than you do."

"So," said James, quickly, and with lowered voice. He puckered his lips into a whistle. "Sets the wind in that quarter? - It's Sara, is it? Go on."

"This is not the place to speak, but since you insist I must be abrupt. How many children have you, James, and when did you see them last? I have a reason for asking. Don't evade me as usual."

"I will not. I have two children, a boy and a girl. The boy I don't remember particularly; he was a good infant, but profoundly uninteresting, both to his mother and to me—continually reminded me of you, by-the-way. I named him for you. The girl was a little beauty. The last time I saw her was when Sara decided to leave me in France and return to her people in England."

"Was it she who deserted you, then?" asked the younger brother, hopefully.

James shrugged his shoulders.

"It happened so, but if she had not gone then, I should later. I took my family to the steamer in proper marital fashion, and saw them off. I remember that the little girl peeped out and smiled at me through the porthole. She was like the most exquisite miniature. I have never forgotten that lovely child's face, framed in the round setting. In fact, she

is the only one of the party I ever regretted.
Have I told you all you want to know?"

"Was that last remark born of fatherly interest, or artistic feeling only? Would you
really care to see the child again? Good God!
there she is!"

"Who is?" said James, turning.

A chorus of shouts drowned their voices,
and the band above them had burst out into
a tumult of dance-music. The masqueraders
were all crowding into the middle of the room.

"You must pardon me, your Majesty," said
one of the revellers, drawing near with mock
reverences and mincing steps, "but mirth
lagged, and as I by chance discovered the surprise you were holding back for us, I loosed it
at once and here it is."

"Good God!" muttered George again.

He drew his brother to the edge of the circle
which had formed, and thrust a way through
for them both. In the midst of the ring of
laughing, admiring spectators he saw little
Fairy leaping and twirling, her small feet flying, and her eyes glowing with elation, as her
father's had on the mummers' stage. The
heavy beat of the brass band seemed to stimu-
late her to something more than the usual immature grace of childish dancing. The blood
of artist dancers in her veins answered hotly to
the applause and shouts of "Brava!" The motions of her arms and bird-like head and eyes

were in such perfect accord with her weaving feet as to make each step a wonderfully harmonious movement for the whole body. George Schuyler, aghast as he was, paused fascinated, gazing at the inspired little dancer. Adding a final touch to the fantastic scene, the child's flying feet were followed by the little boy, who was vainly striving to catch and hold her. He pursued her about the circle with clumsy motions and groping hands which she easily avoided by springing to right or left, light as a butterfly and mischievous as a kitten. The entire left side of the boy's face was masked clownlike by a coating of thick white paint spotted with red, and his odd clothing, half of one color, half of another, carried out too faithfully the clown appearance ; but despite disguise his face as plainly expressed a distressed determination to hold his sister as hers a mischievous play to avoid him.

"You are a princely king of misrule," said the reveller who had spoken before. "The clown is fair, sir king, but the girl is an inspiration. I ventured to add that touch of paint to the clown's face. We had some difficulty in persuading him to his part until you gave the word, but the girl was wild from the time she heard the music."

"Be careful," whispered George in his brother's ear. "Those are your two children !"

He could not be sure that James had heard

him, for at that moment the little boy caught sight of George Schuyler and ran to his side.

"Oh, did you bring us here for this?" he cried, with the pitiful acceptance of one used to being disposed of as others wished. "They told me you did. I wanted to wait for you, but I couldn't hold Fairy back."

Before George could answer, the king of misrule had broken through the circle and picked up the pursuit where the boy dropped it. He seized the little sprite by the waist in one of her bounds, and, lifting her yet higher, set her on his shoulder.

"Who dares to anticipate my surprises?" he cried, looking around. "Out of my way, there, subjects."

He forced his way through the laughing circle, and then for a moment hesitated, when George, grasping his purpose, caught up the boy and made his way to his brother's side.

"This way," he whispered, as, closely pursued by the crew of misrule, they rushed down the hallway and just in time flung to the door of the little cloak-room between themselves and their followers.

"Now," said James, coolly turning the key in the lock, unmindful of shouts from without and blows rained upon the door. "Now, I suppose I am in the bosom of my family, if what you say is true."

"Look at them, and tell me what you think."

James dropped into a chair with little Fairy on his knee and took her flushed face between his two hands. There was admiration, but nothing paternal, that George could detect, in his look. However, he stooped and kissed the child before he set her on the floor.

"That's the same little face that looked out of the port-hole," he said. "Run off and play with your brother. There are some chess-men in that box in the corner. Wait a moment." This to the boy, whom he caught by the arm as he passed. He laughed and released him after a brief look at the undaubed side of the boy's face.

"More like you than ever," he said.

"So Janet thinks," George answered.

"Janet? What does she know about the children? Has she seen them?"

Mr. Schuyler remembered his wife's message.

"It was she who found them, and she who told me to bring them to you with her love as her Old Christmas gift to you."

"Dear old Janet," said the brother-in-law, with more feeling than he had yet shown. "She is the only woman in the world whom I respect, and she's the only being in this world, I honestly believe, who respects me or expects any good of me. Be sure you thank her for me, George. Don't forget. And now, how did she find them?" he asked, curiously. "What are they doing on this side of the water? Have you got Sara hidden somewhere behind the arras?"

It was not very much that George knew, but that little he told with all the quiet passion of his nature, dwelling on his wife's discovery of the unfortunate condition of the children, the neglect and evident unhappiness of the boy, and the education of the girl as a public dancer. He was indignant when, as he ended, James burst into a peal of loud laughter, evidently long suppressed.

"Oh, Sara—Sara," said the amused husband. "It's the same old Sara. Clever is no word for her. And dear old Janet has played straight into her hands. It's queer how strong a weakness can be. I always had a weakness for Sara, and I feel it again now. You can't understand? Well, no, you wouldn't unless you knew Sara. She's tired of this way of living and wants me back again, that's all. She's followed me over here. No, she doesn't need money. She ran through all I left her in short season, to be sure, but she's been banking on my lawyer with my permission and connivance ever since. Lately she hasn't asked for money, so I knew some scheme would develop sooner or later. This is it. Mark my words. The girl was sent to Madame Jeanne purely because Sara discovered that your wife went there. The lesson was timed to follow hers. It's all a careful plan of Sara's. That boy's clothing, too—look at it! A mere ruse to catch Janet's compassionate eye. Those are no remnants. Sara deliberately bought the two pieces off the rolls."

He spoke with a certain pride, which George answered with horror in his voice.

"Do you mean that you think your wife has deliberately sacrified both your children to a ruse to gain your attention, when she could as well have openly sought you?"

"That's about it," said the undisturbed father, "but Sara knows me better than you do. I like cleverness. I might not have been found if sought openly. As it is, the boy she wouldn't have hesitated to sacrifice—she never cared for him — and the girl will only be improved by knowing how to dance like a fire-fly. I think I never saw such child-dancing."

He glanced at the corner where the two listless children were obediently pretending to play with the chess-men. Their docility hurt George Schuyler, as it had his wife.

"What will you do with the poor little things?" he asked, compassionately.

The father stood looking at them, thinking with a lazy slowness.

"Do you know," he said, " I have almost decided to be amiable and play into Sara's hands as meekly as Janet did? Suppose I were to steal the children to-night and take them home with me. I can send word to Sara that I have them. I suppose you have her address?"

"Yes," answered George, shortly.

"Good. She will then play the frantic mother, I the newly awakened father. Neither will be able to bear parting with the children, and so in a day or two, perhaps, we shall all four sail for Europe together, and come back after several years, respectable members of society. What do you think of that programme?"

George rose from his chair.

"I think," he said, "that the whole affair is about as indelicate and unfeeling as anything I ever heard. Why can't you go to your wife and talk with her?"

James rose also, with undisturbed good-nature, his hands in his pockets.

"I don't expect you to see it our way," he said; "but you ought to remember that, after all, Sara and I are not a very delicate or feeling pair—at least, not as you and Janet are. Sara does not know how to come to me or I to go to her. It takes all kinds of men and women to make a world. To be honest, if it is any comfort to you, I have a sneaking feeling of pleasure in thinking of becoming a family man again. I told you I wanted something to do. Neither Sara nor I are so young as we once were. We shall quarrel less, I fancy. I have the idea, from hints my mediating lawyer has dropped, that each of us has been for some time stabling a calf bursting with the fat of forgiveness, all ready for the *other* to eat, but each of us, you see, wanted his or her own calf eaten. I know I feel kindly enough towards Sara, and I think she has arranged to avoid eating either calf rather cleverly. I am grateful to her for it."

A large clock outside in the hall struck twelve with booming strokes, aided by heavy echoes from the brass kettles of the band.

James held out his hand to his brother.

"It's the opening of another year for me," he said. "I am in earnest in my way, George. You can't write clearly on a blotting-pad, and that's the stuff I'm made of. But I am tired of this old leaf, and evidently Sara is also. We'll flutter over a new leaf. I can't promise much for it, either, but we'll try it. I'll purge and live cleanly as a gentleman, and I think I shall enjoy the little girl. She shall dance for me at night, after coffee. Tell Janet I appreciate her gift."

"And the boy?" asked George, still holding his brother's hand. "Janet had more anxiety for him than for the girl. He has not even been taught his letters."

"Well, if he doesn't even know his a b c's, I think a boarding-school will be best for him. Yes, you can tell Janet that the girl will sail with us and the boy will go to a boarding-school. I hope I play the thoughtful father to your satisfaction, George. What a pity you lost your boy. You and Janet are born parents. She has never been quite the same since then, has she?"

George Schuyler's face changed. He dropped his brother's hand.

"Suppose—" he began, quickly, then checked himself. "Never mind. I wish you a good voyage, James, in all its meanings. I will give your message to Janet. Good-night."

. He turned to the door, unlocked it, and went out abruptly.

For a moment James stood perplexed. "Now, what was George going to say?" he thought aloud. "What upset him?" Suddenly he hurried to the door and flung it open, calling down the hall, "George—George—I have something to propose to you."

Between George Schuyler and his wife there was but one subject of real difference, and that lay in a lower drawer of her bureau, to which she kept the key. More than once, coming into the room hastily, Mr. Schuyler had found his wife dropping tears upon some little garments that lay folded away in that drawer, and more than once he had threatened to turn the lock and keep the key himself. It was before this forbidden drawer that Mrs. Schuyler was sitting alone when the clock struck twelve on Old Christmas night. On her knees lay one tiny tumbled garment, which she touched now and then with a reverence that was like passion. In the sleeves of the gown were fastened a pair of gold armlets like those little Fairy had worn. The drawer was full of such garments, all white and immaculate; only this one bore slight marks of wear, and Mrs. Schuyler was sitting with it on her knees as by an open grave. She had so sat since her husband left her, wrapped in her memories. It was his returning footsteps on the stair outside that at last roused her suddenly. She closed the drawer with guilty haste, looking in the mirror at her flushed face, but had only time to wipe the fresh tears from her cheeks when the door opened. Forcing a smile, she went to meet her husband. Her voice trembled as she asked, " Did all go well ?"

Mr. Schuyler did not seem to notice her emotion. He came to her, took her two hands in his, and then she saw the agitation in his own face.

" What have you there ?" asked Mr. Schuyler, looking down.

The tumbled garment which had lain on her knees, and which she had forgotten in her haste, fell to the ground between the husband and wife. With a hurt cry Mrs. Schuyler stooped to lift it, but her husband held her.

" Let it lie," he said, tenderly.

He looked closely at her. " So you have been

grieving to-night again. Look up at me, dear-est. I have something to tell you—something to show you. Are you strong enough to be surprised?"

Without waiting for an answer he hurried to the door and opened it. On the threshold outside stood the little boy, still in the clown costume, with his small face stained with tears and paint, and his lips quivering as pitifully as when Mrs. Schuyler had first seen him in Madame Jeanne's dancing-hall. He looked up at them with swimming eyes.

"This is the return Christmas gift James sends you," said Mr. Schuyler, excitedly. "Do you understand, Janet? James sends him to you."

Mrs. Schuyler glanced from him back to the child, bewildered.

"To me?"

"To you," repeated her husband, deliberate-ly. "As a free gift to you, offered freely and unconditionally, unless it pains you to accept him as yours. Shall you want to take him, dear?"

"Oh, do take me!" wailed the child, sudden-ly. "Don't anybody at all want me?"

He was trembling from head to foot with unchildlike emotion, and with a cry of compas-sion Mrs. Schuyler fell on her knees, gather-ing him into her arms and rocking him like a baby on her breast, taking him to her with broken words that did not need to be articulate. Her husband started as he recognized the mother-note in her voice. Once before he had heard that tone, and believed he never would again. He looked back at the little garment forgotten on the floor, then, moving softly, lifted it and hid it away in the drawer.

He smiled as he heard his wife's glad voice calling him.

"Oh, come," she cried. "What are you waiting for? I want to share my Christmas gift with you."

"But, my dear," said the admiral, "your aunt would surely be more helpful to you here than I."

Marion looked out of the window, across the green grass of the campus, down the terrace, and over the sea-wall, from which the waters of the river spread away like a royal purple mantle, picked out with silver sails of pleasure-boats and straggling sloops. Before she replied she had mechanically counted over all the sails in sight.

"I don't know, uncle. I seemed moved to speak to you. But if you would rather not—"

"No, no, my dear; not at all. I was thinking only of you, and that a woman might better understand how to advise with you. However, I will endeavor to be as womanly as one avowedly a man of action may. And so young Arnold covets you, does he? He must have done so almost at first sight. Well, I don't blame him."

He smiled into his niece's serious eyes, but

her face remained unchanged, and the admiral went on with more gravity:

"If I had been blessed with daughters of my own, I should know better how to speak to you. As it is, you will have to help me a little. Should I draw you out gently, or straightly question you? What would you like me to do?"

"I should like to know all that you can tell me of Mr. Arnold."

The admiral lifted his eyebrows slightly. His favorite cat had been sitting on the table by his elbow, and he whisked her away with his handkerchief, then straightened the papers which lay before him, and set his stick of sealing-wax, his pen, and paper-knife in a methodical row.

"I suppose," he said, dryly, "that the young woman of to-day is more sensible, and that I am an old fogy. In my generation she was the 'lovely burden'; and if the burden sometimes outweighed the beauty, we at least had the theory of romance. To come to business, Marion, as I warned you on your arrival, I know but little of any one here, my present duty being still new. Regarding Mr. Arnold, I think it probable that you know more concerning him than I. Had I dreamed of his representing more than one in the dozen hovering about you, or had he spoken to me first, it would have been different. For his present,

I can only tell you that he has led his class statistically and in spirit, and that he has passed through the furnace of a social favoritism unscathed. For his future I can prophesy as useful and brilliant a career as the government permits to an officer of its navy ; but of his past, his people, and his private means, which is just the information I suppose you want, I know nothing whatever."

As he ended, the admiral looked up at his niece's profile. She was sitting motionless on the couch opposite him, her hands folded on her lap, her eyes still gazing out of the window. There was an expression which he did not understand upon her face. The admiral's voice softened.

" I can, of course, find out all you wish to know concerning Mr. Arnold, Marion ; but, except on one condition, I have no reason, no right, to pry into his affairs, and I am old-fashioned enough to feel that no one has the right to ask you the question which I must now ask, except the one being to whom your answer means everything. To me a woman is as the sphinx—to guess her heart's riddle is to dash her from her heights." He rose to seat himself on the couch by Marion's side. " Your having no father, Marion, and the fact that your mother intrusted you to your aunt and me, only after many misgivings, make me doubly responsible. Therefore — will you let

me ask you if you love Mr. Arnold, my dear?"
It was the admiral who blushed. Marion looked into his face with the same unbroken seriousness.

"I don't know, uncle."

"You do not know! What does that mean,
my dear? Do you want more time for consid-
eration, or do you wish first to learn if it would
be wise to let yourself love him?"

"I already know that nothing on earth could
be more unwise for me."

"Then, as I said, you know far more about
him than I. Do you be my informant. Come,
help me a little, my dear. I am only a rough
old sea-dog, you know. You must teach me
to be womanly with you. As an individual I
believe in Mr. Arnold. Is it his parentage that
is at fault?"

"Yes, his parentage."

The admiral shook his head doubtfully.
"Well, then," he said, with a half-smile, "you
know just what you would have to face in your
mother's opposition. To tell the truth, I should
a little dread taking my share of it. 'Thou
shalt have ancestry' is her eleventh command-
ment."

Marion moved restlessly. "I know. She
would never give her consent to Mr. Arnold."

The admiral held his gray-mustached upper
lip between his finger and thumb, looking out

thoughtfully at his niece from under his white eyebrows.

" How bad is it, Marion ?   After all, the service is a cloak for many sins of birth.   I suppose Arnold himself confessed this shortcoming to you ?"

" No ; I learned it from his mother and sister."

" His mother and sister, eh ?   Are they here?"

" They came yesterday for a week's visit."

" And you have seen them ?"

" Yes ; I saw them to-day."

Certain little lines that the admiral had noticed about his wife's eyes and mouth when in bodily pain he now recognized drawn in Marion's face, where they disturbed him.   He raised his hand involuntarily as if to smooth them away, but Marion withdrew quickly.   Her lip quivered.

" Not yet, please, uncle."

" Go on, my dear," said the admiral.   " I understand.   What were the mother and sister like ?"

" It would be easier to tell you that they were unlike anything that might have been expected.   You have probably seen them walking about the grounds—they are conspicuous enough.   The daughter is a tall, unwholesome-looking parody on her brother.   Her costume this afternoon was a number of ribbon-bows tacked together, apparently.   She might as well have worn a crazy-quilt. The mother is a large woman. She dresses in black, and every article she wears is too small or too short. Her sleeves do not meet her gloves by three inches; the flesh sticks out between them like red bracelets. Her bonnet is too small also, and is tied tightly under her chin; her face seems to gush out between the strings—"

"Marion!" the admiral remonstrated. "Marion!"

His niece laughed unnaturally.

"I wanted you to see it all just as I did. If the bare description shocks you so deeply, what do you suppose the reality was to me?"

"I think I am more bewildered than shocked. I did promise you that I would try to be womanly; but not being a milliner, and, indeed, peculiarly ignorant of woman's dress, your description conveys about as little to me as the price of the materials would. And then, my dear, I did not expect to have to remind you that dress is not a criterion. These women may be provincial, and yet of good enough standing."

"I thought of all that, but they are not from the provinces. They come from a large city."

"You have talked with them, then? When did you meet them? Tell me your story in your own fashion. I will not interrupt you again."

"I met them walking in the grounds when I

was strolling this afternoon with Mr. Arnold.
They were in a distant path, and he could easily
have avoided the introduction. It was of his
own seeking. He seemed fond of them."

"Do you place that to his discredit, Marion?"

"I don't know. I am not able to connect
him with them as yet; they seem of another
flesh and blood."

"Is that all that you have to tell me about
them?" asked the admiral.

His niece had paused. She went on slowly:

"No; that is not all. One of the officers
passed us, and drew Mr. Arnold away for a
few moments' talk. While he was gone the
sister began telling me how they had planned
their visit as a surprise to her brother, and how
her father had meant to come with them, but
some people 'dropping in' had detained him
at the last moment. I said that I was sorry,
and all the rest that I should have said. I really behaved well, uncle."

"I don't doubt that, my dear," replied the
admiral; "I don't doubt that for a moment."

"I said I thought I should have let the people wait, and then she said no, I would not;
for they had come to negotiate some rather
important loans."

The admiral's face brightened. "A broker!
Come, that's not bad at all. There's nothing
disreputable there, anyhow. Even your mother would have to acknowledge that."

"So it seemed to me. I was thinking just that while the girl was speaking. She was mentioning further that her father was a property broker when the mother, who had moved aside, turned back again to tell me of her husband's disappointment, and how his eyes had filled with tears, when they left him behind. They seem an affectionate family. She said he had to stay at home, for—" Marion lifted her eyes desperately to her uncle's face. "She said," she repeated, "that he could not leave home because"—her voice rose hysterically—"because 'a couple of folks that couldn't wait dropped in,' and that a jewelry store was 'a precarious business, anyhow.'"

"What!" exclaimed the admiral, starting to his feet. "A property broker—a jewelry store! But that can only mean pawnbroking! it can't be, Marion."

"It is, uncle. The 'properties' were jewelry. The mother seemed unconscious that she had betrayed a secret, but the daughter was deeply embarrassed. She tried to pass it all off, but—oh, it was horrible!—she only made the truth plainer."

"A pawnbroker! And you tell me that his son has dared ask my niece to marry him?"

"No, uncle, no; pray listen to me. You yourself could not have been more careful than Mr. Arnold has been of his honor."

The admiral paced the room, his eyes flashing. His face was on fire; his hands were alternately tugging at his white mustache and ruffling his thick white hair.

"His honor! What the devil do I care about his honor when my niece is in question? I beg your pardon, my dear; I spoke in heat, but, indeed, with provocation. A pawnbroker! Good heavens!"

"But, uncle, Mr. Arnold has never asked me to marry him. When he joined me again, we left his mother and sister, and he and I walked on together. He knew nothing of what had passed, but I was foolish and shaken, and had to rest on a bench finally. I said it was the heat. I am afraid I was a little hysterical, for I startled him, and he had let me know that he cared for me before he realized what he was saying. Afterwards he was as dismayed as you are now. Indeed, you must not blame him. He was terribly agitated, and asked nothing of me except that I would forget all that he had no right to say until he could speak to you. He is coming to you to-night. Uncle, what shall you say to him?"

The admiral's walk ceased abruptly. "Say to him?" he repeated. "Poor boy, what can one say? If it were anything else on earth!"

Marion covered her face with her hands.

"You pity him," she cried, sharply; "you only pity him; but I—I—" She laid her arm on the side of the couch and bowed her head into it. The admiral paused before her. For a moment his hands hovered irresolutely above her shaken shoulders; then, throwing his palms outward with a gesture of helplessness, he straightened himself and walked away to the window. His back was still towards the room when he spoke:

"My child—" He cleared his throat and began again—"My child, we must take the world as we find it, not as we would like to make it. Mr. Arnold loves you, and if you love him, the question is, What can I do to comfort you? What can I say to him that is not too cruel?"

Facing his niece again, the admiral went on: "You see, I am perilously near being woman-ish when I promised you to be only womanly."

As Marion raised her face, he seated himself on the couch near her, his hands on his knees, his head bent towards her. Though not touching her, his manner had tenderness sufficient.

"If it were any other occupation," he reflected, aloud; "if it were anything less grotesque and absurd, less the subject of ghastly pleasantries—"

"You can remind me of nothing that I have not already considered, uncle. It was the hideous absurdity of it all which made me ill out in the grounds. As I thought of it suddenly from that stand-point, I burst into hysterical laughter and tears. That was the beginning of my weakness and Mr. Arnold's self-betrayal. Oh, uncle, you don't think he ever helped his father, do you? I keep imagining him as a little boy doing the little things—making out the tickets, and arranging the shop-window. Do you think I should ever grow used to those associations, ever be happy in mingling with his family?"

The admiral started, and sat very erect upon the couch.

"Marion," he said, "does this mean that you are seriously considering such a step?"

"I don't know, uncle. As I told you at first, I seem to have lost the power of thinking."

"My dear child, if you have come to me to think for you, I can only repeat your own words to you, and repeat them with most solemn belief. Nothing on earth could be more unwise for you. It is an impossible position."

"Yet you said the service was a cloak for many such sins of birth. Other officers have come from the people. This would be our world, and it has seemed to me not over nice in such matters."

"You have not been here long enough to see what underlies the veneer of official civility. Some things might be forgiven or concealed, but poor Arnold's disability is as a bar-sinister that admits of neither. Your taking such a step is not to be considered. It means misery from the first. You, who are daintiness itself, and who have been protected from every wind that blows, can have no conception of the coarseness that you would have to endure daily. You could not stand it. Your every effort would be to wean your husband from his natural ties of affection, and from the hour you succeeded you would despise him. No, my dear; it is not to be thought of. If the utter sacrifice of yourself is not a sufficient reason to restrain you, remember your mother, and the blow it would be to her hopes for you."

Marion's face hardened. "Mamma! Her hopes for me will be blasted at anything far short of a coronet. She has not yet forgiven me that I am not the wife of a possible heir to one, with a sot for a husband."

"In that matter you had my warm support, Marion."

"I know I did, uncle. You have always been kind to me. Of course mamma would violently oppose Mr. Arnold; and do you know, I am ashamed that it is so, but the thought of the struggle with her nerves me when I might otherwise falter—why, I don't know."

The admiral drew back a little, scanning Marion's flushed face. Her features were exceedingly delicate; the force with which she had spoken had not brought out a coarse line.

"My child," he said, "do you mean that? If your love alone does not nerve you to con-

sider this step, nothing else should—least of all
a mother's opposition."

"Mamma's opposition would not be for love
of me. Mamma ought to have been born a Ce-
lestial. As it is, I should have been piously
sacrificed on· her ancestral altar but for you,
uncle, and what she still terms my wilfulness."

"I know," said the admiral. "And yet this
would break her heart, Marion. It cannot be,
my dear, both for her sake and for yours. It
is quite out of the question."

He spoke gently, and the words were not
commanding. It was a certain finality in his
voice, born of long and undisputed authority,
that his niece answered with spirit.

"I think I shall decide to break mamma's
altars, at which I do not worship, rather than
my own heart."

The admiral looked up quickly. Their eyes
met. He spoke shortly, almost sternly.

"You have decided, Marion?"

"I am deciding now."

She sat with her finger pressed against her
lips, her face grave, and her eyes downcast.

The admiral rose to pace the floor, quarter-
deck fashion, his arms folded on his breast.
His favorite cat, uncoiling herself from a warm
corner near the fire, ran to rub her head against
his leg, as was her wont. Until her sharp wail
roused him the admiral did not know that he
had crushed her tail beneath his foot; even

then, with an absent-minded "Excuse me," he passed on, absorbed in his thoughts. Marion was wondering if, as it seemed to her, her presence was forgotten, when the admiral's walk ceased, and he seated himself at his table, where she had first found him. He spoke without looking up, his fingers occupied with a bunch of keys which he drew from his pocket

"Marion," he said, "I have been thinking that, while a man attains his majority at a given period, as a rule, a woman comes of age, early or late, with her first heart-burn. You know it is a time-honored custom that a son of the house should be introduced to the ghost or the skeleton of the family the day he comes of age. The rule might as well apply to a daughter. I mean now to show you our family ghost ; but first, can you tell me the special line on which we hang our family pride?"

"The Eeliott line," Marion answered, "spelled with two *e*'s and two *t*'s."

Her voice was mocking, and the admiral smiled. He had selected a key from the bunch.

"You know your lesson well," he said, dryly. "The name might as well be spelled with three *c*'s and three *t*'s, while we are about it. It is the skeleton of the Eeliott family that you are to see. I keep it locked in this cupboard with this key."

He unlocked the door of a closed compartment under his table, and drew out a long box of curious and irregular shape, covered with dull red leather, on which were stamped quaint arabesque figures in burnished gold. The odor of age about the case was strong. Marion drew back as the admiral laid it in her lap.

"You needn't be afraid," he said; "it is only a paper ghost. Open the box, Marion."

The inner-case lining, of heavy, gorgeously tinted silk, decorated with a sprawling pomegranate pattern, protected a roll of parchment as yellow as ivory. Attached to the roll by mixed red and silver ribbons were two red seals. Marion touched the faded ribbons softly with her finger tips.

"The Eeliott colors," she said. The admiral tossed them to one side with a short laugh.

"Yes," he repeated; "the Eeliott colors. Unroll the paper."

As she lifted and unrolled the parchment Marion uttered an exclamation. The page shone out with all the glory that emblazoning gives in colors as fresh as the day they were painted. The text, broken here and there by rich initials, was crowned with the royal arms of England, the rose, and the royal ermine. On a corner of the skin, surrounded by festooned roses, hung the painted shield of the Eeliott family. Marion looked at the shield critically.

"Those are surely the Eeliott arms," she said; "and yet isn't there something a little wrong about it?"

"A little," said the admiral. "Read the writing, my dear—read it aloud."

Marion read the text from the top of the gorgeous page to the written signatures at the end :

To all and singular

to whom these Presents shall come Isaac Heard Esquire Garter Principal King of Arms and Thomas Lock Esquire Clarenceux King of Arms of the South East and West Parts of England from the River Trent Southwards send Greeting. Whereas Marion Eeliott wife of the Honorable Francis Herbert, by Letter to the Most Honorable C—— D—— commonly called Earl of A—— Deputy with the Royal Approbation to his Father the Most Noble A—— D—— Duke of C—— Earl Marshall and hereditary marshall of England requested the Favor of his Lordship's Warrant for an exemplifying and confirming to her and her Descendants the Arms of her reputed Father John Eeliott, Lord Knight of the Kingdom of Ireland deceased with such Variations as may be necessary according to the Laws of Arms.

And forasmuch as his Lordship did by Warrant under his Hand and Seal bearing date the twentieth day of March last authorize and direct Us to exemplify and confirm the said Arms accordingly. *Know Ye therefore* that We the said Garter and Clarenceux in pursuance of the Consent of the said Deputy Earl Marshall and by Virtue of the Letters Patent of our several Offices to each of Us respectively granted under the Great Seal of Great Britain do by these Presents exemplify and confirm to the said Marion Eeliott the arms following that is to say *Paly of six argent and gules a Bend Sinister engrailed counter-changed*, as the same are in the Margin hereof more plainly depicted to be borne and used for ever hereafter by her the said Marion Eeliott and her Descendants according to the Laws of Arms without the Let or Interruption of any Person or Persons whatsoever.

> In Witness whereof We the said Garter and Clarenceux Kings
> of Arms have to these Presents subscribed our Names and
> affixed the Seals of our several Offices the sixth day of April
> in the twenty —— year of the Reign of our Sovereign Lord
> George the Third by the Grace of God King of Great Brit-
> ain France and Ireland Defender of the Faith &c : and in
> the year of our Lord One Thousand and seven hundred
> and ——

The skin rolled itself together strongly, as though it still had life, as Marion laid it down.

"What does it mean?" she said. "I don't understand a word of it."

"Your great-grandmother, Marion Eeliott, understood it," said the admiral. "She understood it so well that she kept this locked in her closet to the day of her death, where I, as executor, found it. Why she did not burn the document is one of those things which are inexplicable. That no one in her lifetime saw it save herself, I am almost positive. Since then I know that my eyes alone have seen it, and now yours."

"What does it mean?" Marion repeated.

The admiral bent forward to open the roll. He read a line aloud:

"'The arms of her *reputed father*.' Reputed father! Don't you know what that means, Marion? Your great-grandmother, known as Marion *Eeliott*, had no such maiden name, and her crest might as well have been a bar-sinister couchant, or three balls rampant, or anything else she chose to carry. You surely know the meaning of a bar-sinister, my dear. We are not a mushroom family in the maternal line, but toadstool—old enough, in all conscience, and poison at the root."

Marion drew the parchment towards her, looking again at the emblazoned shield with its fatal lines from left to right. The color rose in her face.

"Do you mean, uncle, that we are not—not legitimate?"

"I mean, my dear niece, that on our grandmother Eeliott's side we are not low-born, but base-born. That high name on which we hang our chiefest pride is our shame. That Lord Eeliott was the father of our ancestress is undoubted; who her mother was, the Lord, or more likely the devil, only knows. Would you care to hear the whole story, Marion, or does this kind of truth shock you? I thought you rather scornful of ancestry."

"This is different, uncle. I thought we were at least of honest blood. I want to know all that you can tell me; but—no, I don't like it; it does shock me."

"This story," said the admiral, "has also a kind of humor about it, almost as grim as the story of Mr. Arnold's order of bar-sinister. Your namesake and maternal ancestress did not like it, either. She was brought up in her father's American home as his daughter, pre-

siding over his household, and arrogantly foist-
ed upon the community, who accepted her for
their own reasons, I suppose. Probably .they
were ignorant of her true position. When I
found this document hidden away in the old
lady's closet, among her silks and laces, I was
sufficiently stirred to look up every scrap of
writing bearing on the subject. Among a heap
of old letters belonging to Lord Eeliott, I un-
earthed one from his father, written in England, and rather sardonically urging his son to
sow all his wild oats on this side of the water,
that the crop might not come up in the old
country. Our ancestress was one of those
blades. How many others there were of Lord
Eeliott's crop, who knows? Before leaving
America Lord Eeliott married his daughter to
your great - grandfather, with a bribe thrown
in of so many thousand pounds down. That,
too, I read between the lines of the papers I
ran through. Ancestors are not unlike sleeping dogs, Marion. It is better to let them lie,
as a rule. If the first Marion Eeliott had been
wise enough to do so, she would have been
spared the mortification of this parchment.
You have seen her portrait, my dear?"

"Yes; and I cannot imagine her humbled.
Uncle, are you sure that all this is true?"

"You have the parchment before you. I
have to look at it to convince myself sometimes, after listening to your mother's talk of

our family history on the Eeliott side. Old
Marion Eeliott grew to think it could not be
true,.and that humility and the pit whence it
came were not for such as she. Others had
forgotten, and she would forget. After her
father's death she evidently conceived the idea
of quartering his arms with her husband's.
She must have written to England, to the Her-
alds' College, claiming them. Heaven knows
what influences and what money she brought
to bear. That the college is incorruptible is
well shown here. What do you suppose were
her feelings as the covered parchment unrolled? *Her reputed father, and a bend sinister.*
Do you think she saw the grim humor of it,
Marion?"

Marion was looking seriously at the parchment.

"I cannot tell, uncle. To me it is only shame-
ful. And so this is what mamma has been wor-
shipping all these years. Why did you never
tell her?"

"Why should I overthrow her altars? Up
to this time there has been no reason for doing
so. And so you see no humor in the story?
Well, perhaps Mr. Arnold may, as we recognize
humor in his. Here, my dear; you have my
permission to use this parchment as you choose.
It is your weapon, and with it you are well
armed for your battle with your mother."

He rolled the parchment as he spoke, and

returning it to its box, laid the case in Marion's hands. She received it mechanically, looking up surprised.

"I—what am I to do with it?"

"Marry Mr. Arnold, if that is what you really desire. Why not, now that you know the truth about yourself? Before you opened that case you had a certain family tradition to live up to; now you are freed. If you care for Mr. Arnold enough to forgive his three balls rampant, and submit your bar-sinister couchant for his forgiveness, I don't see that any one can interfere. If your mother opposes you too strongly, you have only to lay this before her to seal her lips."

Marion lifted her eyes searchingly to the admiral's face.

"Uncle," she asked, "why have you done this?"

The admiral winced slightly. "Why, my dear?" he replied. He rose and laid his hand on Marion's head, meeting her earnest gaze. "Why? Because I want you to realize that it is wholly in your power to marry Mr. Arnold or not, just as you desire. If he were not a gentleman by nature, I would not have run this risk. He is a gentleman, if to be one is to know what is due to others and to render it, to know what is due to himself and to expect it. Beyond a certain point, parents can do nothing if their child chooses to marry the hangman or the man to be hanged. As for you, Marion, if you wish to marry Mr. Arnold, what renders it possible lies there in your hands. Take it away with you, my dear, and make your own use of it."

As he spoke he pointed to the case, which still lay loosely in his niece's grasp.

Without a word, Marion lifted her eyes, for a moment looking full into his. There was no wavering on either side. With a quick gesture she caught up the box and laid it on the table by her uncle's hand; yet the movement was curiously deliberate. She did not look up at the admiral as she passed him on her way from the room.

The admiral sat motionless at his desk, the case before him, and his favorite cat climbing up to his knee. As the door closed he slowly leaned back in his chair, drew a deep breath, and wiped his brow with his handkerchief.

"'Twas as I thought," he muttered: "opposition was her buoy. A shred of it left her to cling to, she'd have plunged in headlong."

He laid his hand on the cat's furry head, more as if gaining comfort from the touch than bestowing it. There was a kind of shame in his fine old face.

"And I promised her to be womanly!" he said, aloud. "I was feline! Pussy, I crave your pardon. You at least show your weapons in the moment of scratching, don't you?"

ONCE when I was a little girl visiting my grandfather, his barn on the hill-side caught fire, and I was the first one who thought of the danger to my grandfather's beloved carriage. I can see it now, hideous, lumbering old vehicle that it was. I rushed to the barn, tore open the great doors, grasped the shafts of the carriage, and started down the hill. For the first ten feet I ran the carriage ; from there to the bottom of the hill the carriage ran me. I have never forgotten the sensation. When my grandfather died and the farm fell to Penneniah and me, the carriage episode repeated itself. For some weeks we ran the farm ; from then the farm ran us, until the bottom of the hill and ruin stared us in the face.

It was all Uncle Elijah's fault ; at least, Penneniah and I so felt it to be. He knew, and we knew, and all the neighborhood knew, that grandfather had not intended leaving us the farm and no money with which to keep it in order. During the last weeks of his illness a stock company that every one had believed in failed suddenly. When the will was read our portion proved to be the old home farm and a number of valueless stocks in the ruined company. Everything else went to Uncle Elijah, who already owned a large farm, which grandfather had given him on his marriage, years before. All the neighborhood thought Uncle Elijah would make up the value of the useless stocks to his dead brother's children. Penneniah thought he would, and Joseph, Uncle Elijah's step-son, was sure of it. I said nothing, for I was sure of the contrary, and I was right. The only move Uncle Elijah made in the matter was to send us a written offer of ten thousand dollars for the farm. Pen sat looking at the letter in dismay. As the elder sister by fifteen years, she opened our joint letters.

"Annie Tousey," she said—she always gave me the benefit of my full name — "Annie Tousey, Uncle Elijah must know that the farm is worth fifteen thousand if it is worth a penny."

I was feeling very guilty.

"Penny," I said, "I must confess something to you. I have done a stupid thing. I should have known better. The day that the will was read Uncle Elijah asked me if we should sell the farm, and I said, 'Knowing how grandfather loved it, I should feel it dishonest to sell to any one outside of the family.' Now, you see, Uncle Elijah is the only living relation we have. There is no one to bid against him that we would accept, and he knows it. Penny, I was very stupid, and I beg your pardon for it."

"You needn't feel so badly," said my sister, "for he asked me the same question and got the same answer. But even if he did buy the farm, he has no one to leave it to but Joseph, and that would be leaving it out of the family, unless, Annie Tousey—"

"He's not going to buy it at ten thousand dollars," I interrupted. "We will write to him that we hold the farm at fifteen thousand, and see what he does then."

But we did not see; for Uncle Elijah did nothing, not even replying to our letter. Yet we knew he received it, for Joseph told us so. Penneniah and I talked the situation over, and finally, in the face of advice from all the neighborhood, decided to try making the farm support us, with itself, aided by a small yearly income which our father had left us. The result was as I have narrated. We and the farm ran steadily downhill. It was long before Penneniah and I would fully acknowledge to each other that our experiment was a failure, and I don't know how long this reserve would have held if it had not been rudely broken.

Open speech between us came about in this way: We were preparing to go into town and make some purchases for the farm (we purchased for nothing else by that time), when

Penneniah came into my room half dressed, with one shoe on her foot and one in her hand. She said, "Annie Tousey, look at this slit in my shoe."

" Is it on the outside or the inside ?" I asked. " If it is on the outside, wear your left boot on your right foot, and *vice versa*. I managed my last pair in that way."

" I thought of that, but they are not reversible."

" Then wear them as they are, and when we get into town we will buy a new pair," I said, . desperately.

" I'd like to know where the money's to come from, Annie Tousey. We must buy chicken feed to - day. The hens have almost stopped laying. I won't buy a pair of shoes until they begin again."

Penneniah's facts were undeniable. I examined the shoe carefully. "Penny," I said," snip off those ravellings sticking out of the slit, and black the white lining. Then, if you wear a black stocking, perhaps the hole won't show."

Penny listened, and followed my suggestions. By the aid of several like manœuvres we really looked so nice that after our business in town was completed I proposed a visit to the neighborhood of fashion, where lived a connection of ours known to Penneniah and myself as the " Favored of Fortune."

" We had better go now, Pen," I said ; " we

may never have another chance. Dear knows what we may look like the next time we come to town !"

Pen dislikes remarks of that kind. She prefers to ignore ignoble particulars, even in the bosom of the family ; but she saw the force of my argument, and assented. Just opposite the home of the Favored of Fortune lies a little park. As we crossed its stone pavement I heard an exclamation of horror from Pen. I turned to see her extended finger pointing to the ground.

"That," she said, in a tragic whisper—"that is *toe*."

I looked. There it was, undeniably. It had punched a way through the black stocking, and was poking out from her black shoe like a little white terrapin head. Its expression was so funny that I sat down on a bench and laughed until the tears rained down my face. A sense of the ridiculous is the little hobby-horse that has carried me safely over many a muddy road, but Penneniah will rarely mount him behind me.

"Annie Tousey," she said, severely, "it is not your toe, or you wouldn't laugh."

I disagreed with her, but it was not the time to say so.

"Pen," I said, "you will have to ask the Favored of Fortune to lend you a pair of shoes."

"I will walk home barefoot first," returned Pen.

And I knew she would; she's just that proud.

"Pen," I said, "what makes you so proud? I believe the marrow in your bones would stand up alone. If you won't ask help you will have to sit down on this bench and turn your stocking wrong side out. That will throw the hole on the other side."

"And have the police speak to me! Annie Tousey, have you lost your mind?"

"He won't see you. I will hold my skirts before you. You'll have to choose between him and the Favored of Fortune, Pen."

She chose the former.

"Do you know where I am going now?" she said, when the performance was safely over. "I am going straight out into the country and offer the farm to Uncle Elijah for thirteen thousand dollars."

"Agreed," I answered, and we went forthwith. Daniel, our black factotum, was waiting for us with our carriage (that same that ran me). Daniel was a legacy from our grandfather along with the farm. Penneniah reposed an absolute confidence in him and his experience. Mine had received some shocks.

"To Uncle Elijah's, Daniel," said Penneniah, with unnecessary decision, as we entered the carriage. When we reached our uncle's home, Joseph came out of the house to receive us. His mother had died years before, not long after her marriage to our Uncle Elijah, and Joseph lived alone with his step-father. Uncle Elijah had not much patience with Joseph, who openly believed in theoretical farming, and wore gloves.

Uncle Elijah's creed was that a man should advertise his profession by trade-marks upon his person.

"When I buy a horse," he would say, "I look at his teeth; with a farmer, I look at his hands."

Joseph's white hands were as thorns in his step-father's side.

"Father is on the back porch," said Joseph. "He's buying eggs of a man. Did you ever see father buy eggs? You'd better take a lesson. It's a kind of retroactive thing. The man sells the eggs, and father sells the man."

We found Uncle Elijah on the back porch with a basket of eggs before him. A wooden ring was in his hand. Any egg which would go through the ring he rejected; only the eggs which stuck came up to his standard for buying. Uncle Elijah nodded to us, and went on with his purchasing.

"Penneniah," I whispered in her ear, "ask him twelve thousand five hundred for the farm, not thirteen thousand."

"Annie Tousey," Penneniah replied, in the same tone, "you said on the way out that you wouldn't come down a single penny."

" I hadn't seen that ring then," I answered. "Pen, I really think you'd better say twelve thousand."

"Very well," she answered ; and when Uncle Elijah was ready to give us his attention, that was the offer Pen made him. Uncle Elijah had one habit of awful fascination to me. Whenever he talked on business matters he remodelled his features with his fingers, one after the other, in a kind of innocent, pensive way, not to his personal advantage.

He remodelled his nose and lips on this occasion, but not his heart. He would only repeat his offer of ten thousand, which Pen refused as absolutely.

The interview was short, and conducted on my sister's side with some asperity, which Uncle Elijah met with forbearance as aggravating as it was unyielding. On these terms we parted.

" Penny," I said, when we reached home, " what on earth are we to do? Of course we can't sell the farm outside of the family, as Uncle Elijah knows too well, but how are we to keep, not rings, but gloves on our fingers and shoes on our toe—"

" I wish you would not refer to that again, Annie Tousey," said Pen, with dignity.

"Very well," I answered, "I won't ; but we must have some ready money or starve ourselves—and the live-stock too, which is worse.

Suppose we reduce the live-stock, Penneniah? We might sell off half of what we have and feed the rest on the proceeds. We'll see what Joseph thinks of it."

Joseph happened in the next day, and not only thought well of it, but offered to be auctioneer for us, so Pen and I decided to have a sale.

" There's a good deal to sell, you see," said Pen. "We don't want all these farming implements ; we have about forty head of cattle, plenty of ducks and chickens, and, above all, the Berkshire pig, with her nine young ones."

Now this pig and her young ones were the pride of Pen's heart. I believe she prized their pedigree more than her own. Theirs certainly was the longer, but it came more trippingly from her tongue. As the day of sale drew near, Pen visited the sty daily, lavishing every attention on the inmates. She expected to realize more from them than from anything else. Alas! it was not to be.

One morning my sister rushed into the house with the announcement that there were but six little Berkshires in the sty.

" In my opinion," said Penneniah, " the fox has taken them. It might be possible."

" Are you sure it was not a mink ?" I asked, satirically.

Earlier in the year, Pen, assisted by Daniel, had arrived at the conclusion that it was a mink which nightly entered the chicken-house to steal the chickens bodily. She persisted in this belief in Daniel and the mink, even when faced by an old almanac found in the garret which defined a mink as "a small animal of the weasel species, that sucks the blood of its victim and leaves the carcass." No carcasses were left in our hen-house.

But the present fact to face now was that by some agent the little pigs were gone also, and the next day three of their brethren followed them. Pen and I stood by the sty looking sadly at the three remaining relics.

"I am sure it is a fox," said Pen.

"How can you be so foolish?" I replied. "If it is a fox it is a two-legged one named Daniel. The little pigs have gone the way of the chickens. Do you really suppose, Pen, that the old pig would let a fox walk off with her young ones? She has teeth, too, hasn't she?"

Alas! she had. Pen, poking about in the straw with the point of her parasol, found an unexpected answer to my question. The murder was out. Daniel was vindicated, but the cherished Berkshire was a cannibal. Under the straw lay the half-eaten scraps of her children. Pen was made ill by this discovery, and not only from a moral point of view.

"She ain' no mo' use as a breeder, Miss Pen," said Daniel. "After they wonst tas'es peeg, they's a-goin' t'eat 'em ev'ry time."

I remembered having heard something of the same sort told by missionaries, and began to say so, when Pen begged me to stop.

"I suppose it's only one of Daniel's lies," I said, encouragingly. "You remember the mink—"

"It might be possible," Pen interrupted ; and when Joseph came to talk over the inventory he said it was not only possible, but certain.

"Then it would be dishonest not to mention the fact at the sale," said Pen, sadly.

"No farmer would buy her if you did," said Joseph.

"It must be mentioned," replied Pen, with the air of a Roman father.

I followed Joseph into the hall when he left. "Look here," I said ; "about that pig. So you mention the fact of the eating, it won't matter how you express it, I suppose. If you say that part of the litter were killed in the last *snap*, would that do ?"

Joseph looked at me, and I looked at Joseph. The corners of his mouth approached his ears. "Yes, Annie," he said, "that will *do* somebody," and we parted with a mutual understanding. Pen is honest always. I am as honest as the times permit.

The morning of the sale came at last, and was like a nightmare. The live - stock would not be collected ; and when they finally were, they would not stay where we put them. First the chickens got out. Those for sale had been locked in the hen-house the night before. In the morning Pen gave the key to Daniel's boy, with repeated instructions to "feed the chickens *in* the hen-house." Half an hour later Pen opened the trap-door of the hen-house and peeped in curiously.

"Hen, hen, hen," she called. Pen would never say "Chicky, chick." She thought it vulgar. But it made little difference, for there was not a chicken present in the hen-house.

"'Deed, Miss Penneniah, you done tol' me ter feed de chickens what ware *in* de hen-house, an' I let um out an' fed um," said Daniel's own son. "I 'ain' done nothin' but what you said."

Pen admitted that "it might be possible," and for the rest of the morning the little darky had the delightful and previously forbidden occupation of chasing chickens.

For the ducks, every one supposed the other had locked them up the night before. "I seen um dis mornin'," said Daniel's son. "A-head-in' up de stream dey was. Dey's got a feedin'-groun' 'way up de country yander. 'Tain' no kin' of use lookin' fur um."

To crown these discoveries came another. An Alderney calf, aged twenty-four hours, was missing, and the mother was lowing wildly in the stable.

"Hit sartinly was shet up las' night wid de

res'," asserted Daniel; "jes as shore as you live, ladies, de bull eat it."

"I never heard of such a thing," replied Pen, tentatively; "did you, Annie Tousey?"

Daniel took serious umbrage at my reply.

"*Ex*cuse me, miss. I don' like to contradic' you, madam, but indeed, miss, I hev known bulls what eat calfs."

"It might be possible," said Pen, and Daniel looked at me reproachfully, supported by her faith; "and if he has," Pen went on, "he will be as useless as the Berkshire, I suppose."

"Daniel," I said, "if you are too lazy to hunt the calf yourself, let that poor cow out of the stable, and she'll find it fast enough. It was no more locked up last night than the ducks were."

Daniel departed, swelling with injury.

"Pen," I said, "how can you be such a fool? I wouldn't trust Daniel tied with a string. Who ever heard of a bull eating a calf?"

"Annie Tousey, you know nothing about it. If a pig eats her young, it might be possible to a bull. You hurt Daniel's feelings just now."

A little later Daniel appeared in the doorway. He was rolling a bit of straw about in his lips sheepishly. He generally carried a sample of the crop in season in his mouth.

"De calf done foun', Miss Penneniah," he said; "hit's ma went right to it. Hit ware out in de parsture, jes as snug under de bushes where she done hid it las' night. How come I ter furgit it is 'cos I bin combin' my hade at nights here lately. They say ef you combs yer hade at nights, you fergits. That's what's got to me."

"Well," I said, "you were very careless, Daniel, but I am thankful the calf is found and safe."

"'Tain't safe," said Daniel, solemnly. "Hit's done foun' dade."

With all my dismay, this was too much. The sublimity of our misfortunes rose to the ridiculous, and I laughed until Pen became really angry.

I will not dwell longer on the confusions of that morning. Despite the ill luck which seemed to pursue us, we had everything fairly in order when Joseph arrived, and, passing all over into his hands, Pen and I retired to the house, where we awaited results impatiently.

When the sale was over, and most of the people gone, Joseph came in to tell us that he really thought he had done rather well for us. "All the farming implements you wanted to sell are gone," he said; "but, best of all, the greater part of the live-stock has been bought in by one man, named Smith."

Pen bounded from her chair.

"Frank Smith!" she cried. "Did he pay cash? If not, he mustn't have one of them."

Joseph said the man gave his note, and

"'THEY SAY EF YOU COMBS YER HADE AT NIGHTS, YOU FERGITS'"

added that he thought "a bird in the hand was worth two in the bush."

"In the case of Smith, his note represents the bush birds," I replied. "Joseph, you can't mean to say you didn't know that Smith has no credit in the county? Well, I see why you irritate your poor father."

I really had reason to feel troubled ; for, with Smith refused as a purchaser, when the ducks came back at nightfall, there was almost as much live-stock cackling and quacking and lowing about us as there had been before the sale.

That night Pen and I sat again looking at each other despairingly.

"Pen," I said, at last, "this is a crisis. We have been working the farm together ; now I suggest that you take what small proceeds there are from the sale, wear my shoes into town to-morrow" (she had been wearing rubbers over hers to hide the hole), "buy yourself a pair of shoes, and the things we must have to live, while I stay here trying to think out a plan."

Pen consented, and went into town the next day. All that morning I sat thinking, and all that afternoon I still thought, seeing before me more and more plainly but one hateful conclusion—to sell the farm to Uncle Elijah for two-thirds of its value; yet by the time Pen came home the problem was solved otherwise.

"Well, Annie Tousey," she said, "has any thought come to you?"

"Yes," I replied. "It didn't come until late in the afternoon, Penny, when I was sitting alone on the front porch; then it opened the gate and walked up the path, with a bucket of paint in each hand. Now, Penneniah, before I tell you anything I want to make a bargain with you. You know we decided that working together we had made a failure. I want you to promise me that you will not interfere with any of my decisions about the farm for a month. Then if I have not succeeded I will turn the farm over to you, and you can do what you like for a month. If we both fail we will hand it over to Uncle Elijah for his ten thousand dollars. Will you agree?"

"Yes," said my sister; "that seems fair."

"No interference for a month, mind, no matter what I do. Do you promise that?"

"Yes," answered Pen, and I knew she would keep her word—that's Penneniah. Then I said:

"I will tell you what I have done. By noon to-morrow the roof of this house will be crying out in large letters, white upon a red ground, 'Use Camphorated Compound Cramp Cure.' As we are on a hill and near the railroad, hundreds of people will have read it before nightfall, and we shall have one hundred dollars in our pockets."

Penny dropped into the nearest chair. She

did not speak; but it would have been a waste of breath—her face was enough.

"I am glad you remember your promise," I said, quickly. "I was afraid for a moment that you were going to forget it. The man came up the path to say that if I would let him paint his advertisement on the roof of the barn he would pay me twenty-five dollars. I told him no—of course not. He was going away, when a thought struck me, and I called him back.

"'What would you pay me,' I said, 'if I let you paint it on the roof of the *house?*' He looked from one roof to the other, and said, as they were of about equal size, he would pay the same. 'No, you won't,' I told him. 'You know you never advertised on the roof of a handsome stone house before. You will pay me three times as much as for the barn, or none at all.' I wished I had asked him more; for he grabbed at it, and the bargain is closed—twenty-five dollars for the barn and seventy-five for the house—one hundred dollars in all, where we had nothing."

Penneniah burst into tears. "As I promised, of course I can say nothing," she sobbed, "but I shall never forgive you, Annie Tousey—never."

"I am very sorry you feel so badly about it," I said. "It seems to me best—conscientiously best, Pen. But, you know, I am to have but thirty days as my share of the management, and so I only rented the roofs for that term. Then you can have them painted over if you desire."

"The first day," sobbed Pen—"the very first day of my term."

"It may be possible to paint them over before then," I said. "Something may happen."

But as Pen would not be comforted, and as I was not moved sufficiently to withdraw from my decision, our relations became a little strained. In fact, I had to stand quite alone in the matter. The next day, when the white letters glared out on the red roof, and all the neighbors checked their teams at the gate to stare and laugh, Pen shut every window-blind, and would not cross the door-sill.

"I said I will not interfere, and I will not," she said, "but I feel exactly as if a demon were sitting on the roof."

Even Joseph saw fit to remonstrate with me on the subject.

"Annie," he said, "upon my word, I don't wonder Pen feels badly. I can't think what you're doing this for. It's not worth it."

"Joseph," I replied, "I advise you to go home and pull your thinkers up by the roots and plant them again. That's what I did the day Penny went into town. They got a new start that way. What does Uncle Elijah say?"

"He's pretty angry, Annie. And, to tell the

truth, I don't blame him for it—or Penneniah
either."

This was the first day. The second day
Joseph came again to tell me that his step-
father had been to see his lawyer.

"He came home more outraged than ever,"
Joseph said, gravely. Then he began to laugh.
"By - the - way, Annie, last night, after I went
home, I did what you told me to. I pulled up
my thinkers by the roots and planted them
again. They are growing very fast now."

"What did you say?" asked Penny, wiping
her eyes. She had been wiping one eye or the
other ever since the "Compound Cure" had
brooded over our roof.

"Nothing important," Joseph answered. "All
the neighbors called on father to-day, Annie—
casually, you know, just to pass the weather.
You girls and the roof were mentioned by each
one incidentally." He began to laugh again.

"Joseph," I said, sharply, "you had better
not aggravate your father by coming to see us
just now."

Joseph shook his head solemnly. "He'll be
here himself before long. You see if he isn't.
You had better be mixing your war-paint and
collecting your feathers, Annie."

With this warning he left me.

"I can't think what ailed Joseph," said Pen,
when he had gone. "He is usually so considerate and sympathetic. He must have seen

I was in trouble to-day, yet he kept bursting out laughing in the oddest way at nothing at all. It was not like Joseph. Do you think Uncle Elijah is really coming here, Annie Tousey?"

On the third day of the reign of the "Compound Cure" on our roof Pen's question was answered by Uncle Elijah himself. Joseph was the first to see him, from the window, coming up the path to the house door.

"Annie," said Joseph, "are you ready? He's here."

Both Penneniah and I knew whom he meant. Penny was sewing, and as she dropped her work and her hands together on the table by which she was sitting, her thimble positively rattled with apprehension.

"Joseph," I said, "I don't want Uncle Elijah to find you here. You have just time to slip out of the back door."

Joseph shook his head emphatically. "When I have been hanging about here for three days to see this ! No, indeed, Annie ; you can't make me go."

"Stay, Joseph," pleaded Pen ; "I should feel safer. Annie, let him hide in the closet. Do, Joseph."

"I will if I may have the door on a crack," said Joseph. And to this I had to consent, for Uncle Elijah was already knocking at the front door. I went to let him in myself, and when

I brought him back to our sitting-room with me only Pen was to be seen, sewing at the table with stitches which had all to be picked out afterwards ; but the closet door was ajar.

"Penneniah," said Uncle Elijah, deliberately, as he entered—he had ignored me, save for a brief greeting in the hall—"Penneniah," he repeated, standing accusingly before her, " I have come to speak to you regarding the indecent way you arc treating the home of your grandfather and your own father. Both would turn in their graves—"

" No, Uncle Elijah," I interrupted—Pen was already dissolved in tears—"Penny didn't do it ; I did."

Uncle Elijah turned to me. "You, Annie Tousey?"

"Yes," I replied. "Penny is the elder, of course, but you know how we keep our word when we once give it, and she has promised me that I shall run the farm, and that she will not interfere with anything I choose to do."

"Only for thirty—" Pen began to sob.

"Penny," I cried, "hold your tongue! You agreed not to say one word. Now keep your promise."

And my sister bowed her face into the white work she had been sewing.

"Uncle Elijah," I said, "if you have anything to say, please say it to me. I am in charge. Won't you take a chair?"

Uncle Elijah looked from the seat I offered to me, and then back again to the chair, into which he finally sank. I sat opposite him, and we looked silently at each other, until he had to begin.

"Annie Tousey," he said, "when you first told me that you would not sell the farm out of the family, I supposed you had some feeling for the old place."

"So I had, Uncle Elijah," I answered, "and so I have. That's why I rented the roof out to the 'Compound Cure' rather than sell it."

My uncle put his hand in his pocket and drew out his check-book.

"Now, Annie," he said, "it's not worth while for me to tell you that this is a great personal inconvenience to me, nor to enter into a talk on values. You have one mind as to the price of this farm, I another. I have offered you ten thousand dollars down for the property; you have offered it to me for twelve thousand. I came over this afternoon prepared to make a compromise. Get me pen and ink. I will write you out a check for eleven thousand, which will split the difference."

He laid his check - book on the table and opened it.

"Uncle Elijah," I said, without moving, "I am very sorry you feel it so about the 'Compound Cure.' I had tried everything else to make the farm pay before I came to that. And

I am sorry, too, that I must refuse your eleven thousand dollars; but I am in charge of affairs, and I wouldn't feel it just to Penneniah."

Penny took her head out of her work to open her mouth, but I frowned it shut again.

" I must absolutely refuse, Uncle Elijah," I said.

" Very well, then," he answered ; " if you are so obstinate over one thousand dollars, Annie Tousey, I will yield it."

He got up from his chair, found pen and ink for himself, and brought them back to the table with him.

" What are you going to do, Uncle Elijah ?" I said, as he drew the check-book towards him. Uncle Elijah looked up at me and began to remodel his features.

" I accept your offer," he answered ; " but it is a large sum to pay out, Annie Tousey."

" What is a large sum ?" I asked.

" Twelve thousand dollars."

I shook my head.

" I can't sell the farm at twelve thousand, Uncle Elijah. I can't conscientiously do that."

Uncle Elijah laid down the pen and stared at me.

" What do you mean, Annie Tousey? That was your own offer. Penneni—"

" No, Uncle Elijah," I said. " Pen has promised to leave all this to me, and you know she will. We did offer you the farm at twelve thousand, but that was before we—or rather I—had developed this advertising industry. We can afford to hold the farm now, and I mean to hold it at its full value—fifteen thousand dollars."

Uncle Elijah closed his check-book with a snap, which his eyes and mouth seemed to imitate.

"Then you can hold it," he said; "but understand, Annie Tousey, no matter what straits and what disgrace you run yourself and Penneniah into, don't look to me for anything, for I wash my hands of you."

"We won't get into any straits, Uncle Elijah," I answered, firmly. "I see plain sailing ahead of me. I have thought out ever so many plans for developing an advertising industry. Our being near the railroad and on a hill is a great deal in our favor. I have decided to run a flagstaff up the side of every chimney we have, and rent out the flags. Of course wooden scantlings set up in the fields are nothing new, but that will yield something. I have a crowning plan of setting a scantling on the top of the house as high as it is safe. We live on a hill, but we don't have heavy winds. I mean to create here an advertising farm that people will come from far and near to see. I shall ask fancy prices for the advertisements, and I shall be inventing original and startling methods all the time."

Uncle Elijah lay back in his chair staring at me. I did not dare to look in Pen's direction.

"Annie Tousey," said Uncle Elijah, "do you actually mean to do this disgraceful thing on the old home-place?"

"Uncle Elijah," I answered, solemnly, "I pledge you my honor I mean every word of it. I am sick of spending every penny we get on the farm. Now the farm has got to do something for us. If you can think of any better paying plan, short of selling the farm out of the family or selling it for less than fifteen thousand dollars, I should be delighted to hear of it. Otherwise this advertising industry will go on. I can see no help for it."

My uncle forgot to mould his features; he forgot to dip his pen in the ink until he found it would not write in his check-book.

"Here, Annie Tousey," he said, tearing out the check he drew up, and laying it loose on the table before me, "do you go and have a deed of this farm made to me. Of all the disgraceful things I ever heard, this is the most disgraceful. Get me the deed, I say, and two witnesses."

I looked at the check. It was for fifteen thousand dollars.

"Annie Tousey," said my Uncle Elijah, as I took the check and he rose to go, "I will do you the justice to say that I believe you do not realize what you have done. As a woman, you cannot understand how it appears, but if you were a man, Annie Tousey, I should say, without a moment's hesitation, that you had deliberately played a very close and—a—very doubtful game. Annie Tousey—"

What my uncle saw written on my face I am sure I do not know. I opened my reticule quickly, and shut his check inside. When I looked up again my uncle was vigorously modelling his features, and watching me so curiously that I was glad to glance at Penneniah. Pen was also looking at me, with an expression of doubtful awe. At that point it seemed to me that I heard a distinct and suppressed chuckle. I glanced at the cupboard door anxiously, but the sound did not come from that direction. As it was repeated, I turned involuntarily towards Uncle Elijah. He was no longer modelling his features, but they wore an expression quite new to me.

"Annie Tousey," he said, slowly, "you ought to have been a man"; and when he said that I knew that he felt himself paying me the highest compliment in his power, and also that in pocketing my uncle's check I had pocketed his respect.

"I am very sorry, Uncle Elijah—" I began, but he stopped me.

"No, you ain't, Annie Tousey. You needn't think I bear you a grudge, though, for I don't. Lord, it's a pity you ain't a man. It makes me sick when I see what ought to be a man having to walk about this world in woman's skirts, but it makes me sicker to see what ought to be a woman in man's trousers. Now there's my wife's Joseph— By-the-way, Annie Tousey, I have thought—"

The closet-door creaked, and I broke in : "Never mind about Joseph, Uncle Elijah. I am glad you don't feel hardly towards me, and we can move away in a week, if that will suit you."

Uncle Elijah held out his hand. There was a curious smile on his face.

"It was a close deal, Annie Tousey," he said ; "but as a deal it was square, and I can't complain. I'll tell you what, though, I'd rather have you on my side than on the other. You needn't think of leaving this farm for very long. I look at it this way : It takes two halves to make a whole, but you can make it out of three quarters and Joseph. He— Well, I wouldn't take away the big pieces of furniture, Annie Tousey."

"It isn't as if I cared for any one else. I think you know that. It's only that I—"

"That you don't care for me."

"You put words into my mouth. I had not meant to say exactly that—still, if you prefer it should stand so—"

"I do, if you are thinking of our long row home, and so are tempering the wind for my shearing. Won't you speak with brutal frankness? When a woman has refused a man directly and indirectly as often as you have me, he may suffer each time a gamut of emotions, but really he ceases to be embarrassed."

The woman who had spoken flushed a little.

"That was not a nice speech. I have always been honest with you."

"Yes, but never quite so far from covert. If I were not I, and you you, the prospect ahead might be awkward for an hour or so, and awkwardness means anguish to your mind. You are a symphony of social accords. I have never yet made a discordant scene, I think, but being repeatedly refused with such unfailing tact

and courtesy is having its effects on my nerves.
I am more irritable than I used to be. It would
be easier if you were rude to me."

"I know it." The answer came quickly.
"It is all wrong between you and me. May I
speak very plainly?"

"I beg that you will. I think I have almost
the right to demand it; and you can speak
the naked truth and still be artistic, you know.
I learned that early in my art career. One
day, when we were all in the studio painting,
my old master came behind me and leaned
over my shoulder to find that I had boyishly
draped my figure in a floating gauzy veil. 'Mr.
Satterly,' he said, 'if you want to paint draped
figures, paint them, and if you want to paint
nude figures, paint nude figures, but spare me
shimmerettes!' Won't you spare me shimmerettes to-day, Annette?"

Satterly looked up, smiling, and his companion laughed, but she was still uneasy, as her
very attitude showed. The two were sitting
together in a deep stony hollow formed in some
wave-smitten rocks, which were at once the
breakwater and rugged bluff of a small island
that lay green with its pine-trees in the midst
of a deep cove. The site was too exposed to
winter gales for verdure, but in place of grass,
nature, fertile in expedients, had laid down
matted pine-needles season after season, until
the net-work underfoot was more dense than

the prickly boughs crossing overhead. Winds and storms had filled all the nooks and corners of the red crags with this fodder-like pine, making a veritable rookery of warm nests in among the rocks. It was in one of these nests that Annette and Satterly were sitting.

"I and my shimmerettes seem to offend you to-day," said Annette, after a long pause. "Do you know that we close our cottage to-morrow? I asked you early in the summer to give me quiet freedom while I stayed here to think it all over, and I meant to be decided when these last days of October came. I have tried to be so all along, but I hoped you understood why I could not be too vehement in my denials."

There was a genuine sweetness and an unusual softness in her tone and manner that one less a lover would have found hard to resist. Satterly moved to lay his hand closely on the hand of the woman he loved, with a quick touch which had in it so much earnestness and so little of a caress that she did not withdraw from him.

"Forgive me," he said, "if I am soured; indeed it is not your fault. However this talk between us ends—and I feel that there are to be finalities in it—you must believe that I acquit you of any blame whatever. You have been most exquisitely patient, womanly, and kind to me from Alpha to Omega, if Omega it is to be. Now, while I can speak calmly and with unbiased truth, I want you to write it in the tablets of your memory that I told you this. Don't you let anything—anything that I may be provoked to say or do hereafter—make you believe that I really think differently."

He was sitting at her feet, and could see, as she looked down at him, all the little flecks of warm brown in her eyes that on near view made them seem hazel. Her lips were parted and quivering slightly. To Satterly her face perfectly expressed her character as he had learned to know it. Her underlying nature was as the tendernesses of her beauty—those brown lights of the eyes, those soft curves of the lips—visible only when studied as Satterly was then devoutly studying them. She turned a little from his fixed gaze on her face, and looked over the waters at the low wintry sun hanging red above the red rocks. The movement drew her hand softly, as if unintentionally, from Satterly's grasp. He fell back with a laugh.

"Everything you do is characteristic of you. Here you have let me sit as another woman would not have dared trust a man madly in love with her, but you know exactly to a mathematical nicety the line of safety. Did you know that for two foolish moments just now, because a squirrel in the tree made you start, and again because the sunlight shifted on your face, I half believed that your fingers caught mine, or that your expression altered? Was that why you drew your hand away? No—pardon me—another woman would have done that—you only let it melt from mine."

"Yes," she answered, frankly; "and you are thinking, too, that my horror of 'scenes,' as you call them, is the cause of whatever is wrong between us. No, don't stop me. Something is wrong; but my real inability to decide and end this finally one way or the other has been due to my inexperience—"

Satterly laughed outright. "Inexperience! In what, pray, are you inexperienced—men or manners? Dear one, don't be troubled to find *reasons*. You don't love me—that's all—and enough. Why should you? Because I can't forget you—things stick in my heart as in a dog's —is no reason that you should be annoyed."

"I am glad you are willing to understand," she said, gently, "but you don't quite do so yet. I mean what I say of my ignorance. Most women of my age—I am no longer an immature girl—have some experiences to guide them, but I have never really cared for any man in my life; and as a woman has to be a little—well—susceptible herself, you know, to thoroughly enjoy playing at love, I have never even had flirtations to teach me. I have come nearer to both love and flirtation with you than with any one else." She paused, as if doubting the wisdom of such plain speech.

"Go on," he answered; "this is just what I wanted."

"You see now why I asked you for these free months. I have had nothing by which to gauge myself. Other men have loved me. You know that, so there is no harm in my saying so. I have been ashamed that I could hear them with not even a throb of answering emotion. With you it has been a little different. Sometimes I have thought that I did care for you because I hate to make you suffer, and because I can talk to you—well, as I am talking now. But neither of these is love. I want to ask you an odd question. How did you know that you loved me?" She flushed under his look of amusement, but did not explain further.

"How do I know I love you?"

"That was not what I asked. The tense makes all the difference. I said, how *did* you know. I think I can understand diving deeply after plunging, but plunging in, it is quite another matter."

"Yes," he admitted, "it is. I have often wondered how women got the impulse to dive into marriage, lacking the stimulus of the chase."

Annette looked her assent.

"You understand me wonderfully well. It must be partly your artistic temperament that teaches you how a woman feels. You could never have sent me a Japanese oak, for instance, though you do think me a worldling. I think I want to tell you about my Japanese oak, and how I almost married the man who gave it to me. It was a long while ago. I was little more than a *débutante* then, but I thought it high time I married. The idea of never marrying had not then occurred to me." She waited again for Satterly to speak; but he was silent, and she went on: "I was never really engaged to the man I decided to marry. Something held me back from the final step; but he had reason to believe it would soon come to that, though I never pretended to love him at all; and his first gift to me, a young, sensitive girl, was—what do you think?—a morbid Old World plant—a Japanese oak! Did you ever see one?"

"I think so. They look like weary, wizened old men—don't they?—and never grow larger than a little bush."

Annette spoke with suppressed feeling. "They don't grow because you deny them every natural condition. You keep them in a pot too small for them, with cruelly little water, too little sun, and too little air. They live for a century, and cost, I forget what, but small fortunes. It was a gift I was very proud of for a day or so. Then I began to hate it, and the man who thought I could be hard enough to enjoy it. I was, as he had reason to know, a rather cold woman, but not then, or now, I hope, a hard one. I set the poor thing in a great pot of earth, and put it in a south window, and drowned it with water, and flooded it with air. Of course it died. When I broke my engagement, if I can call the half-agreement such a name, I said that I did so because the oak had been made a gift to me, and because that proved an utter lack of comprehension of me. But that was not my whole reason. I did not tell him how I had learned to realize that if I married without love I should grow, or rather stop growing, just like that miserable, starved little tree. He had unconsciously given me an object-lesson, you see, and I have never forgotten it. Worldly, as you and he—yes, both of you—think me, the ghost of that oak has again and again stood between me and a loveless marriage." There was a long pause. Annette broke the silence, speaking slowly, as if feeling her way to an understanding with herself as well as with her listener. "I am not a cold woman, whatever I seem. If I were, I should have married long ago. A marriage of love, genuine, tender love, is what I call beautiful, and I will have nothing less lovely. But how is one to know? How am I to know, for instance, that you can give me the sunshine, space, and free air of a love-marriage? I know—all this is hard for me to say—that I shall never marry any one if I do not engage myself to you to-day, for I can never again expect to meet a man whose comradeship I so enjoy or with whom I feel such freedom, and who—it is even harder to say than I thought—who so nearly stirs my heart." Satterly looked up quickly, but she would not meet his eyes. She had to steady her voice to go on, and the words came more firmly. "I confess I shrink from the thought of parting with you finally ; yet, I do not, no, I do not feel that irresistible impulse to bind myself more closely to you which, I suppose, would mean that I really loved you. I don't know how better to test my heart, and you don't help me."

She ended with a little catch in her breath and more emotion than Satterly had ever seen her show. He replied instantly.

" Frankly, don't you think you are rather unreasonable ? How am I to test your heart for you ? As I understand, you paraphrase the old agnostic's prayer : ' O Love, if you be my Love, touch my heart, if I have a heart.' Perhaps you don't realize that you are asking me to teach you exactly what I have been vainly striving and slaving to make you learn, lo, these many moons. What more can I do ? I do melt my own tested heart for you to drink as Cleopatra did her pearl. But that hasn't taught you, my Princess—Princess I-Would-I-Wot-Not."

Annette's face changed. She looked down with a quick turn of her head.

"Princess I - Would - I - Wot - Not," she repeated — "I-Would-I-Wot-Not." She recited
the title over and over, as if it fascinated her.
"Is that descriptive of me? Yes, I suppose it
is. How discontented and fretful and peevish
the name sounds — I would I wot not!" She
interrupted Satterly's murmured protest. "I
don't mind; it's entirely true. But don't you
know that I would give the world to wot what
I do want—to know my heart as others know
theirs—as you do?"

"Yes," said Satterly, dryly, "there's no doubt
whatever about my knowing. I am not intro-
spective enough to be a doubter. I'm simply
an old-fashioned lover on one knee before you
offering my simple heart for what it is worth as
frankly and as perpetually as an old-fashioned
valentine picture. I have known unfortunately well just what I wanted — not ever since I
first met you—I am not practised enough to
pretend I have always loved you. I don't think
I quite liked you when we first met, did I?"

"No," said Annette, laughing; "you thought
me a worldly woman, and once deliberately told
me so. I don't think I have ever had to complain of what you call 'shimmerettes' with
you."

"You never will, I hope. The first time it
ever occurred to me to love you was when we
were walking one day under a grove of pine-
trees just like these, and the ground was springy

in the same way with the old and new shed needles. Do you remember that walk? I don't suppose so, but I was as I thought making myself agreeable to you, and talking cynically of what money could do, what I knew my own money had bought me of the world's favor, when you stopped short and dug the point of your parasol into the mat of pine-needles. 'Bah! You haven't the money that would buy a carpet like this!' you said, scornfully, and you could have knocked me down with one of those same needles. I looked at you, and then somehow it seemed to me that I saw your beauty for the first time. I thought, 'Why, this is a woman to love!' But frankly it wasn't the first time I had thought that of a woman, and, according to experience, it seemed to me an unimportant discovery. Only I thought it again shortly, and again in a segregated kind of way, until at last the thought dropped down so often it grew as this pine-needle carpet must have grown, slowly but surely overlapping everything else. I can't tell you how I know I love you any more than the pine-needles know what made them fall, or why they keep on falling."

Satterly was speaking with apparent calmness, but, as Annette looked aside, the excited contraction of his eyes told a different story. Annette had been listening earnestly, now she leaned her hand on the stone by her, and with a restless gesture rose to her feet.   She spoke slowly.

"I have always dreamed that if I ever fell in love it would be so deeply and overwhelmingly that I think I may have been, and perhaps I am now, afraid to loosen my hold on myself. That may be the trouble.   But whatever the reason is, that hold is still there, Mr. Satterly.   You have taught me nothing, and I am still my own.   If I *had* to marry you"—she turned to Satterly with a smile so sweet and so frank that his heart sank in his breast— "I believe I could make you fairly happy, and you me, but I can be sure of nothing more ideal than that, and that is not very ideal, is it?   As I said, if I *had* to marry you, I think it would be in all probability best and happiest for me; but marriages can't be made in that way, and as it has to be deliberate, and as the last word has to lie with me, I cannot take the responsibility of making it yes—it must be no."

She paused in a sudden embarrassment, looking away from Satterly over the edge of the rocky nest down on the curved beach at the foot of the bluff.   As she stood she shivered slightly.

"It grows very cold," she began, conventionally.   Suddenly she interrupted herself, crying out in another voice, "Look! look! our boat!"

Satterly sprang to his feet beside her.   He had left their flat-bottomed sharpy beached on the sands with the oars drawn into it ; now it was floating free on the water, each moment drifting farther, and already some distance away. The stealthy tide, rising and falling softly and rapidly, had washed off the light shell. They both stood staring helplessly after it.

"Can we do nothing?" cried Annette, aghast. "We might as well be in a prison with our key drifting away."

In answer Satterly flung back his head suddenly, looking full in her face with wide-opened eyes that fairly spoke, though she failed to read the thought behind. An overwhelming sense of something trembling in the balance seized her, but a moment later he had turned from her as if with a wrench of will-power, and began to climb from the deep nest to the rocks above. His foot was on the upper ledge when Annette, following him, caught his arm.

"What are you thinking of?" she cried, sharply. Her upturned face was suffused with color, her lips were quivering, her eyes terrified. Satterly had never seen her so beautiful or so womanly.

"The boat," he answered, simply, looking down at her. "I can overtake it."

"You must not try. I implore you! These waters are always bitterly cold. Now they are icy. They will send out a search-party from home after nightfall, so we have only to wait," she went on, resolutely, as his arm seemed to stiffen under her grasp. "I am not afraid, and I am woman enough, Mr. Satterly, and proud enough, to be indifferent."

Satterly broke from her hold.

"I am not," he said. "Go to the back of the rock. For God's sake don't follow me with your eyes! If I should fail, you could do nothing whatever to help me." He drew himself up and over the edge. His footfall sounded on the hard stone fainter and fainter. Annette stood for a moment motionless, then dropped down into the hollow, crouching against the wall, her face hidden, her eyes and ears sealed—waiting.

A half-hour later the low sun, hanging like a red disk over the water, shone blindingly into Annette's face as she sat in the stern of the boat facing Satterly, who was rowing. She was utterly silent, and he noticed that the glow in the sky, sea, and air failed to warm her pallor. Her face was grave, her manner serious.

"I am sorry," said Satterly, apologetically. "It was a careless trick on my part. I should have remembered what a thief the water is; but, indeed," he went on, laughing, "you need not take it so solemnly. Except for your sad fright and a little wad of wet underwear in the locker, there's no harm done. It was not so bad at is looked. The tide was with me, and the water was not too cold."

Annette dropped her hand over the side of the boat, trailing it in the water, and drew it out again blue with the chill. Her voice was shaking, but she spoke with a cold precision.

"You risked your life. The tide could have swept you out and the cold have cramped you. It is a marvel that neither happened. I shall never as long as I live forget those moments I spent crouching down among the pine-needles at the back of that rock. I was afraid to see or hear. I tried to bury myself alive."

"I know," said Satterly; "I had almost to shake you awake when I came back. It was like a disappointment, wasn't it, with such preparation for horrors?"

The recollection of her terrors and his light manner seemed to double Annette's annoyance.

"What right had you to impose such an experience on me? I am not speaking of any duty to yourself."

Satterly did not answer. She went on restlessly:

"I can't forgive you for any of it. I am weighed down by the obligations you persistently thrust on me. It is not generous."

Then he looked up, his brow reddening.

"On the contrary," he answered, quickly. He rowed less strongly, and the tide swept heavily against the bow of the boat until his face was in the sunlight, and Annette could see plainly his look of indignant repudiation. "On the contrary, you are now under no obligation of any kind. You are not Princess I-Wot-What-I-Must, as you might have been. You are still Princess I-Would-I-Wot-Not."

Annette's head rose proudly.

"You think, then, that I did not mean it when I told you on the island I was willing to wait for rescue?"

"You thought you meant it; but as I was I, and you you, if the chance of escape had been one in a million, and I had but half a life to risk, I ought to have risked it."

"Why?"

But Satterly had already regained his composure and his usual easy good-humor.

"I refuse to answer," he said, laughing. "Just now you stung me into saying a great deal more than I should."

"You may as well go on, as you have said so much. You think, in a word, that with the publicity, the hue-and-cry of a search-party looking for us, I should not have been exactly in a position that forced me to marry you, but where it would have been more comfortable to my worldly-mindedness to do so, and so, worldly to the end, I would have married you as a mere escape from annoyance."

Satterly showed that he braced himself for

what he saw had to come. "It is what you would have done," he said, firmly, "and what indubitably I should have grasped at your doing, and far better have died than been party to. You are very angry with me, I see. I don't wonder. I hardly think it will mend matters for me to tell you that I worship you just as you are, worldly-mindedness and all. You are not worldly at the core of your heart, but you have—you can't deny it—you have lived and outlived some things that other women have yet to fathom. You know, for instance, exactly how valuable the world's opinion is, and what it means to run even a little counter to it. I mean to tell you the whole truth now; it is better. When I saw the boat drifting off, I remembered that you had just told me you could marry me if you *had* to do so, and be fairly happy. I knew—forgive me—that you *would* consent to marry me because of that accident of wind and tide, and deep down in my heart I knew all in a moment that I should not be strong enough to resist such a temptation. My only salvation was to plunge in at once, and come back with the boat, or never come back to you at all. You must see that."

"You risked your life, then, to save me from yourself?"

Satterly laughed, and shook his head. "I don't know. I am getting out of my depth now. I tell you I haven't the kind of mind that untangles metaphysical confusions. I only know that I love you, and I stand now where I stood before the boat drifted away—with a fair field, but no favor whatever."

"You risked your life to save me from yourself," Annette repeated. Her voice was hard and mechanical. "You knew me better than I knew myself. Yes, I would have married you. It was very nobly done."

Satterly replied by silence only, which Annette made no effort to break. He bent to his oars, rowing strongly, while the sun sank and twilight settled on the waters. It was dark when the homing boat with its two silent occupants wove its way through the shipping and touched at the landing-pier. They could see the old weather-worn boat-master standing on the floating wharf with his lantern lit, peering out over the harbor, waiting for them. He had heard the splash of oars, and this was the last boat out. Satterly took the lantern from him, crossing the seats to the stern where Annette sat. As he lifted the light, and it fell full on her face, he paused in amazement, his hand extended to help her. It was Annette who spoke to the boatman, bidding him bring her some wrappings from the boat-house.

The man turned away, and she rose, taking the hand Satterly was still mechanically offering. As she stood beside him, the lifted light showed plainly her flushed and tear-wet cheeks.

Her voice was soft with emotion, low with earnestness. All the tenderness of her beauty shone on Satterly as through a mist. It was the same imploring face that had looked up at him from the rocky nest.

"I sent him away on purpose, because I can't let myself leave this boat without speaking. Don't try to help me. I ought to say it alone. I know I am not worthy of a man like yourself—no, don't speak. But I have learned one thing from you to-night, and you'll teach me more. I know now that I never shall learn what love is except by loving and sacrificing as you do. It is with you that the last word lies, but you must never again call me Princess I-Would-I-Wot-Not, for now, though I don't know just what it means, just as you do, I wot what I want."

The old boatman, limping down the pier with the wrappings, broke into a run as he heard a crash and saw the light fall and disappear from the rowboat. When he reached the wharf, Satterly was stumblingly helping Annette over the broken glass of the lantern and the seats of the boat. They were bcth groping and laughing.

"Lost your light, sir?" came the unnecessary question.

And Satterly's voice, strong and exultant, rang out from the darkness: "I? Oh no! I've only just found it."

IT IS THE CUSTOM

A TRUE STORY OF LITTLE RUSSIA

IT seems a far call to the village of Evanovka, in the heart of Little Russia, and a farther call yet to the heart of the Little Russian
moujik living there ; but, while the sun rises in
the east and sets in the west, there will be
nothing new under the sun.

All the youth and jollity of Evanovka—
Heaven knows there is little enough of the
latter—are assembled together in a one-room
isba which it will not tax the eyes of the imagination to see. It has but one door and one
small window, both cut in the same wall. A
great oven, built of stone, juts out from the
opposite side, its chimney, also of stone, rising
from floor to ceiling, almost a wall in itself.
The furniture consists of a rudely made table
and a couple of long wooden benches. The
light of the home-made tallow candles, which
stand on the table stuck in old bottles or with
only their own drippings as candlestick, falls
on a circle of young girls variously employed.

Some are weaving bits of carpet which they will wear as skirts, others are spinning coarse linen, and others again cutting and sewing the linen into garments. There is not an article of dress worn in the room which is not in a state of reproduction under busy fingers.

By law of comparison, the day of labor is over. This work does not prevent laughter and jesting with the young men of the village who have crowded in and sit on the floor or where they can. They are mere boys of eighteen or nineteen, but grinding poverty and unremitting work may induce maturity even more rapidly than the sunny side o' the wall.

Each wears his high fur cap and is wrapped in his sheepskin *schuba*, the untanned skin and rough stitches on the outside, the fur in.

According to a time-honored custom, the young people have come together to spend the night in work and play. They meet thus in this *isba*, which is set apart for the purpose, once or twice a week during the winter months, as did their fathers and mothers before them, and as will their children after them, and think no evil.

As the voices and laughter merge together occasionally in a swinging peasant chorus, the curious rhythmic air—always in the minor key —is supported by a full contralto voice; and it is the same voice, almost guttural in depth, but singularly rich, which creates an audience whenever it is raised to speak. This is Nëila, the village beauty. She is speaking now.

"I tell you it is true that the Princess works, and as hard as I do, Masha, or you."

In answer to the general laughter which followed her remark, Nëila dropped her sewing in her lap, leaned her elbows on the table, and rested her chin in her hands, overlooking the room with her large brown eyes.

"I tell you it is true," she repeated, deliberately.

A young *moujik*, who was sitting on the floor near her, did not join in the laughter. This lowly attitude at the feet of their women had its root in convenience, and began and ended in its literalness with the young peasants of Evanovka; but Dimitri, better known as Mitia, the diminutive of Dimitri, was an exception, as Nëila well knew.

"Who has told you that the Barina works, Nëila?" he asked.

Nëila dropped her eyes on him for a moment. Apparently she was never conscious of Mitia's exits and entrances, but when she wished to single him out there was no hesitation in her glance, however crowded the room.

She answered his question to the company at large, and with an air of indifference.

"The Barina told me herself."

As they stared at her, open-mouthed, Nëila explained further. "It was like this. It was in a warm week in the last summer, and the Princess would bring her papers into the garden, and she would sit in the shade of the apple-tree just by the flower-bed I was weeding, and she would write, and she would write and write."

With a quick motion the peasant girl lifted her work from her lap and folded it in book-shape on the table, scribbling over it with an imaginary pen which she dipped into an imaginary inkstand. Her companions watched her with absorbed attention.

"Every day I would weed the bed and make the end in each line run close by her Excellency's side. Every day I thought I should like to ask her what she was writing and writing about."

She paused for an effective moment, and helped herself to a dried sunflower seed which she selected from a pile which Mitia had poured on the table before her.

"You asked the Barina that, Nëila!" exclaimed Mitia.

"I did," answered Nëila, cooly blowing the husk of the seed from her lips. "I said one day, 'Will your illustrious Highness pardon me for approaching you, but will your Highness tell me what you are writing?' And the Barina was pleased to smile at me most graciously, and told me what I did not understand, and so, of course, you cannot. She said, 'I am writing my diary.' 'What is diary?' I asked her. 'I write down in this book all that I do every day,' she replied to me; and then I said, as you have said, 'But your Highness does nothing,' and she laughed a long time before she answered me at all. At last she asked, 'What is your name?' and when I told her she explained to me that, although she did not weed and dig and water as I do, she also worked in ways which she would tell me of, and she told me for a long time; but if it took the Princess herself to make me understand, it would be useless for me to try to explain to you. Yes, the Princess works, I tell you, only she works in her own way, which is not our way—not at all."

As she ended, Nëila caught up her sewing again, and while her audience discussed her experience with true *moujik* heaviness and deliberation, she stitched on with marvellous rapidity as if unconscious of the sensation she had caused. She had thrown aside her *schuba*, and, thus unencumbered, her strong, graceful figure, a little above middle height, showed freely as she moved. Masha, the girl seated nearest to Nëila, sighed enviously as she looked at her. Nëila's *kaftan* was trimmed with rows of gay ribbons, her skirt was of bright calico, and her heavy braids of brown hair were tied with three ribbons where Masha's were tied with but one. Masha fingered discontentedly the clumsy carpet-strips which hung from her waist.

"Why is it that you will not wear carpet skirts as I do, Nëila?" she asked, aggrievedly.

Nëila moved restlessly. She stretched out her booted feet, kicking them a little. It was an added aggravation to Masha that the boots had bright red tops.

"I like to be free, and if I can work fast and make money, I may buy what I choose."

Masha sighed again as she watched the swift fingers. Nëila could drop her work and hold the attention of the entire room, and yet she had more finery for the present, and more laid by for her trousseau, than any girl in the village. She was then decorating a Sunday *rubashki* (a garment which serves as chemisette and skirt) with drawn-work at the top and bottom, and about the neck and sleeves. There were no patterns to copy. Nëila was designing for herself, drawing out some threads and catching others together with a button-hole stitch. The every day *rubashki* she wore was embroidered simply with the national embroidery—a cross-stitch in blue and red thread on the white linen.

"Is that for your trousseau, Nëila?" asked Masha, nodding her head towards the new garment.

Every peasant girl expects to marry, and prepares her trousseau accordingly. For what else is she born!

Nëila replied, with a shrug of her strong shoulders, "I shall not marry at all!"

She lifted her work as if to examine the pattern, with the candle-light behind it. Through the network of threads Mitia's blue eyes sought hers, reproachfully and sheepishly. Masha and the other girls looked at him and laughed. They were fond of laughing at Mitia. He was the water-carrier for the garden where they worked in summer, and they had even seen him take Nëila's water-pot from her hand and water her part of the flower-beds after his own labors were over. They had not been spoiled by such civility themselves. It struck them as amusing.

"No one ever comes for me," sighed Nëila, coquettishly—"no one. In the name of all the saints, what is that?"

She half rose, pointing with extended arm towards the little window cut near the door. All eyes turned in the same direction. Framed in the sash, and pressed close against the glass, they saw a bearded face surmounted by the inevitable high fur cap of a Little Russian *moujik*.

The light of a lantern which the intruder held in his uplifted hand showed his features with ghostly dimness, and also showed that he beckoned with his free hand.

"It is you he calls, Nëila," whispered Masha, crossing herself, fearfully. "You have wished for some one, and he has come for you."

Nëila, braver, but not less superstitious, crossed herself also with pious fervor.

"May the Mother of God forbid ! It is only a *moujik;* but his look is not true. It is you that he beckons, Mitia, not I."

Later, Masha's words were remembered. Fatalism is religion with the *moujik.* Ask him why he makes no effort to contest his small plot of land with the locust when that scourge sweeps his all from him, and he will reply to you, raking his heavy fingers through his heavy hair as if to stir the heavy brain beneath, "God sends it—let it be so."

In response to Nëila's suggestion, Mitia rose from her side and approached the window. As he opened the little glass door cut in the inner part of the double frame, he found himself face to face with the new-comer. The corresponding door in the outer frame was already unlatched and open.

With an exclamation, Mitia wrapped his *schuba* more closely about him, pressed his fur cap down over his ears and hurried from the door.

"How have you come here, Trophime?" he called. The figure moved from the window and joined him. Both men removed their caps and kissed each other on the lips in greeting.

"I have been to the horse-fair, Mitia. Unless you will take me in for the rest of the night, I must walk over thirteen versts to Ragazan."

Mitia welcomed the belated wanderer heartily. Visitors were a pleasant novelty ; for life was given for work, and the villages lay very far apart. Ragazan was called a near neighbor.

"Wait for me here," said Mitia. "I must say one word inside first, and then we will go to my father's hut together."

Trophime checked him, glancing again through the window.

"Why should we go yet, Mitia? They are having a good time in there, those others." He jerked his thumb towards the *isba* as he spoke. Mitia hesitated.

"If I took you in there they would be angry. You know it is not allowed to a stranger."

"Who knows what is allowed until he tries? You were always bragging of your girls last summer. Let me see if they are as pretty as ours."

The challenge told. Mitia still shook his head. "They will never allow it," he repeated, but he opened the door and made the attempt. Nëila's voice rose above the discussion which followed his proposition.

"What does he wish to come in here for?" she asked.

Mitia looked at her consciously.

"He is a good fellow. I worked a field with him on the farm last summer. He wants no harm."

Nëila glanced at him with a quick, sidelong look.

" How do you know that? What does he want, then ?"

Mitia removed his cap and scratched the mat of fair hair which he wore combed straight down over brow, ears, and neck. It was useless to contend with Nëila. She turned his soul inside out as easily as he did his *schuba*.

" He wishes to see if our girls are as pretty as the girls of Ragazan," he blurted out, reddening.

" Oh, let him come," replied Nëila, dryly.

Seemingly, she lost further interest. Her needle flew under her fingers. The question lay with the rest. Finally the permission was granted, and Mitia brought in Trophime.

Dazzled and blinded by the lights after the darkness outside, the stranger stood for a moment in the centre of a circle of curious eyes. He was a handsome young peasant, magnificently animal, with his powerful frame, strong jaw, full eyes, and coarse, vigorous hair. As his vision cleared, the first object it held was Nëila, yet the other girls had all looked up from their various employments.

Her eyes alone remained glued to her work. One sleeve was pushed back to the elbow, perhaps for greater convenience, and the bare, well-moulded arm moved backward and forward, following the needle.

Trophime stood gazing at her blinkingly. Nëila looked up. Her eyes were as brown as berries, and her teeth, as her lips parted over them unexpectedly, were like young corn.

Trophime crossed the room and sat down on the floor by her side.

One by one, as the night wore on, the occupants of the hut rolled themselves up in their *schubas* and stretched themselves on the top of the stove, where they soon fell asleep in the warmth. When the stove was full, the others, less fortunate, laid their wearied limbs on the floor, but as the floor would probably have been their bed at home, they did not complain.

Trophime and Nëila alone talked on and on ; a dull excitement was taking the place of sleep in Trophime's light-gray eyes, and Nëila's brown eyes shone on him like the stars in the night he had left outside.

For Nëila, a new conquest was a new conquest. She could sleep to-morrow.

Mitia had watched with them for a time, but the conversation had resolved itself into a dialogue, and the dialogue into whispers. His body was tired after his day of labor, and his soul was not much troubled. It was nothing new to see Nëila coquet with other men. To-morrow she would smile in his face again, would be his partner if there were dancing, eat sunflower seeds from his pocket, and at the next meeting in the hut she would let him sit at her feet and look up at her as he sang his love-songs. And then, if the coming harvest were good and he could prove to old Anton, her father, that he was able to support a wife —why, then— Mitia was fast asleep in his *schuba*.

"Let him sleep," whispered Trophime. "My God and my Lord! are the men of this village without eyes, that you are yet unmarried?"

"God has given them eyes to see their hands with, and hands to do their work with," Nëila replied, sharply, pushing away Trophime's encroaching arm.

He drew back, laughing.

"Tell me who he is, then. Which one of them here has asked you to fix the day?"

Nëila lowered her lids. Beneath her long lashes she looked down on Mitia's slender, sinewy figure stretched out on the floor near them.

"No one," she replied, smiling—"no one. I I am too ugly."

Trophime laughed loudly. Nëila hushed him with lifted hand.

"Be quiet! You will wake the others. Why are you laughing?"

Trophime drew nearer to her, whispering: "Come now, my beauty, suppose I should ask you to fix the day?"

Nëila threw back her comely head with a smothered laugh, which she caught in her throat with her hand. The rows of beads twisted there on the warm skin, above the loosely gathered *rubashki*, clattered together.

"It is very well," she said, nodding with mock solemnity. "Very well, indeed! We will fix the festival of Christmas. It is two weeks off, and you are not to forget me when the time comes."

"That would be likely, indeed! But a bargain is no bargain without the seal."

He caught her arm as he spoke and bent his face towards her for a kiss ; but strong as the young *moujik* was, he had not reckoned on the unexpected force with which Nëila met his advances.

"Take that !" she cried, warningly, as her vigorous arm sent him staggering back against the table. The jar shook down one of the bottle candlesticks, which rolled over and over and fell to the floor with a crash of breaking glass. The sleepers started up, complaining and muttering.

Mitia, roused also, rose and spoke with a rude dignity.

" My father's hut is close by, Trophime. We will finish the night there. Come."

Trophime turned from him angrily, but, in the face of the general discontent, submitted in sullen silence. Nëila would not glance at him again.   As he bade her good-night she turned her shoulder to him, muttering a proverb—"Measure the cloth ten times before you cut it once."

Mitia heard.   His face softened ; he touched Nëila's hand awkwardly, as it hung by her side near him.

"May you sleep well, Nëila !" he whispered, and went out, followed by Trophime.

The next morning, before the village was astir, Trophime, his brief visit over, had set out on foot for his home.

One noonday, a week before the coming festival, old Anton, the head herdsman of the Prince, sat in his *isba* contentedly eating his dinner.   He felt that he had reason to be content.   He had earned it.   His hut had two rooms, and in the inner room there was a bedstead covered with blankets and sheepskins where he might sleep if he wished.   It happened that he preferred the top of the stove, but that was of choice.

The *isba* was a model of neatness ; the table and benches were scoured thoroughly, and the stove was newly whitewashed, ready for the Christmas festival.   The *kasha* (a thick gruel of grits) which he was eating, the black rye-bread, the sour ·cabbage-soup, and the salted cucumbers were all prepared to a nicety. True, it was Nastasia, his wife, whose work

this was, but had it not been he who had selected her for this purpose?

In regard to Nëila, his only child, Anton felt
that he had done well also. Not because she
was the handsomest girl in the village, but because she knew how to work and earn money,
of which she gave him a faithful proportion.
What he had himself laid by in the pouch hidden in the patron image was nobody's affair
but his own. There was, however, one matter
which, while not exactly troubling him, lay on
Anton's mind to arrange. He was thinking of
this when he looked up at his wife with his little sunken eyes.

"Where is Nëila?" he asked.

"I hear her coming now," answered Nastasia, quickly.

She watched her husband's eyes always with
the timid, fluttering manner of a bird which a
cat fascinates. She looked threescore, and was
in reality scarcely forty years old. But in this
there was nothing unusual.

The footsteps which Nastasia heard outside
paused at the door, and were followed by a
loud knock.

"Go to the door," said Anton, and his wife
obeyed with a start. Lifting the latch, she
peered out timidly through the crack of the
door.

"Does Anton live here, *Matiouska?*" said a
voice outside.

"That is my name. Who is it that wants me?" answered Anton himself. "Open the door wide, Nastasia; he is not the wind, to come through the key-hole."

Nastasia threw open the door hurriedly, and Trophime, bending his tall head, entered. He walked straight up to old Anton's chair, and bowed low before him.

"*Batushka*," he said, "I have come to ask your daughter's hand of you. She has promised to marry me after the Christmas festival. I am here now to answer whatever questions it pleases you to ask."

Anton looked the bold speaker over from head to foot. Trophime's *schuba* was evidently quite new, and was belted in with a new scarf. His fur cap was new also, and his boots creaked loudly as he walked. He bore inspection.

Anton pushed a wooden spoon towards his guest and pointed to the large wooden bowl in the centre of the table. From it he and his wife were dipping the cabbage-soup.

"Sit and eat with us. Talking is hungry work. What is your name?"

Trophime dipped his spoon into the bowl and ate without hunger. He did not wish to save his breath for his porridge.

"My name is Trophime Evanov. I live at Ragazan, and have an *isba* of two rooms as large as these to take my wife to. My mother is dead.

There is no woman there to quarrel with. My father is old, but not much trouble. The land is rich, and, by the help of God, I have saved a little. Now you know how it is with me."

Anton's little eyes grew smaller, and almost disappeared in his wrinkled, parchment skin. His large, white teeth, perfectly preserved by his diet of rye-bread and salted cucumbers, glistened curiously as he smiled.

"You are Evan's son, then," he said. "I remember him and his *isba* and his land very well. You look as strong as your father was before you. We will talk it over."

Nastasia was eating nothing. She withdrew to the stove and sat there trembling and watching the door. The two men were talking together with loud-voiced satisfaction.

She alone heard when the latch lifted, and a strong, full voice on the threshold cried out some laughing defiance to a companion who passed on.

Nëila pushed open the door and took one step into the room. The poor bent figure by the stove trembled yet more. Nëila stood still in surprise, the smile yet on her lips, as Anton and Trophime looked up at her.

"Nëila," said Anton, rapping the table with his short fingers at each word, "this is your husband."

Nëila stood looking from one to the other, but she was no longer smiling.

Trophime rose and advanced towards her.

"You remember our bargain, Nëila," he said, holding out his hand. "I have come."

Her brown eyes alone answered him. Trophime quailed a little, but held his ground. Nëila passed him and strode to her father's side.

"What has he told you?" she asked, huskily.

There was no quailing on either side here. Old Anton's gimletlike eyes fastened on his daughter's piercingly. He boasted that he never needed to beat his women.

"My word is my word," he said, shortly, stroking his long, square beard as he spoke, "and yours shall be yours. You marry at Christmas."

Nëila turned fiercely on Trophime.

"You are a liar!" she cried. "A black-hearted liar! That is what you are. If I have promised any one it is Mitia, and Mitia alone."

Anton laughed in her face.

"Mitia! with his old father and mother, and the children like fleas in a sheep's wool, all settled on his back!"

He pointed to Trophime, his stubby fingers spread out.

"There stands your husband; you understand me?"

Nëlia's passionate eyes were the only color in her face.

"You may kill me," she muttered. "Kill me, but I will not marry him."

She glanced at her mother as she ended. Nastasia half rose from the bench with an imploring gesture, then sank back again. Her trembling seemed to communicate itself to her child. Nëila fell on the floor at her father's feet. Anton turned away indifferently, leaving her prostrate.

"She is yours, Trophime; take her," he said, over his shoulder.

As Trophime approached her Nëila rose slowly. There was no trace of tears on her face. Nëila was never known to weep. She motioned to Trophime to follow her, and went out of the room. When he joined her outside she was leaning against the wall of the hut, her body pressed close against the rough logs, her hand curled into a crevice supporting her. The bright red of the kerchief on her hair seemed repeated in the depths of her eyes and in the ragged patches of color on either cheek.

As Trophime laid his hand on her arm she shuddered closer into the wall.

"You know well that it was a jest," she said, hoarsely. "How have you dared to come for me?"

"It is no jest to me, Nëila. Listen to me. You shall live like a princess. You can set your foot on the neck of every girl in Ragazan.

A hut with two rooms, and you the only woman, is surely better than—"

Nëila turned on him fiercely, wrenching her shoulder from his hand.

"Once for all, Trophime, hear me. I would rather live with Mitia in a barn than with you in the great house of the Prince. I will marry Mitia, or no one."

Trophime's face altered. "Gently, gently, my beauty," he said, warningly.

He took a step nearer to her, and bent until his lips almost touched her ear. She could feel his hot breath on her neck.

The wind, which had been blowing down little showers of dry snow from the roof above, had teased a strand of Nëila's straight hair from under her kerchief and twisted it in a dark line about her throat.

Trophime caught the hair necklace in his finger, drawing it closer. "Like that I have you, my little bird," he whispered. "You know well I can say that of you which will keep you from being wife to any other man."

Nëila flung back her head scornfully. Her throat arched as a serpent's about to strike.

"I!" she cried, "I can call a dozen to witness for me—a hundred—"

She checked herself suddenly. Trophime's eyes were fastened on hers with a triumphant question. As if reflected there, she saw the scene in the *isba* at their first meeting: the sleeping figures ; even Mitia unconscious at their feet ; saw, with a quick, terrifying foreshadowing, her father's credulity and fury, a marriage arranged within the hour, and herself thrust into Trophime's sledge on the road to Ragazan before the sunset.

The hair necklace at her throat seemed to tighten chokingly, although Trophime had withdrawn his finger. She fell against the wall with closed eyes.

"But come, now, my little queen," urged Trophime. " Marry me quietly and all will be well. You will never repent it. Tell me to come back at Christmas, Nëila."

Nëila looked up.

"Christmas is a week off," she thought, rapidly, "and to-day is to-day. I will say yes, and trust in God and Mitia."

She dragged herself to her feet and moved away from the wall.

"Shall it be Christmas, Nëila ?"

"Yes," she answered, deliberately, "it shall be Christmas."

"I may tell Anton that it is all arranged ?"

"You may tell him."

As Trophime stretched out a covetous hand towards her, she avoided his touch, and, doubling like a hare, passed him, gained the open road, and broke into a swift run.

Trophime returned to Anton's hut slowly, hesitating, and watching her over his shoulder.

"Where is she off to?" he muttered, but Nëila herself could not have told him. When she stopped running she was in a large field, far from the *isba*, with a vast expanse of white all about her and a dull leaden sky above. There were tall, shadowy pines standing out in occasional groups. At the other end of the field stood an ox-sledge, the tracks of the wide runners and the feet of the oxen marking their way in the snow.

Nëila followed blindly in the same path. There was no one with the oxen when she reached them, and she stood before them looking into their great brown eyes and wondering dully of what they reminded her. Suddenly she recollected how Mitia had once told her that her eyes were like those of the oxen he drove, and how angry she had been. She remembered, too, that he had said he would be working in this field all day, and then she woke to the realization of what she had flown from and to whom; she turned, and saw that Mitia was close beside her.

Nëila spoke without preface.

"Mitia, Trophime has come to marry me."

The blood rushed over Mitia's face.

"What have you said, Nëila?" he asked, quickly.

"Trophime has come to marry me. He says he had my promise."

"You gave Trophime your promise!"

" No, it is a lie."

Mitia turned to his sledge, and swung himself up into the seat. He bent down, holding out his hand to Nëila.

" Come," he said, shortly.

" Where ?"

" We are going to find him," he answered, between his teeth.

Nëila did not move.

" I have more to tell you. He is with my father, and my father consents."

Mitia sprang from the sledge to her side.

" Mother of God ! Anton consents ! Nëila, what more ?"

" I have said I will marry him at Christmas, and I love thee ! I love thee as I hate him."

Defiant, coquettish, alluring, and evasive he had known her. Now that she confessed herself his, the present was enough.

Mitia's hand trembled as he smoothed her ruffled hair with awkward tenderness.

" If thou lovest me, Nëila, thou art mine— mine, I say. No one shall claim thee. Why hast thou promised this to Trophime ?"

As he drew her to him, Nëila turned away, hiding her face.

" Wait, Mitia," she panted. " I promised, to gain time ; but wait and listen first."

Mitia bent his ear closer. As he heard her broken whispers, he started violently and his open face darkened.

"Go on," he said, hoarsely, as she faltered once ; and Nëila went on.

"They will believe it all in the village, Mitia. I have no witness to speak for me. My father will take Trophime's word ; but thou, Mitia, as thou hopest for mercy from thy God, believe in me."

Mitia did not speak. Nëila knew that he had lifted her face in his hands and that his gaze was devouring her features. Her lids were weighted down over her hot eyes.

Mitia's lips touched her quivering mouth.

"What I know, I know, Nëila. The December snow is not more pure than thou, and thou art mine alone."

It was the final touch. As the strain lifted, Nëila burst into a passion of weeping. Mitia rocked her in his arms, comforting her.

"We have a week yet, Nëila, my heart's blood. We will bide here together until Trophime leaves the village, and to-morrow we will go to the church, and as soon as the service ends I will go to the pope and tell him all. I will throw myself on my knees before him and pray him to marry us at once. Take courage, my little pigeon, my little dove ! And for Trophime—but no one will believe his base story."

Nëila shook her head.

"Some would be glad to help blacken my name," she said, simply. "My tongue has been as sharp as my needle, and my laugh as ready as my trousseau. Mitia, if I have worked my trousseau for Trophime I shall tear it in pieces."

Mitia wiped the tears from her face with the back of his toil-worn hand.

"It shall not be, Nëila. Come, what shall I say to the pope? Do thou be the *Batushka* now, and let me plead with thee; then I shall know better what to say, and be less frightened when the time comes."

Nëila smiled through her tears, throwing herself into the part with quick reaction.

"Yes, I will stand here," she said, "with my arms folded, and the back of the sledge shall be the door, and thou must come in there, Mitia, and fall at my feet. Yes, that is well; and now what wilt thou say?"

"*Batushka*, I love Nëila devotedly, and she adores me—"

"Who said that I adore thee?"

"And Nëila loves me."

"Yes, that is better."

"Let me get on, Nëila."

"I will, but could I let thee begin with a lie to the little father?"

"Nëila loves me, and is waiting in the church, but unless you will marry us now, Anton will marry her to a black-hearted devil—"

"Art thou mad, Mitia? The pope will excommunicate thee forever! Thou must say,

'*Batushka*, I entreat and implore you to marry us. I will live on the ground at your feet. I will fast forever. I worship Nëila next to the holy images and yourself, *Batushka*, and she worships me.'"

"Is that true, Nëila?"

"Never mind now. The little father will hold out his hand thus, and thou must kiss it—but not so many times, Mitia. Thou mightest vex him. He will say, 'Come, then, my son, I will marry you as you wish, and she wishes; for Nëila has always been a good girl,' and then they will hold the silver marriage-crowns over our heads, and they will sing—'Isaiah, enter into happiness.' And now begin all over again, Mitia."

They were not unhappy. They loved each other and had confessed it. God was very good, and if they made their prayers to him and to the saints, what might not happen in seven days!

Again and again they repeated their rehearsal until Mitia was perfect in his part, with Nëila as priest and prompter, the snow-covered field as stage, the sledge as setting, and the brown-eyed oxen as audience.

The next morning they were kneeling side by side in the church, praying the same prayer—that the silver marriage-crowns might be resting above their heads within the hour.

The little church where the services were

held was built near the house of the Prince, and was connected with it by a private avenue, down which, as on this morning, the Princess often walked to take her part in the prayers.

She knelt apart in the corner railed off for the Prince's family : for the building was the orthodox Greek Church, and the worshippers stood or knelt ; there were no pews.

She lingered a little after the service to pray before the gorgeous patron image of her household, and she paused again at the door, speaking, with kindly condescension, to a mother who had brought her baby to church with her, its little bekerchiefed head sticking out of the folds of her *schuba*.

The avenue had been swept free of snow, and the Princess, a graceful, fair-faced woman, walked slowly up the path, looking idly at the snow-hung trees above her. Even the little twigs carried each a frozen load, which the wind rocked to and fro heavily.

Suddenly the Princess started and looked down.

A flying figure had darted noiselessly across the snow, and now lay on the ground before her.

"Who is it?" said the Princess, gently, "and what do you wish? Ah, I remember your name now. It is Nëila. What do you mean by this, my girl?"

Nëila rose to her knees and humbly kissed the white hand extended to her.

"Will your Excellency ever pardon me? It was the holy image that belongs to you that sent me to you. I was kneeling in the church, striking the ground with my forehead in my grief, when I caught sight of it, with the beautiful shining stones hanging all about it, and I remembered that when the Barin was talking with Death even, the pope had only to carry the image to his bedside and he was cured, and then I prayed to it—ah, how I prayed!—and then the thought came to me quickly, 'Go to the Princess,' and so I have come. I have not stopped for a moment. If your Highness will only deign to help me!"

"What is your trouble, Nëila?" asked the Princess, gravely. "Stand up and tell me. Is it one where I can help you?"

Nëila blushed and hung her head. The Princess encouraged her kindly.

"You need not be afraid to speak now. You may walk by my side to the house; but, first, have you asked advice from the pope?"

"The pope, your Excellency!" Nëila's lips opened, and the story of her troubles rushed forth: Trophime's ill faith—her father's cruelty—Mitia's love. "And for the pope," she ended, bitterly, "first, your Excellency, he has asked Mitia what fee he could offer for marrying us, and Mitia has nothing. *Then* he has said that without my father's consent he will not marry us, for it would be wrong."

The Princess turned away her head. Her short upper lip curled irresistibly. She did not herself love the little father.

"He is your pope, Nëila," she said, reprovingly, "and your father is your father. He has the right to your obedience."

Nëila bowed her head respectfully. She was watching the gentle, thoughtful face and the slow-moving figure intently.

"And are you sure that you really love Mitia, my child!"

Nëila's shyness returned. She burrowed into her *schuba* until little but her reddened brow was visible.

"*Eh-heh*" (yes), she replied, in a smothered voice.

The Princess smiled. Her own marriage was a love-match.

"Very well, then," she said. "I will send for your father, and will myself speak to him for you. You may go now."

She held out her hand and smiled again as Nëila covered the jewelled fingers with passionately grateful kisses.

There was not a year's difference in the ages of the two women ; both were beauty's daughters, and both had learned their own hearts. But those were the only points in common. In reality they were as far apart as the cold North and the warm South.

Perhaps the suggestion of such a thought

visited the mind of the Princess as she stood watching the girl's light figure walking easily down the path despite her heavily booted feet. Still thoughtful, she moved to the house and dispatched a messenger for the head herdsman, bidding him come to her in the avenue, where she continued her walk.

The summons reached Anton in his *isba*, and he listened with respectful surprise, but his piercing eyes rested on his daughter with instant suspicion. Nevertheless the event was an honor, and he appeared before his mistress weighed down with servility.

The Princess cut his salutation short.

"Anton, I hear that you are forcing your daughter to marry a man from another village. Have you had opportunity to know him?"

Anton again bowed himself before her.

"Your Highness is too good to take this interest in our humble affairs," he said, slowly.

The Princess continued:

"Are you sure that this stranger is a good man?"

"He is a thrifty *moujik*, your Highness, and he has no family to speak of. He will make me a good son in my old age—I, who have only a daughter."

"But will he make your daughter happy, Anton?"

Anton dropped further pretences. It was evident that his mistress knew all.

"Your Highness, it is time the girl married, and that Mitia has nothing to offer her, nor can he have anything until the next harvest, and the good God above knows what may happen by that time!"

"Anton, Trophime cannot be a nice peasant to force the poor girl into marrying him in this way. He will make a bad husband, and your child will be miserable."

Anton took off his fur cap and scratched his matted hair before he answered.

"Every man has his way of courting a girl, your Highness. She will get used to Trophime's way. Girls must not have their own heads too much; they must abide by their father's word; and your Highness knows well that peasant girls cannot let a comfortable two-room *isba* and a rich bit of land slip through their fingers for nothing. That is not offered every day."

"And the pope, have you spoken to him? Does he approve this, Anton?"

Anton wet his lips with his tongue, and spread out his short hands deprecatingly.

"He knows how it is with us poor peasants, your Highness," he said, with elaborate innocence. "He will approve when he understands all. Mitia is a beggar. Trophime can give twice the corn and potatoes that Mitia could give as a marriage fee. But if your Highness disapproves, it is enough. Your Highness has but to speak."

The old man bowed low again. The Princess hesitated. What she had already done was without precedent, and opened a wide door. Anton was only following the peasant rule of life. Nëila's story had been that of hundreds of others, and would be again. None ever dreamed of enlisting the sympathy of the Princess. They all submitted—was it not the custom !

Anton was watching his mistress keenly between his protestations and prostrations. He knew what was passing in her mind. Paternal authority was a creed not to be lightly overturned. The Princess moved away, waving her hand in haughty dismissal.

"It is on your own head, Anton," she said, sternly.

Anton raised his bowed figure and looked after her, laughing in his beard. Even the Princess had her limitations, and recognized them. Custom was custom, and iron to high or low.

On Christmas Day Mitia and Nëila met once more in the field where they had first exchanged their vows. They walked hand in hand, leaning against each other. Nëila's face was white and tear-stained, Mitia's gloomy and drawn.

"God will not let it be, Mitia," Nëila was saying. "I have prayed and prayed my heart out to Him. Something will happen yet."

Mitia shook his head.

"No, God wills it to be so, Nëila. He will not let the pope help us, nor the Princess. What can we do? When misfortune enters, throw the door wide open."

"God is good, Mitia. Trophime may not come."

"He will come—and then, Nëila—"

Nëila shuddered.

"Mitia, if he comes, thou wilt promise me one thing—thou wilt not follow us to the church."

Mitia struck his hand violently on the trunk of the tree by which they had paused. He muttered a curse under his breath; his eyes turned desperately about him over the landscape, a frozen plain. Did they steal away together, where could they go, to what, and with what means. There was no escape.

"May God kill him like a wolf!" he cried, savagely; "and He will. I pray for it night and day."

Nëila crossed herself hurriedly. She laid her fingers on Mitia's lips.

"May God forgive thee, Mitia! What art thou saying?"

"The truth only, Nëila. I will work my fingers to the bone. I will never marry. Remember, I shall be always waiting for thee, and always ready."

Nëila's answer was a new outbreak of grief. One by one their plans had failed, and they walked on over the frozen field supporting and consoling each other with vague hopes, which each knew had no foundation.

The day after Christmas, punctual to the appointed hour, Trophime drove into the village dressed in his new *schuba*, belted in at the waist with a bright green scarf. The sledge in which he rode and the horse which drew it were both his own. He stood up, driving himself. When he reached Anton's hut he flung the reins on the horse's back, and, descending, rapped loudly.

Anton himself opened the door and came out.

"Is it you?" he said. "You are in good time, and welcome."

He was followed by the nuptial godfather (the master of ceremonies), who, after exchanging greeting with the groom, at once took possession of him and drove him in the sledge to the church. Anton stood looking after them, until some girls who were passing pointed at him and whispered indignantly together. Then he turned and re-entered the hut.

No one had seen Nëila since the day before. The door of the *isba* had been bolted from the early morning, and only the nuptial godmother (the mistress of ceremonies) had been allowed to enter. Anton walked into the inner room, where the nuptial godmother was putting the finishing touches to a wreath of paper roses on the bride's hair. She had dressed Nëila in all her finery, her beads and ribbons and red-top boots, unassisted and unhindered.

Nastasia was rocking her withered body to and fro in the corner, but the girl herself sat like a stone.

"Come," said Anton, shortly. "Trophime has gone to the church."

The nuptial godmother helped Nëila to her feet and led her from the hut. Anton and Nastasia followed behind them. Nëila moved on slowly, her eyes fixed before her. When she entered the church she glanced about her once fearfully, as if seeking some one, and then sank into apathy again.

Trophime had met her at the door, but she had not looked at him. He stood by her side at a table set below the altar. On it the priest's cross and books lay ready. As the door of the Holy of Holies opened, the congregation prostrated themselves. The priest entered and moved towards the bridal party at the table and began the ceremony. At the same moment two of the young peasants came forward with the silver marriage-crowns, holding them high above the heads of the bride and groom. It was then only that Nëila seemed to rouse for a moment from her trance of despair. She shrank from under the crown and again prostrated herself on the floor before the priest. The ceremony went on monotonously, and she rose again as she had fallen. She followed the service through, blindly, a mere automaton. With a scarf twisted about her wrist, binding it to Trophime's, she was led three times around the table by the pope. Trophime placed a silver ring on her finger, she kissed the cross extended to her, and she and Trophime were man and wife.

"Nëila will have her white veil," whispered Masha, to her companions; "no girl in the village has been more virtuous, but I could almost wish the nuptial godmother would deny it to her. Then we should see old Anton disgraced. It would be fine to see him driven through the village with a halter about his neck, if they would let poor Nastasia off. Ah, but I would help to scoff at him, brute that he is!"

Brandy and gingerbread were set out in plenty in Anton's *isba*, but with this spirit in the air towards the host, and with the bride sitting like a statue in the corner under the image of the patron saint, not even replying when spoken to, appetite was lacking. It was customary and proper for a bride to weep, but this was something else.

One by one the guests dropped away, and the wedding party was left to make merry alone, with what merriment they had. Trophime rose and stood before Nëila.

"What has my wife to say to me before I go?"
he asked.

Nëila's eyes darkened. She looked at him in
silence. Trophime was about to seat himself
beside her, but Anton drew him away.

"Come," he said, "why should you talk with
a woman? Let her be. When you come back
for her at the week's end you may do as you
choose ; but now, if you wish to be home before
morning, you had best be starting out."

Trophime withdrew reluctantly. As he looked back again from the door Anton laughed at
him loudly. "Your turn will come," he said,
pushing his son-in-law before him. "Come, to
your sledge with you, and home. In a week
I shall expect you to fetch her."

During this last week in her father's home,
no one in the village saw Nëila's face. She
shut herself in the inner room of the *isba*, and
would not be comforted. As for Mitia, he had
disappeared from the village on the morning of
the wedding, and his whereabouts were not
known.

At the end of the week, when his son-in-law
came driving into the village again, Anton,
angered at the failure of the wedding feast,
would make no second attempt at a merry-
making, but a few of the more curious peasants
straggled into the *isba*, unasked and unwel-
comed. Trophime left his sledge standing at
the door while he hurried through the final cer-

emonies, pouring a handful of copper coins on the table, and setting beside them a loaf of black bread and a dish of salt. He glanced eagerly about the room, but Nëila had not yet appeared and Nastasia was absent also.

The sound of a woman's weeping came from the inner room.

The dislike and curiosity in the faces about him irritated Trophime.

" There is the price of my wife, and there lie my witnesses that I will support her, and her parents too, if need be," he said, impatiently. " Now for your part, Anton."

Anton rose in silence and went to the inner door. As the nuptial godmother appeared leading Nëila, whose face was buried in her hands, a murmur of sympathy ran around the room. Anton attempted to carry off the scene with a high hand.

" That is well," he said, loudly. " It would be a disgrace for a girl to leave her father's house laughing. Take her, Trophime."

He flung open the door as he spoke. Trophime stepped forward and set his powerful hands on the waist of the weeping girl. He lifted her from the floor and swung her into his sledge as lightly as he might have lifted a child.

" There's a man for you !" said Anton, looking around.

In spite of himself his voice was defiant.

Nëila's bowed head fell against the side of the sledge. Her hands were still clasped to her face, and the tears dropped through her fingers. The nuptial godmother climbed into the sledge beside Trophime.

Anton threw two patron images, which the pope had previously blessed for him, into her lap. He had provided these for the home of the new couple, as a pious parent should.

Trophime jerked the reins, and they slid rapidly out of the village.

The Princess was walking in the village street, talking with her husband, on whose arm she leaned, when the sledge passed them.

Trophime and the nuptial godmother both saluted respectfully, but the Princess did not respond. She had seen beyond them a beautiful tear-stained face, and two helpless, imploring hands that were stretched out towards her. She pressed her husband's arm and uttered an exclamation of pity.

"Oh, see, my husband, it is poor Nëila! I told you her story."

The Prince glanced after the sledge indifferently. .

"It is the custom," he replied, with a slight shrug. "She will accept it by to-morrow."

He drew his wife with him down the road, and returned to their interrupted subject; but the Princess, looking back over her shoulder, did not hear him, and Nëila's last vision in the village where she left her girl life was the pitying face that watched her until out of sight.

The next day even the nuptial godmother deserted her, for, having settled her charge in her husband's home, her task was over, and she returned to Evanovka.

Nëila was left alone with Trophime and his father and her new duties.

"She is a fine wife for you, Trophime," said the old father, after a few days of trial. "You have chosen well. She has been with us but a little while, and the *isba* is as clean as the snow when it falls; and for her cooking—!"

The old man smacked his lips. He loved his creature comforts, and his wife had been dead a year.

"Yes, you have done well," he repeated. "She is a good girl, too The pope gave her the white veil at the church to-day."

Trophime shook his head. He was not so satisfied. He went into the hut and left the old man sitting on the bench outside.

Nëila, with the white veil of purity still on her hair, which was now coiled close as a married woman's, was sitting by the table, her head resting in her arms. Trophime went up to her, frowning. As he touched her shoulder she raised her head, but did not speak. She drew a bowl of potatoes towards her and began to prepare them for cooking. Trophime stood looking at her, still frowning. Nëila's face had altered in those few days.

"What is it?" he said, harshly. "What are you fretting for? You have more than any girl in Evanovka, or Ragazan either, for that."

Nëila glanced around the comfortable *isba* indifferently.

"I told you how it would be," she answered, listlessly.

Trophime sneered.

"So that is it. You would rather live in a rabbit-warren?"

Nëila's eyes flashed. He knew how to rouse her. "Then I might be able to breathe," she muttered; "here I am choked and smothered."

She moved her hands as if pushing away the walls about her. Trophime advanced towards her threateningly.

"Have a care!" he said, warningly. "Thou swimmest in shallow waters."

Nëila rose to her feet before him. She spread out her arms.

"Strike!" she cried, passionately. "Beat me to death. Then I might breathe."

Trophime lifted his hand, advancing yet nearer. She stood unwincing, her eyes defying him. With a quick movement, before she realized his intention, Trophime, laughing loudly, flung his arms about her.

"Aha! my wild hawk, I know how to tame you. What! must a husband fight for a kiss?"

Nëila struggled violently.

"Let me go!" she panted. "Let me go before I kill you!"

From the doorway the old man laughed a dry, cackling laugh.

"Fighting already!" he wheezed, in his cracked, high voice. "Does a peasant girl love her man until he beats her? No."

Trophime again laughed loudly.

"Do you hear that? Mother of God! how strong my wife is! Have done, I tell you!"

"What did I say?" croaked the old man.

He was a Little Russian *moujik*, and had his own ideas of humor. "Beat her, Trophime, and she will kiss your boots."

Trophime raised his hand, still laughing boisterously. He struck Nëila a sharp blow on the arm, and she ceased struggling instantly.

"That fetches love, does it?" said Trophime, triumphantly. He bent his face to hers as he spoke, but with the same unexpected vehemence with which she had repulsed his first kiss at that fatal meeting in the *isba*, Nëila placed her hands on his breast, thrust him staggering from her, and fled from the door.

At the back of the town grew a thick wood, pierced by a path which led through it windingly. It was into this refuge that the flying figure plunged. She ran like the wind—anywhere, so that it was away from the hated *isba* and Trophime.

There was no pursuit ; she did not expect it. Trophime knew as well as she that every flying step must be retraced. Yet Nëila ran on and on, her white veil fluttering in the wind. The sharp report of a gun and the sharper cry of animal pain checked her suddenly. In the path, almost at her feet, lay a brown hare, its limbs twitching in death. A man's figure broke from the brushwood at the side of the path and came towards her.

It was Mitia.

His gun fell from his hand, he stretched out his arms, and with a cry like that of the wounded hare Nëila flung herself on his breast.

Mitia spoke first. His face was as altered as her own.

"I have found work on a farm not a verst away." His voice sank to a whisper. "Nëila, how is it with thee ?"

Nëila withdrew herself from his clasp, her face inflamed with fury. She struck back the sleeve from her arm with a passionate gesture and held it towards him. The arm above the elbow was bruised and angry. Mitia caught her back to him, uttering a stifled cry.

His arms trembled as they held her, drawing her closer to him.

The white veil, loosened from its fastenings, fluttered from her head to the ground, where the blood of the hare stained and soiled it.

"I hate him!" she whispered, fiercely. "God in heaven! I hate him!"

Alas! Undisciplined, half-civilized, unmoral rather than immoral, could there be but one ending? The whispers which soon crept about the village became open rumor, the rumor certainty, and popular sympathy was with Mitia and Nëila.

There were some who believed that Trophime might have made a good husband had that been permitted him; however it may have been, curses and blows seemed to render Nëila but more openly reckless.

In the Greek Church divorce is not allowed; however wronged the husband, however guilty the wife, they must live out their lives — the mockery of a unit.

One cold day in the following autumn, as old Anton stood in his doorway, he saw a woman's figure come toiling over the snow towards the *isba*. She did not speak, but fell on her knees before him, with trembling, uplifted hands.

It was Nëila. She had walked over the thirteen versts from Ragazan alone and through the snow. Was this the same Nëila who had left that door not a year before? Anton had not recognized her.

"Back you shall go!" he cried, furiously. "Myself, I will throw you in the cart and drive you back."

Nëila did not reply. She closed her eyes and shuddered.

Nastasia came out from the hut and whispered entreatingly to Anton.

She lifted her child from the snow and led her in.

That night Nëila's child was born.

God is very merciful. When the spirit is high and will not bend or break, however bruised and tortured by man, He will often render the body frail, and open a way by which the overtaxed soul may escape.

With the morning, the whole village knew that Nëila lay dying in her father's *isba*. Word was sent to the other village, but Trophime did not come.

Later in the day, Mitia crept into the room and sat by the bedside, his face buried in his hands. He had run over the thirteen versts which Nëila had toiled through the day before, and he was in time.

"Let them be," whispered Nastasia; "what harm now?"

But Anton, shaking his head obstinately, laid a rough hand on Mitia's shoulder and pointed to the door. The young peasant raised his face for a moment—and Anton moved away from him into the outer room.

Mitia did not stir from the bedside.

When the end came, Nëila's last breath was breathed in his arms; her eyes were set on his face. Mitia laid her back on the sheepskins and staggered from the door.

He stood before old Anton and spoke thickly.

"Anton, if you and Nastasia will keep the child, I will pay you for it. Is it agreed?"

"It is agreed," Anton answered. He knew then that all was over.

When the funeral procession wound through the fields it was followed by all the village, and Trophime was walking after the coffin as chief mourner; but it was on Mitia that all eyes were turned with sympathy, and Trophime was looked at askance.

He saw, and resented sullenly. When the poor body was prepared for burial, marks had been found upon it as damning to the husband as the writing on the wall.

With no word spoken to him, and himself speaking to no one, Trophime mounted his cart and drove to his home.

There he married shortly after, with little trouble.

Mitia has never married. Broken and old at twenty, he lives, but lives only to minister to the wants of Nëila's mother and Nëila's child.

Thus the story of Nëila ends, to be forgotten in time among a hundred others more or less similar.

'AND so, sister dear, you want to hear the whole story of our boy Hal and Wilhelmina? I don't see why I should not tell it to you, as the years when it hurt us all are far behind. For a long time I couldn't even think of it with any composure, but now—if I had known that I should ever feel able to tell the whole history to you, actually smiling over parts of it, I suppose I should have felt less bitterly at the time. And yet I don't know. It never comforted me very much, when a child, to be told that a cut finger wouldn't be hurting by the time I was twice married. Pain is pain. While it lasts it hurts, even if you do forget some of the pangs by to-morrow.

In the case of Hal and Wilhelmina, I was doubly distressed by the miserable feeling that I had, as it were, cut my own finger ; and you know to be suffering with only yourself to blame makes everything just so much harder to bear.

Of course, though you have never heard all the story, you know that Wilhelmina was, at one period, *our cook*. Time does much for us, my dear, but it cannot and does not spare me a pang as I make this plain statement. Yes, she was our cook ; and while my share of the blame came later, the engaging of Wilhelmina Schroder as a servant of our house seemed at the time the right thing to do. It came about in this wise :

Wilhelmina's father was a plain, thrifty, German farmer. He lived up the county road on his own farm quite prosperously until he indorsed a note for a friend. The friend failed, and Schroder was called upon to pay heavily. The first thing he did on hearing this bad news was to drive down to our farm and ask counsel of my dear husband ; for, as you know, everybody in the county comes to him for advice when in trouble. Schroder wanted to mortgage his farm and work off the claim by degrees, but my husband does not believe in mortgages.

"Make your sacrifice now, Schroder," he said ; "don't think of mortgaging. You will never catch up with life again if you do. Sell, and buy a smaller house somewhere in the neighborhood. You can then hire out yourself and your team by the day. Don't spend the little capital you have."

I was afraid he might have offended Schroder by suggesting that he should work as a hired man ; but my husband said that Schroder was too sensible for that, and so it proved. Within a week he had moved into a little house not far away from us, and not only was he at work himself, but we heard that his three daughters were also looking for what they called "service places." Schroder had no sons.

As it happened, shortly after Schroder's visit I received a letter from my Mary, telling me that she and her children were coming to stay with us for a time ; and the very day the letter came my cook gave warning.

When the cook gives warning in the country, you know what that means. I felt quite distracted.

Then I thought of Schroder's girls, and wondered if one of them would answer as a cook. When I suggested this plan to my husband, his amendment was that we should take all three of them into our service.

"As they have never lived out before, it would be easier for them to start together," he said. "Our second girl has been unsatisfactory ; send her away, and turn over the whole establishment to the Schroders."

" That would mean taking an extra woman," I said ; "can you spare the money ?"

"Better than Schroder can," said my husband, laughing ; "and, besides, you won't find three women any too many after Mary's children come."

So it was settled, and my husband drove down to the little house, engaging the three girls that same afternoon. They were very glad to come, and I to have them. In fact, I was never so comfortable in all my house-keeping as when I had those girls with me—Wilhelmina as cook, and her sisters working about the house. They had been splendidly taught. I really had to raise my own standards of cleanliness to meet theirs, and pretend that I was used to the furniture being moved out and swept under, in place of being only swept up to—you know what that means. My husband says I actually cried when Mr. Schroder came over some months later and very abruptly took his girls away from me. He was "on his feet again," he said, and able to keep his daughters at home, where their mother, who was ill, needed their services. I have never seen Mr. Schroder but that one time. He talked with a strong accent, and was a round-faced, honest-looking Dutchman, with large, ruminating, blue eyes. Wilhelmina inherits her eyes from her father, but not her beauty—that comes to her from her mother, whom I never saw but once either. She chanced to hear one day that Wilhelmina had hurt her finger and so could not milk the cows, which was one of her duties, and her pleasure as well. Neither of the other girls understood milking. Knowing this, Mrs. Schroder came over, very kindly offering to help us by undertaking the milking herself. She proved a beautiful milker, my husband said, and I could see that she had been a remarkably pretty woman, but had grown stout and heavy and stupid. That is the only time I ever saw her closely. Even then I was glad to note that Wilhelmina had not the same tendency to heaviness, though I almost believed her beauty could stand a greater handicap.

So much did I admire her that, while she was with me in the capacity of cook, I was so foolish as to find excuses for myself to visit the kitchen. She did look so pretty at her work. You know, dear, what a weakness I have always had for beauty. You remember how long I bore with a certain other cook, the one who drank, just because she had such a pretty face. It was the same way with Wilhelmina. I don't mean that there was any reason for dissatisfaction with her, for she was a treasure in every way. Indeed, she had and still has a lighter hand for pastry and cake than I myself. I loved to watch her, with her sleeves rolled up to her pretty white elbows, kneading dough or sweeping, with her light curly hair twisting out from under her mob-cap, her blue eyes earnest as if she were always saying her prayers.

I shouldn't have felt blameworthy if I had kept my admiration of Wilhelmina to myself, but my old tongue was so long, what must I do but prate of her beauty to others !

I told you it was her duty to milk the cows ; and she had a healthy farmer's-daughter enjoyment of the barn-yard. I used to note the little added spring in her gait when she stepped from the kitchen door-sill to walk down the barn-yard path to the open-air work she loved. My own Mary was pretty enough, yet I knew that she could not compare with Wilhelmina. It was not only that the girl's face was beautiful, but her lithe, noble walk was something that to see simply delighted your eyes.

The barn-yard path passes near our old west porch, you remember, where we used to sit together an hour or so after supper to watch the sunset, the boys and my husband smoking and all of us chatting over the past day. Every night sitting there I used to watch Wilhelmina's feet tripping by, helping to wear the path, and see her figure cross the setting sun. Every night I used to say, " Oh, Mary, my child, I do wish you had Wilhelmina's figure," and then they would all laugh at me.

How foolish I was to do this I never awoke to realize until one night, only a week before Schroder came so unexpectedly to take his daughters home, I looked up to see Rowland also craning his neck around a porch pillar to see Wilhelmina pass. Of course I never called attention to her after that, but I felt vaguely troubled. Hal was sitting beside Rowland on the night I speak of. I noticed that he did not even raise his eyes. They rarely do the same thing, my two dear boys ; there were never two sons born of one woman so unlike as mine.

People have always said that Hal was my husband's favorite. That was only because he was so little a favorite with others. He has ever been shy, and hated company of any kind, as you know. " He is inarticulate only," my dear husband used to say, and he always reproved our Mary seriously when she grew vexed with her brother or called him stupid, as she would at times—girls think so little.

Hal's greatest joy was to be riding about the farm with his father ; that was enough to content him.

My husband used to say laughingly that I loved Rowland best because he was beautiful ; but you, my dear sister, know that was not true. Rowland has always been a great favorite with every one because he has pleasant ways, and is genial and undeniably handsome ; while my dear Hal is heavily built and slow— yet good-looking enough in his way.

Rowland's quickness and grace have been of great disadvantage to his older brother, by reason of the contrast. You know how discouraged you'd feel yourself with some one near you always brighter and gayer and more of a favorite, no matter how hard you strove.

But to go back to Wilhelmina. Before she and her sisters left me, something else happened which again made me vaguely uncomfortable.

One evening, after we had all left the sunset porch, I thought I would go down to the barnyard to look at the new Alderney calf, which I had not seen. Perhaps, too, I wanted a glimpse of Wilhelmina with her skirts caught up from her pretty feet, her face happy and flushed as it always was when she was working among the farm animals. I waited until the milking-hour was over, for my husband never liked any one but Wilhelmina about the yard then. He said confusion distracted the cows, and then they did not give milk so well. Under his rules ours certainly do give a great quantity.

When I reached the yard I thought at first I was too late, and that no one was there; then I saw Wilhelmina leaning against the closed lower half of the stable door. The upper half of the door was wide open. I was about to call to her when I realized that Wilhelmina was speaking to some one just inside the stable. Her back was half turned from the opening, and her head was bent. The moment I saw Wilhelmina's attitude and her drooping face I recognized something unmistakable. I said to myself in my sentimental old heart:

"I am going to lose the best cook I ever had, for Wilhelmina is surely listening to a love-

story, and she does look too pretty for anything."

Though I longed to know who was the man,
and hoped it was not our second coachman, for
he was unworthy of her, I was slipping off
softly when Wilhelmina caught sight of me.
She stepped forward quite quietly.

"Did you come to see the new calf?" she
asked; and before I could answer, the lower
half of the door swung open and my Hal
walked out!

Oh! sister dear, I suppose Hal showed me
the calf; but when I got back to the house I
could not have told if it were red or white, had
any one asked me. My first thought was to
go at once to my dear husband and tell him
what I had discovered; but on thinking it
over in the quiet of my room I soon saw that
I had discovered nothing. Wilhelmina had
stood by, calm and just like herself, while Hal
showed me that wretched calf. He had been
rather silent, to be sure; but if Hal had been
garrulous, that would have been unusual for
him. Altogether, the only evidence I had of
a secret between those two lay in the look of
conscious happy listening which I thought I
had caught on Wilhelmina's face. This was
no evidence at all, coming as it did from a
foolish, sentimental old woman like myself.
I therefore said nothing to any one, but, watching closely, never saw a word or look pass be-

tween Hal and Wilhelmina from that time to a week later, when her father came to take her and her sisters home. Their abrupt leaving was inconvenient to me, of course, and under other circumstances I should have resented it. As it was, far from crying, as my dear husband believed (how little our best-loved know us!), it was the greatest relief to me to see the Schroder team drive out of our gate with Wilhelmina on the front seat by her father's side.

How mistaken I was to rejoice in that sight!

Not two months after, as I was sitting one morning placidly sewing in my bedroom, my husband came in, and, taking a chair beside me, began turning over the contents of my work-basket. You know that he is not what one could call a "fidgety" man. If I find my work-basket in disorder, I know something has sorely troubled my husband, and that he has been turning over the matter in his mind, along with my spools and scissors. No one else ever dares touch my work-basket.

"What is it, dear?" I asked; and he answered:

"Have you noticed that Hal has been much away from home of late?"

My heart sank unaccountably. "I thought he was out on the farm with you," I said.

My husband turned over my spools a little more, then said, slowly: "No, he has not been with me. Can you guess where he has been?"

I was shaking like a leaf as I answered, "With Wilhelmina Schroder. Oh, my dear boy!"

"Have you suspected something there?" asked my husband.

And then I told him of the scene in the barnyard, saying that I had not mentioned it before, because it seemed such a straw to build fears upon.

"I am afraid your straw showed the way the wind was blowing," said my husband, and then he told me something which he in turn had been keeping from me.

A few days before, one of the neighbors had met my husband and mentioned to him seeing Hal at Farmer Schroder's.

He spoke so significantly that my husband asked him outright, "Have you a motive in mentioning this?"

Our neighbor, who is also an old friend, said frankly that he had, and added :

"Hal visits the Schroders frequently ; I think you ought to know it."

My husband shook his head when I urged that Hal might have been consulting the farmer about the crops.

"I think you had better hear all," he said. "I have more evidence at hand. To-day I learned something from Schroder himself. He was walking on the roadside with a friend, and did not hear my buggy-wheels on the soft earth. He was talking loudly of his good prospects, ending, as I came up, with : ' An' den, t'ank Gott, Wilhelmina ish besphoke !' "

My husband laughed a little as he quoted this, but I burst into tears.

" It does look rather badly," said he.

I thought it looked wretchedly, yet, knowing that Hal loved his father as he loved no one else on earth, I did not feel hopeless, and implored my husband to speak to the boy. "If you forbid it he will give her up," I cried. "I know he will !"

" I know it, too," answered my husband, " but I cannot forbid this, my dear. Once before Hal entangled himself in a love affair of this same kind, and I interfered ; he has never been happy since."

" I was not told of that !" I cried.

" It was not necessary to trouble you," said my dear husband, "for Hal was very young then. The girl was of the same rank of life as Wilhelmina Schroder. Evidently that is Hal's taste, and he is a man now, he should be able to decide. I do not think he would be happy with a woman of his own rank of life. Has he ever been happy with his sister and her friends ? They are all too cultivated, too dainty, for him. Hal has a slow, uncultured nature. He is frightened by the refinements even here in his own home. We must thank God that the boy's tastes are not low, as they well might be in his case. Hal wanted to honorably marry the first girl; nothing else occurred to him. We can't drive him too far; he is no boy now."

My dear sister, what could I say? This was a long, long speech for my husband, and he was right in every particular, but where did our boy get a nature that only a Wilhelmina Schroder could satisfy? I began to feel as if he were a cuckoo in our nest, though I don't believe the mother bird ever pushed the changeling out of the home tree and heart, do you? Some father birds would, I know. My husband was not of that kind.

"Let me speak to Hal," I urged; but no, my husband would not consent to that either.

"I dare not interfere," he said; "nor ought you to do so. We must watch and wait and be silent. The boy will speak to me before long; and, after all, he might do worse, far worse, than marry Wilhelmina Schroder."

Of course I cried out at this, as any mother would. In the bitterness of my heart I said a wicked thing; comparing my two boys, and crying:

"Oh, if Hal were but like Rowland!" My husband smiled.

"Oh, my dear," he said, "Rowland may be more like Hal than you know, and Wilhelmina must have great natural refinement, or I should not have been obliged to go to Schroder and tell him he must take his girls home. A coarse woman would not have attracted Rowland. It is all safely over now, and Schroder came for his girls, as you know; but you did not know, did you, that Rowland came to me in sore distress, entreating that Wilhelmina might be taken out of his sight before it was too late? Like Rowland, was it not? Careful as Hal is careless."

Sister dear, imagine my feelings; learning in the same hour that both my boys had fallen victim to my—to Wilhelmina!

For the moment I was very angry; and yet, as Rowland had honorably spoken to his father, stamping out his passing passion, my husband was right in telling me of this. It did comfort me to have it so proven that Wilhelmina was not wholly unrefined; for Rowland is almost too fastidious. The girl he has since married is dainty as a flower, body and mind.

It must have been Wilhelmina's beauty that first singed Rowland's heart; and then she did have a wonderfully quiet, queenly manner.

I say that I found some comfort in my husband's argument; but that is as I now look back on it. In those hard days it seems to me I found comfort in nothing. I could only sit in my room, weeping and weeping over the utter sacrifice of my boy. My judgment quite forsook me. I could only give myself up into my dear husband's hands and do whatever he bade me—which was to do nothing.

As his father had prophesied, Hal's confession soon came. Perhaps the sight of my unexplained sorrow hastened it. He spoke to his father as they rode over the farm together one morning, and was told that, while it was impossible for his parents to approve such a marriage, nothing would be done to oppose it.

"You are now twenty-six years old," said my husband. "You refused the yearly allowance I offered you on your coming of age. I will now increase that sum, and offer it again to you on your marriage-day, with the one provision that you and Wilhelmina make a home for yourselves."

When my husband repeated this speech to me, I was as nearly angry with him as ever in our married life. It seemed to me that he was simply smoothing the way for our boy to run down-hill.

"Do you want Hal and his wife settling with the Schroders?" asked my husband. "Marry they will, one way or another. Do you want our grandchildren brought up as a part of that family?"

He was right, as always, dear sister; but I could hardly see it so when Hal came to my room, where I was then spending the greater part of my days, and told me that, owing to his father's generosity, he was able to marry at once.

"I won't ask you or father," he said, "or any of our family to be present at my wedding. You wouldn't want to come. It is to be as quiet as can be, in the old church where you and father were married, and where we children have all been baptized."

Oh, what memories those words brought to me! This was a long speech from Hal, and I knew to have made it he must have been feeling deeply; so I tried to answer, but could only kiss him and cry foolishly. He seemed to be satisfied, however, and this was all he told us of his plans.

Though Hal did not mention when his marriage was to be, we knew the date, as families do know these things by instinct. We learned afterwards that at Hal's request none of the Schroders were present at the ceremony either. In all but the one vital point he proved unusually careful. His only witnesses were our clergyman's wife, the sexton, and—whom do you think?—our old, old coachman, who taught Hal to ride, and his father, too, for that matter. He has been like a member of the family so long that he had the same power to divine the day and hour of our boy's marriage. There he was when Hal reached the church, a wedding-favor in his button-hole, a nosegay in his hand, ready to open the door, bow his young master through, and respectfully follow him and Wilhelmina up the aisle. My husband said that Hal had tears in his eyes when he told him of this. We were all touched by it. But to think that our eldest son should have had as groomsman only a faithful servant following him !

Still, it was best so. We could not go to that wedding, and Rowland would not. He was very angry with his brother. I knew he had yet another reason for this than family pride alone. He had trampled out that same fire, and believed his brother could have done so with as little cost. I don't know myself. Hal has few roots; those are strong and go deep.

Rowland was married before the half-year was out; such a satisfactory marriage in every way. It was a great comfort to us in our trouble to have this joy come breaking through; for although we thought ourselves unhappy before Hal's wedding, it was after its accomplishment that the real trials began. How were we to meet Wilhelmina, and she us? Remember, my dear sister, my last parting with her had been at my *kitchen door*.

Fortunately, I had little time to think of the meeting. A short while before the marriage my husband had bought a little cottage some miles down the road which passes our farm. He asked me to help him in furnishing it from garret to cellar. I knew, of course, without asking, why this cottage was bought, and for whom ; but my husband said nothing, and I could not bring myself to open speech. We used to call the place " the little cottage " when we talked over the arrangements.

I think if I had not had the furnishing of that cottage to distract me I should have lost my mind during the interval between Hal's confession and his wedding. Perhaps my dear husband knew this ; he understands most of those things taught by tenderness.

It was hard work to have all in order by the date my husband set, Hal's wedding-day, but we did; and when it was done, tired as I was, I wished I had it all to do over again—carpentering, furnishing, painting—so restless was I.

The last nail was driven, the last curtain hung the morning of the marriage ; and that night, for the first time, my husband called the " little cottage " by its true name.

I could see that he, too, was somewhat restless, walking from window to window and looking out into the moonlight.

" Come," he said, at last, turning to me ; " it's as bright as day outside ; suppose we have the colt harnessed to the buggy and drive down to Hal's cottage to meet them, get it over, and go to sleep in peace."

We did not talk much during that drive ; the colt always behaved badly in harness, which engrossed us both ; I knew my husband had selected the colt intentionally.

I don't like to dwell on that meeting, my dear. We were received by my boy and his wife ; and though it was their home, it was we who showed them through it, opening every room and cupboard. When we came to the store-closet, which I had filled with preserves and groceries from my own stores, Wilhelmina turned gratefully to me. She was about to speak, but either I shrank back or she faltered, so not one direct word passed between us that night. My husband and Hal talked for four.

When I dared look at Wilhelmina, I could see that she had been crying. Her eyelids still kept swelling with unshed tears which she would not let fall. She showed great self-control, was quiet and subdued in manner, yet not without dignity. It was a trying half-hour to us all.

When we left them at last, my husband laid his hand on Wilhelmina's shoulder, saying what I had been trying to say all the while.

" This cottage is your wedding-gift from us, my child. May you be very happy here, and God bless you !"

Wilhelmina broke down then and covered her face with her hands. I liked her for it, but it was none the less bitterly hard to see my boy, so undemonstrative with his very own, comforting this stranger as I never would have dreamed he could.

I found that my husband felt this also.

" Hal will make her a good husband," he said, with a sigh, on the way home. " She understands him ; perhaps we have been to blame that we never have."

" Yes," I said, bitterly ; " we have not been Schroders, and our friends are not of that kind."

" Our friends," repeated my husband, thoughtfully. " I had not considered them."

" No," I answered ; " I suppose not. But there is not a woman in this county who is not to-night considering whether she shall or shall not call on Wilhelmina."

" It is for us to settle that," said my husband, still more thoughtfully ; and then I wished heartily that I had held my tongue. But if I wished so then, I wished it again and more strongly the next day, which was Sunday.

Hal was married on a Saturday afternoon, and on Sunday morning about sunrise I was awakened by hearing some one moving stealthily in my room. Opening my eyes, I saw my husband standing by my bed. I was startled for a moment, thinking he must be ill, until he said, " There is nothing wrong," and added, " I have been lying awake, Mary, thinking over the social question you mentioned last night. I am now about to ride down to Hal's cottage, and, if you approve, tell him we wish him to bring his wife to our pew to-day. I think that will settle everything in the eyes of the neighborhood."

I knew it would, and I knew, too, in my wicked old heart, that I did not want matters so settled. I suppose I think entirely too much of what my neighbors do and say. It seemed to me that I could forehear the whispers and see the smiles of our best friends—for best friends will do that—when calling upon poor Wilhelmina, whose manners were nil, and whose English was remarkable at times.

I did not urge my husband against doing what he suggested, simply because I knew it would be useless, if he had lain awake and decided that it was right. Also I knew his deferring the question to me was but a matter of courtesy, which he never forgets or omits. Then, too, if it were really right, I suppose I wanted it done ; but, oh, dear sister, when Wilhelmina and Hal walked up the aisle to our pew that Sunday morning, and I saw the bonnets turning and moving and meeting in every pew in the church, I thought I should die.

I noticed gratefully that Wilhelmina was dressed simply. She was quiet and stately in appearance, looking rather pale and proud with her lowered lids. She has pretty, white eyelids. I don't think outsiders would have suspected anything wrong, but you know there are no outsiders in a country congregation.

My dear husband knew the world better than I. He was again proven right. All the old county families called on Wilhelmina during the following week, and it was far better so.

Wilhelmina told me of these calls simply. She astonished me, too, by saying, humbly, that she had refused herself to every one of her visitors, as she "did not feel ready yet."

Touching, was it not? I felt so sorry for her, and grateful, too. She did indeed have much to learn before receiving any one, or returning calls either. All that could wait. Wilhelmina was a fine, sensible woman in many ways. I think I should have admired her immensely had she been married to somebody else's boy. She was clever, too, and determined. When she found that she was a little old to unlearn the poor but distinct English she spoke, she deliberately dropped into a really pretty German accent, literally translated idioms, and so on. It covered a multitude of sins. One forgives so much in a pretty foreigner. This clever move of Wilhelmina's ought to have amused me then, as it does now, but the subject was a little too tender. I had not much sense of humor at that time.

"She is wonderfully plucky," said my husband. I knew she was, and as time went on and I found in her other virtues as well, I was at the cottage more frequently than I had ever thought it possible I could be.

I always chose hours when I would not meet the Schroders, though I knew they were there but little, as they were hard-working people and lived at some distance. And yet, with all my care, a meeting there was. One unfortunate day I came in unexpectedly and went straight up the stairs to Wilhelmina's bedroom, which I had never done before. As I stood on the threshold, I heard a little scurry inside the room, and, opening the door, I caught a glimpse of a heavy figure hurrying out of my sight by another door. I recognized Mrs. Schroder's broad back.

Wilhelmina came to me with an unusual color in her cheeks; she was subdued and depressed in manner. Somehow the whole episode made me feel sick, disgusted, and degraded. When I went home, which was soon after, you may be sure, I told my husband of my encounter, with tears of self-pity. He only said, "Poor child!" and at first I thought he was speaking of me. I did not like it when I found it was Wilhelmina he meant.

"We separate her from her own kind, and are but little to her ourselves," he said; "I feel sincerely sorry for her."

I tried to look at it in the same way, but I was dreadfully sorry for myself. The only comfort I could see was that the Schroders were soon to move yet farther away, and that Hal was really perfectly happy in his marriage. He still assisted his father on the farm—a business arrangement it had become—and as the farming season grew busy, we saw more and more of him and less of Wilhelmina. I dreaded visiting my daughter-in-law after that chance encounter with her mother, and Wilhelmina came to see us very seldom. I am afraid I liked it thus; for so matters stood, and had been standing for weeks (to my shame I say it), when one day, in the height of the wheat season, my husband came to me looking troubled.

"My dear," he said, "Hal has not complained at all, but something he has said—very little, though evidently from a full heart—has made me realize that his duties are keeping him here with us constantly, that Mrs. Schroder now lives too far away to be anything to Wilhelmina, and the child must be living in a lonely cottage on an unfrequented roadside by herself, day in and day out, except for her negro servant. It is very bad for her. When did you see her last?"

I had the grace to be ashamed to tell him, but I did.

"Oh, dear, dear, dear!" answered my husband.

Then I knew that he was almost angry with me, for that's as harsh a word as I ever receive from him.

In the same afternoon I went to see Wilhelmina, and was shocked to find her looking ill and depressed. She was almost repellent in her manner to me, though perfectly respectful. She was "quite well," she said. You know the proud way a woman refuses sympathy sometimes.

I could not blame her, for I had not striven to win her confidence; but I went home and lay awake a greater part of the night full of trouble. In the morning, the first words I said to my husband were:

"I cannot stand this. I don't know what we ought to do, and yet we must do something. Wilhelmina is fretting her heart out."

"You can't stand what?" asked my husband; "having Wilhelmina so far away, or bringing her nearer? Have you thought of the old Lodge Cottage, my dear?"

"Oh, don't!" I cried; "oh, don't! As if that Lodge Cottage has not been haunting me all night!"

"Well, after all, it is a gloomy old place," said my husband.

"It wouldn't be, if you sacrificed a few trees," I answered; "but it has too few windows."

"I could easily have a few more eyes poked in it," my husband argued, "and run up a porch or so. But the Lodge is very near the house, my dear. It would bring Wilhelmina and our boy close to us in every way. It is for you to consider and decide."

I did not need to ask my husband what his

wish was. His voice told me when he spoke of our oldest boy being close to us. Yet I could not bring my mind or my heart to consent to that closeness with Wilhelmina.

"I dare not risk it," I said. "We must leave matters as they are, and I will try to see Wilhelmina more constantly where she is."

So we arranged to drive down to Hal's cottage that night as a good beginning. It was a brilliant moonlight evening, almost as bright as the night when we first had introduced Hal and Wilhelmina to their new home, months before. I was reminded of that past unhappy time in other ways also, as we drove rapidly down the familiar road. Wilhelmina had become again as a stranger to me. I felt uneasily that I was to meet her on a new and unfamiliar footing.

Nothing turns out just as we expect, does it, my dear? Why we should plan and plan as we do I cannot imagine, when but one little touch of the kaleidoscope changes all the scene. As I imagined things were to be, I had a little speech composed to repeat to Wilhelmina. It was, as I now remember it, coldly kind, a little reproachful, and all that it should not have been. This is what happened as things were in reality.

Hal met us in the road as we turned into his gateway, and stopped me as I held out my hand for him to lift me to the gro nd.

"No, mother," he said, gently; "we heard the wheels and saw you coming. Wilhelmina sent me out to meet you. She says she can't see you to-night. Don't get down, mother, don't get down. Wilhelmina is far from well. She is getting everything ready for me to take her to her mother's house to-morrow for a long visit. Mrs. Schroder was here yesterday, and had made me anxious. Mother, did you think my wife looked so very ill?"

What a jealous old woman I am! I looked at my own boy's face, flushed and quivering, and my first thought was a deep resentment that never in his life with us had I seen him so deeply moved. Wilhelmina alone was able to stir those waters.

I have always been very grateful to my good angel that at least my second thought was for Wilhelmina. Absurd as it was, I resented also that Mrs. Schroder should dare to claim her.

I caught the hands which Hal stretched out to restrain me, and by them helped myself to the ground. Hal was ever slow of motion. I ran straight past him into the house and up the stair to Wilhelmina's bedroom. I did not wait to knock, but turned the handle of the door. It was locked. I could hear a step pacing back and forth, back and forth, inside. It was a sound that made me anxious.

"Wilhelmina," I said, "open the door. I want to speak to you." Then I realized, with a shock, that I had not a single familiar endearing name by which to call my son's wife to me. What I had said sounded as cold as death, showing the tones with which I must always have approached her.

"My dear, my dear child," I cried, desperately, "open the door to me."

There was no answer, but I could hear choked sobs, and the footsteps ceased. My heart was in actual pain, what with sympathy for the poor lonely child and with the lashes of my own accusing conscience.

"Oh, my dear," I urged, "at least come nearer to the door and listen to me."

But only the sobs answered, and it seemed to me that I could stand it no longer. I burst into tears myself. "I don't blame you," I cried. "I have been cruel to you, Wilhelmina, cruel; but I didn't mean to be. It has been terribly hard on us both, but now—I am Hal's mother, I ought to be with you, and I can't stand being locked out."

Then the key turned in the door, and Wilhelmina fell forward into my open arms.

Oh, my dear sister, it was not only the door of her room that the dear child then unlocked to me; all that was pent up in her poor proud heart came rushing out.

"My dear," I said, when I could speak, "you must come home with me to-night, and stay with us until the Lodge Cottage is made ready.

You and Hal are to live there in the future. This is too far away from us; we came to-night to tell you so." Which was not in the least true, my dear, as you know; yet, indeed, at the moment, I somehow found myself honestly believing that it was.

Perhaps you don't understand my sudden change towards Wilhelmina; I could never quite account for it myself. I only know that from that hour to this Wilhelmina and I have known and loved each other. Far from separating me from my boy, she has been to me as the key of his heart, which I could never unlock; for Hal never loved me, save as a kind of matter of course, until his wife became an interpreter between us. Yes; I am very fond of Wilhelmina (in your ear, my dear, fonder than of Rowland's wife, who is a trifle too perfect for my every-day mind). She is a dear daughter to me, a sweet wife to my son, and a good mother to his children. The little ones are almost overflowing the Lodge Cottage, which is not gloomy at all, but a real sun-trap. There they live quietly and happily under our parent wings, the only ones of our nestlings building near us. Wilhelmina does not care for society, and goes out very little, though she might if she wished, as she has spent much time and labor in learning those things which seemed needful. She was pathetically humble over her deficiencies, yet proud, too, in a nice way.

After that first peacemaker baby was born in the Lodge Cottage, I took Wilhelmina with me to return all the county family calls which she had allowed to wait. She looked charmingly pretty, and was so modest and shy as to disarm unkind criticism.

And what a difference dress makes! I designed Wilhelmina's calling costume myself. In fact, on that night when she unlocked to me her door and her heart in one, I said to her: "Take the worry of the sewing off your mind, my dear; I will attend to all that for you." Then I added: "I only promise for this one time, you know—just to start you. I want you to learn to do all such things for yourself."

I said this because I was afraid that I might spoil her; but since then, though Wilhelmina is not in the least spoiled, she hardly knows what she or her children are to wear from season to season.

"Still starting Wilhelmina?" says my husband, when he sees me absorbed with the seamstress; but I know that he loves to find me thus happily occupied. It keeps me young.

You can see from all this, dear, what a united household we are, and also how nearly we escaped something widely different. When I think that these dear little grandchildren of ours might have grown up apart from us and in surroundings most painful to us; that our eldest son might have been wholly alienated from us and our old age have found us sorrowing, I am filled with gratitude for what we have and for what we are spared. I don't even now pretend to say that it was not a hard, hard trial that we passed through. But see what it has brought for us. I have gained a new-made son, a tender, grateful daughter, and, better than all, I can look at my dear husband and know I owe the whole to him; but for his kind heart, wise head, and strong hand, the wrong would never have become the right. He was the salt that flavored the bread of bitterness I was forced to eat, and I do constantly thank God first that he has created those who are as the salt of the earth, and next that he has granted such an one to me.

And now, my dear, you know the whole story.

"Look up, Martin Pope," I said. "Well met. How is Lydia the Fair? and what in the name of all goose-chases are you about now?"

Martin and I understand each other. Neither of us ever evinces surprise on finding that he has been followed by the other; but though I had often sought and found my friend in strange places and most strangely occupied, I had never before seen him quite so curiously employed as when I stood on that green bank overhanging a dusty highway and looked down on Martin skilfully driving a flock of geese before him by aid of a long willow switch.

I thought the creatures were geese, though I could not be sure, as each of the queer waddling objects was swathed in a gray jacket, close-fitting, and patterned somewhat after the blankets worn by lapdogs.

Beyond a welcoming wave of his switch, Martin made no reply to me until he had carefully driven his charges into the rich pasture of the fence corner behind us.

"Sit down," he said, hospitably waving me

to the grass, as one might offer a drawing-room chair; so we sat on the turf together, and without further greeting Martin began: "I suppose, as usual, you want to hear the whole story, from the moment I left town till now."

"Usually I do prefer your stories begun at the beginning," I answered, "but in this case, my dear boy, I shall have to ask you first what those creatures in the fence corner may be, and what you have to do with them?"

"They are geese," said Martin—"dressed geese; but they are the very end of my story, and as it's the best tale you or I have ever yet lived—and we've lived some pretty good ones, eh?—I'd rather take things as they come."

"Then do so," I answered. "The last I saw of you was when you boarded the train which followed Lydia into this wilderness, and the last I have heard is a single rhapsodical letter, written chiefly concerning the veins on Lydia's temple, and the beauties of the homestead where you have secured lodgings near your charmer."

"She lives just a little way up that road." Martin pointed up the highway to a point where the road forked. "The right-hand road leads to Lydia," he said, "and the left to my present home—and Peachy."

"Who's Peachy?" I asked. "You did not mention her in your letter."

"Because she was then away visiting a

neighbor. Her father, a primitive degenerate, whose ancestors once owned about all of the country around here, is a lazy farmer, who adds to his cash by now and then taking in a stray artist boarder or a wandering fisherman, or a loafer like me. He sent for Peachy as soon as I arrived. As I was eating my breakfast one morning I heard a cooing voice on the porch outside the dining-room window. These were the first words I heard Peachy speak :

" ' You, Joey, I thought I told you I wouldn't have potatoes planted there. You thought I was away, did you? Well, I'm home now, and you can just dig them right up. The first thing I plant in my own garden is my own foot, and I want you to remember it.'

" I heard a resolute stamp from the member referred to, and I rose and looked out to see Peachy. Oh, my poor heart !"

"What! that old thing?" I said, crossly. "Don't ask sympathy from me for your battered heart, Martin. I believe you're inventing all this, anyway."

More than once, when there was no story to tell, Martin had invented one with which to meet me ; though, in truth, the actual experiences he managed to fall into were generally stranger than his fiction.

"This time it's all true," said Martin. "You can ask Lydia."

" Does Lydia know of Peachy's existence ?"

Martin's eyes twinkled. "I am coming to that. The first morning after meeting Peachy I helped her to pick the currants in her garden. I spent the afternoon with Lydia. The next day I spent the morning with Lydia and the afternoon with Peachy. So the week passed, and by the time Sunday came the donkey between two bundles of hay wasn't a circumstance to me. I lost pounds running around that fork yonder, going from one house to the other and back again. You see, whenever I was with one, I was afraid I wanted to be with the other.

"On Sunday, after long doubt, I decided that it was Lydia I wanted to take to the country church, and, as luck would have it, there sat Peachy in the pew before us. A white muslin a little open at the neck, a string of White River shells about the whitest throat, and little gold curls about the nape of her neck to creep into the shells !

"That was Peachy. Lydia gave a gasp of delight at the vision—there's nothing mean about Lydia ; she has her faults, but she's not mean. No man could have sat behind Peachy that morning with any safety if she hadn't worn something else. You've seen those ghastly imitation-gold daggers shop-girls stick in their hair? Well, Peachy wore one, and that same dagger was my salvation. I riveted my eyes on it as a counter-charm, and in a fatal moment Lydia's glance followed mine. From that moment her fingers began to twitch in her lap. You know how an inartistic effect hurts Lydia. That dagger was to her as a discordant note perpetually sounded. It hurt her.

"'I can't stand it,' I heard her murmur; and then she swiftly dealt with the dagger as she does with you or me, or whatever offends her. I pledge you my word, she coolly plucked it out — leaned forward and drew it from Peachy's hair. My blood ran cold as I sat there. It didn't make matters any better that she smiled and nodded into Peachy's astonished face, nor that she replaced the dagger with a shell pin from her own hair. That dagger was the only thing which had protected me. When that was gone, it was good-bye, Martin Pope. That night Peachy cried for an hour on a bench in the arbor, while I argued with her through the vines. She wouldn't let me in. The next day I took Lydia's shell pin back to her, and I brought back to Peachy her own hideous dagger, with one of those charming notes which Lydia alone can write. Lydia laughed as only Lydia can laugh when I explained to her that the family were not mountain folk exactly, but decayed gentlefolk, and then she explained to me how she *had* to take out the dagger—explained it so that I admired her more than ever. I don't know how she managed it, but she did. Lydia can explain anything on earth."

"Martin, can Lydia explain you?" said I. "Are you lingering here for the sake of Lydia or Peachy?"

"The Lord knows!" said Martin. "I wish I did—but then," he added, becomingly, "both Peachy and Lydia may refuse me."

"Oh, Martin," I groaned, with a spasm of truth, "well do we all know that Lydia could never bring herself to refuse you and what is yours. She may play with you for a time, but she'll marry you in the end."

"If Peachy doesn't marry me first," said Martin, placidly, "and I pledge you my honor I'm not sure she would. Which road do you advise me to try, old friend—the left to Peachy, or the right to Lydia?"

I looked at Martin, and saw that for one of the few times in his scatter-brained life he was in earnest. For my own good reasons, which are no man's affairs, I did not reply at once. Martin laid his hand on my shoulder.

"Honestly," he said—" you have always been my mentor—which is best for me?"

"Lydia!" I burst out. "Lydia, of course, unless you've been breaking a country heart. Lydia is the only wife for you; she's as irresponsible as yourself. You have the money and she has the brains. You were made for each other. She doesn't love you; I won't

pretend she does; but she'll make you perfectly happy. On the other hand, if you don't
marry her, she'll put up contentedly with some
one of us, and make that one and herself equal-
ly happy. How matters stand with Peachy I
don't know, of course, but you've got to decide
it one way or another, Martin."

"I'm going to decide to-day," said Martin.
"In fact, I've got to decide this hour. That
flock of geese represents the crisis."

"So we have come to them at last, have
we?" said I, with a glance towards the fence
corner, where the ridiculous flock still fed.

"A week ago to-day," said Martin—"and
don't interrupt me again, for the story runs
right on from this—I helped Peachy to clean
the cellar. In these weeks I've learned how to
clean a house from top to bottom, and to work
a garden from potatoes to pease. Well, turning over the rubbish, I stumbled on a stray
bottle of rum, that had lain there since the
days when the place was a wine-cellar, I suppose. I knew the old man had never found it.

"'Don't tell father,' said Peachy; 'he'd sell
it' (the old man would sell his soul for a dol-
lar). 'Don't tell father. Let's make a rum
punch, after my great-great-grandmother's receipt.'

"Peachy has all the tastes that prove an in-
heritance from gouty generations. It appeared
that part of the rum-punch receipt called for

setting the mixture in the hot sun for half a day, so Peachy and I busily made punch, leaving the punch-bowl on the hot grass, ourselves sitting in the cool arbor. So nearly as I recollect, the punch-making ran like this :

"I : 'Why do they call you Peachy? That's not a name.'

"Peachy : 'Some of father's nonsense — because my face is all red and white, he says. I'm sure I wish it wasn't. It makes me look like a doll-baby. I'd like to have proud features and mournful big eyes, and dark hair and an oval face. I've done everything to make myself look like that. I've visited sick people and taught in Sunday-school, but I keep on looking just the same frivolous doll-baby.'

"I, with a start : 'But if you looked like that, you'd be—you'd be Lydia, and then what would I do ?'

"Peachy, innocently : 'Does Lydia teach in Sunday-schools and visit sick people ?'

"I, quickly : 'On the contrary.'

"Peachy, vehemently : 'I hate her ! I do hate her, and I hate her because she's more beautiful than I, and better dressed, and knows more, and because my dagger was hideous and she knew it and I didn't. I know it's hideous now ; don't you see I never wear it ? Did you think it hideous ? Tell me the truth.'

"I, reluctantly : 'Yes, I did.'

"Peachy : 'I knew you did. Of course I hate her.'

" Here Peachy thrust her hand in her pocket and drew out a package of dress samples. 'I want you to choose my winter gown for me,' she said ; 'you know all about these things—no, you needn't match the samples against my hair.'

" So we continued to make punch.

" 'But I can't buy my winter gown,' said Peachy, 'until I sell my flock of geese. My poultry-yard buys me all my clothes. Now my flock of geese ought to bring me—'

" As if answering to its name, a large goose, one of the flock, staggered to the arbor door, turned round in its tracks, cackled feebly once or twice, then fell gasping on its side. Peachy rushed out from the arbor, and I heard a cry. I followed quickly. On the grass before us, in various stages of reeling or collapse, we beheld all the promising flock of geese. The punch-bowl, empty and upset, told the story. What represented Peachy's winter gown lay all about us, tipsy as any ancestor of the house on the old rum. Peachy lifted her voice and wept aloud, while I dashed water over the fainting fowls. In vain — they one by one twirled over on their backs and lay motionless, claws up.

" 'It's no use,' sobbed Peachy. 'They are all dead or dying ; and I was so fond of them !'

Then, practical in her grief, ' Go tell Joey to pick them before they get cold ; at least I'll sell the feathers.'

" There and then I would have thrown myself at her feet, offering myself and any number of wardrobes, but—and I was grateful to her for it—Peachy fled to the house, sobbing as if her heart were broken.

" I called Joey, and together we plucked those geese. When Peachy at last returned, we had quite a consolatory heap of feathers to show her.

" ' But they won't buy a whole gown,' she said, sorrowfully ; ' and, Joey, these geese won't be fit to eat either. You can bury all of them in the bottom of the garden.'

" Joey got a wheelbarrow, and packing the bodies within, wheeled them away, Peachy's eyes following the hearse, filled with tears. Suppose we go to the funeral, I suggested, as distraction. But when Peachy and I arrived at what was to have been the graveyard, we found there was to be no funeral. Terror-stricken Joey was backing away from the wheelbarrow, where a poor stripped goose was quacking feebly, stiffly yet unmistakably moving its bare legs and wings. Soon the whole pile was in motion. They had only been boozy, after all, and the long cool drive had refreshed them, as it would any other gentlemen in like condition. The scene was indescribable as the denuded fowls disengaged themselves from each other and flapped from the wheelbarrow to the ground. Peachy laughed and wept alternately, but a brilliant idea came to me.

"Behind you, in this fence corner, my friend, you see the result of applied literature. I led Peachy to the house, where I selected Cranford from the old bookcase and read aloud those immortal pages where the clothing of the singed cow is described. A hint is enough for Peachy. By nightfall the shamelessly naked flock were as good as ever for market purposes, and all decently clothed in the gray uniform in which you now see them browsing."

I looked at the feeding geese, and ridiculous enough they were; but again, for my own reasons, my face was grave.

"When I told this story of the dressed geese to Lydia, she didn't sit on the grass and blink on me solemnly. Not at all," said Martin.

"'I'd give anything I possess for that flock of geese,' said Lydia, when she could speak for laughing.

"That ought to have warned me, but it did not. Peachy and I went out fishing the next morning, and when we came home the old man handed twenty-five dollars to Peachy.

"'There's your winter gown,' he said. 'I sold your dressed geese for you for a fancy price.'

"If you believe me, Lydia had been over and

"'ALL DECENTLY CLOTHED'"

bought the whole flock and driven it away herself.

"The dagger episode wasn't a circumstance to this.

"'You,' said Peachy, turning to me in a rage, 'must have told her of my geese; she couldn't have known of them unless you did. You can take back this twenty-five dollars to her and bring my geese, or you can go away and never let me see you again.'

"Here's the twenty-five dollars," said Martin, drawing a roll of notes from his pocket, "and, as you see, here's the crisis.

"'If you take my geese away from me,' says Lydia, 'you may follow them and never come back to me.'

"For a week I have vibrated around this fence corner. Neither Peachy nor Lydia will yield. They have made it a test case. It's under which king—speak or die? And then to-day, if I didn't meet the geese free and browsing on the roadside! They have escaped from Lydia's keeping and are in my hands. So now, old friend, to whom shall I take them? Shall I drive them up the right-hand road to Lydia, or the left to Peachy? I leave it to you. This must settle Martin Pope."

I looked at Martin and I looked at the grotesque geese, and I looked into my own soul.

"Why don't you settle your fate for yourself?" I said, angrily.

"Because you've always done it for me," said Martin, and I looked again desperately at the geese.

A brilliant thought suddenly seized me. "Why not let them decide?" I said. "They've been fed for a week at Lydia's—the chance is as good that they'll return there as that they'll go to Peachy. Drive them to the fork and let them lead you."

"I will," said Martin. He started to his feet and herded the noisy geese into the roadway. "Stand there and watch," he shouted. "It's the corner of my life. Shoo—shoo!"

I stood on the bank watching him. I am older than Martin, and I have known him for years. I can never tell, however, how much is earnest with him and how much jest, how much truth he is telling me and how much of lies; but, foolish as his story had been, I had seen that it hid an unusually real feeling, for what or whom I could not decide. My heart beat hard as Martin reached the fork of the road. I wondered if he would subtly direct the flock one way or the other; but no, he was rigorously just, keeping the absurd cackling creatures well in the midst of the highway. At the crucial moment he even dropped his stick and stood with arms folded. The geese browsed a moment at the grass on the fork's wedge, then with slow, deliberate waddle the leader turned into the right-hand road—the road to Lydia.

"Stop that !" shouted Martin. "Stop that, I tell you ! Shoo out of that—shoo !"

The willow rod came down on the back of the leader with a whack that drove him squeaking into the left-hand road, followed by the brood. With shouts of laughter, and one mischievous backward look at me, Martin drove them mercilessly before him. Had he always meant to take that road ? Did he guess something ? I did not stop to wonder. With a spring I leaped up from the bank and walked—no, ran—on my own goose-chase up the right-hand road.

" No, sir, I don't think so. I'm judgin' 'em by my own feelin's. If I was to keep climbin' up to a third story to find a meal, and be poked down to the street just as I got a nibble, I'd be too discouraged to do anything but set on the curb-stone and starve. I shorely would. That's jest the way I think these pertater-bugs feel. Kill 'em? No, I know I ain't doin' that, but I certainly am discouragin' 'em. Yes, killin' would be more final like, I suppose, but then I'd have to lug the water and cans and poison-stuff 'way from the house down here. It ain't hardly worth while, an' it's kinder cruel anyhow. Every farmer has his own way o' doin' things."

Martin Pope stood leaning on the garden fence, watching Farmer Esip at his arduous labors. The old man was dressed like a retired preacher from his waist up, wearing a long solemn-looking black coat and an old stove-pipe hat, but on his legs were a pair of farmer's overalls, worn to an artistic pale blue. He held a little stick in his hand, and moved with

IN THE GARDEN PATCH

lazy patience from plant to plant discouraging the potato-beetles. This was Peachy's father. Martin had wished to ask his permission before making open love to his daughter, which he meant to do within that hour, but somehow Mr. Esip's occupation and costume did not strike Martin's artistic sense as exactly suitable for such an occasion. Therefore he only said :

"You ought to use a longer stick, Mr. Esip. Then you wouldn't have to bend your back like that. Take mine. I've done with it."

"It's more trouble to hold your back up, seems to me," said Mr. Esip, after using the long stick on several plants. "Guess I'll go back to my old way. Where's my little stick ?"

Martin found it for him, and with grave delight watched his efforts towards extermination. There was nothing Martin Pope would not do to enjoy new experiences and a new sensation. His bohemianism was a true strain that in verity knew no law. It had led him into this wilderness, held him loitering in the farm-house, and made him now look on this prospective father-in-law as to costume and character with no more serious feeling than delightful amusement.

"Father ! Father !"

It was Peachy's voice. She was standing looking at her sire with a face that expressed more than her indignant tone. Mr. Esip jumped, and then was plainly angry with himself for doing so.

"I wisht you wouldn't walk so soft," he said, testily. "I've been working to knock one beetle down these five minutes. He's the most set I ever struck, and now I've lost him."

"I call it a shame," said Peachy's clear tones, "bothering those poor bugs. It doesn't help the potatoes one bit, and just worries the beetles to death. No, not even to death. It don't do that much good." She looked her father up and down with a sidelong glance of disapproval. "Father, you *do* look dreadful!" she said.

Mr. Esip moved on to another swarming plant. "I calculate to sometimes," he said, with calm obstinacy.

Martin laughed aloud. Peachy flushed an offended pink that in Martin's fond eyes glorified the whole garden, not excluding Mr. Esip.

"Father," said the daughter, slowly, "you go to the house and take off those overalls and put on your broadcloth trousers, or take off that coat and hat and put on your working-blouse. I don't care which you do, but it's got to be one or the other. I won't have you going about looking like this."

Mr. Esip nodded his head sidewise rapidly and angrily. "I actually—I actually believe you think you run this house?"

"I do run it," said Peachy, firmly.

Mr. Esip took off his silk hat with one hand, and with the other scrubbed his hair over his head, as if perplexed between what ought to be and what was not. "Well, I guess you do," he admitted, pleasantly, and trudged off to his house—his in name only.

"Peachy," said Martin, leaning far over the fence, and half whispering — "Peachy, I've brought home your geese. Here they are, and —Peachy, do you love me?"

Peachy ran to the fence, in her eagerness leaning out as far as her lover had leaned in. She was very close to him. Martin could see every little curling golden hair on her neck and temples. Lydia wore her dark hair off her brow, showing the bluest veins in her temples. It was a shock of pure joy to Martin to *know* in that moment that he preferred the golden tendrils to the blue veins.

"Are they all there?" cried Peachy.

"Every one," said Martin, "just as they left you. I wanted to have their jackets cleaned and pressed before I brought them back, but I thought I wouldn't wait."

Now the history of these geese, and the cause of their wearing flannel jackets, is a long story aforetold, and not necessary to the present tale even in *résumé*. Suffice to say that the safe return of this straying flock had been made by Peachy the key to her favor, and here they were.

"Yes," she said, rapidly counting them over. "Yes, every one," and she turned and beamed on Martin with her blue eyes.

"Now, Peachy, do you love me?"

"Come into the garden," said Peachy. "Drive the geese into the paddock, and I'll meet you at the gate."

She was holding the garden gate ajar for him when he came back, and Martin entered, feeling like the first man in the first garden. He murmured something of the kind to Peachy as the gate creaked open.

"Adam," said Peachy, coolly, "had an easy time in the garden : don't you think so? All his work was done for him, every way. With only one woman in the world, it was easy to choose, wasn't it?"

Then Martin knew that Peachy had guessed far more than he had ever told her about Lydia.

"Peachy," he said, ignoring the insinuation, "do you love me?"

"That's not what you ought to say first, is it?" asked Peachy.

"You know I love you, Peachy," he replied.

"No, I don't; and what's more to the point, I don't believe you do," said Peachy.

"I do," he retorted, warmly.

"How do you know?"

Martin began to laugh. "I'll tell you," he said. "Come sit in the old arbor with me, and I'll tell you just how I know I love you. You see, my mother once gave me a receipt for knowing. An old maid that got married somehow told her how she found out she loved, and it was a good enough test for anybody's use. This was the way she knew: 'Tilly Pope,' she said — that was my mother's name — 'Tilly Pope, when I look up in the sky, Nicholas Gray is there; when I walk out in the woods, Nicholas Gray is there; when I look out in the dark, Nicholas Gray is there. In fact, Tilly Pope, Nicholas Gray is perfectly identified with me.'" Martin flung back his head and laughed until the arbor rang. Then he grew suddenly serious. "It *is* a good test, though, and I ought to know, because that's exactly the way I am about you, Peachy. When I look—"

"How about when you look at—Lydia?" said Peachy, dryly.

The laugh died out of Martin's eyes; he looked depressed. He gazed at Peachy judicially. She was sitting on the arbor seat, where the sunlight fell on her twisting golden hair. Her blue eyes were in shadow; they looked a deeper blue than usual as she glanced up at Martin. Yes, decidedly she was worth it. Martin revived. He began again, this time with a sweet candor.

"I suppose I may as well own up, as you seem to know all about it; but you might let me alone a little, I think. It was hard enough to decide, without your trying to shake my decision after I think it all done. It's been just like playing ' King William,' Peachy. I swear it has. You know how they play it—asking what you want, ices and cake, or locusts and wild-honey, or some such things. I always did hate to decide ; it takes me forever. But, dear, really this time I have chosen. I can't say I don't want the ices and cake, for that man isn't born who could say he didn't want Lydia. But I know I want the locusts and wild-honey *most*. Isn't that enough ?"

Peachy turned away her head, but she left her hand in Martin's grasp.

" I don't understand you. Why don't you talk like other people ?" she asked.

" Because I can't. Peachy, do you love me ? I'm not sure I understand about the locusts myself, but I do know wild-honey when I see it ; and as for the taste of it—" He thought he had her hand at his lips, but Peachy was gone. Martin followed her out into the garden, and caught up with her at the potato-patch, where she lingered a little, looking down, frowning at the stripped stalks and riddled leaves of the potato plants.

" How's a man to prove anything to you if you won't sit still ? I say these modern days are hard," urged Martin. " Here am I, Martin Pope, pining to prove my love for a woman, and the only thing I've been able to do for her is to herd geese! Now if I could rid you of a dragon or so, Peachy, you'd believe I loved you, wouldn't you?"

Peachy was still looking down, disconsolately. "I'd a good deal rather you'd rid me of potato-beetles. Just look at this patch! I declare, it makes me heart-sick."

Martin stood gazing from the potato plants to Peachy and back again. It seemed to him that his brain worked like fire.

"Peachy," he burst out, "I'll make a bargain with you. I can't kill a dragon for you, because I can't find one, but if I rid you of these potato-bugs, and do it in two days' time, will you marry me?"

Peachy flushed to the roots of her hair.

"How can you be so absurd? You couldn't do it, in the first place. Nobody could."

"All the more glory if I do—and the less risk for you. Is it a bargain?"

"Of course not. It's too ridiculous to think of; and then father's awfully tender-hearted. He won't have anything on this farm poisoned."

"I don't care," said Martin, obstinately; "if you'll take the risk of marrying me, I will take the risk of losing you. We'll call it a final test. I'll rid you of the potato-bugs or—or Martin Pope by the mid-day after to-morrow night, and I won't use poison either. Is it a bargain?"

Peachy laid her finger ponderingly on her lips. They were half pouting, half laughing, and she was evidently half angry, half disquieted. "How dare you mix up love and potato-bugs!"

"That's all right," said Martin, radiantly. "If that's all that bothers you, you haven't any case at all ; for, you see, you don't marry me unless I kill off the bugs, and that disposes of them before the love comes, doesn't it? Peachy, don't be stiff-necked about it. Can't you see ?—it gives you a chance to yield gracefully, if you find you want to. And look here, dear, just in a whisper between you and me and the beetles : if I lay every beetle dead at your feet, and then you find you don't want me, you can kick me away, and I won't say a word. Only, if I am to be kicked, my dear, I shall wish to Heaven that the foot doing it wasn't so extremely tiny. I always did dote on a small foot, and yours is the very smallest— No, no, Peachy. Oh, no, no ! Of course you know it. Then why have you called on me to tie your shoestring three times this day ?" and so on and so on, until the potato-beetles seemed wholly forgotten; but in the end Martin had his way, and they were finally made the pivot on which was to hang his fate as a bachelor.

On the day set for Martin's experiment, the potato - patch was a most remarkable - looking field. In the first place, about its not very large area ran a wall made of a bolt of un-bleached muslin. One end of the muslin was tacked neatly to the trunk of a flowering plum-tree, and the other end to a twin brother of the tree that grew but a few feet away. Stakes driven in the soft earth at intervals supported the muslin walls beyond the trees. The narrow space between the two trunks was a natural door. Inside this enclosure lay rows and rows of prostrate potato plants, each stalk pinned firmly to the earth by innumerable hair-pins — supplied under protest by Peachy. Furthermore, with the sweat of unwonted labor on his brow, Martin had by entreaties and exhortations so wrought upon Peachy's mind that she had actually lent him not only hair-pins, but the services of Joey, the hired man ; and lastly, when Martin, so absorbed in his work that he seemingly forgot what was the prize he worked for, rushed into the house imploring, nay, demanding Peachy's added assistance, she really hesitated to remind him of the delicacy of her position, and hastily followed him into the potato enclosure. There, unquestioningly, and for no possible purpose that her imagination could conceive, she feverishly helped him and Joey pin down potato stalks, running a race with the summer light, and beating it by half a row of potatoes.

"We've done it !" shouted Martin, rising, sunburnt and weary, from the last plant.

"Peachy, we've as good as won— No, I've—no—well, it doesn't matter." He looked hard at Peachy, and his eyes suddenly began to twinkle.

Peachy made no reply. She walked into the house in silence, and Martin did not see her again until the next morning. That crucial day found Martin an excited and very tired man. He had told Peachy that he wished, for the furtherance of his plans, to have in his hands the control of the whole farm for the time being, and to this she consented the more easily because there was no control to hand over. Farmer Esip, as he said, had his own ways of farming. He did not know of the change of dictatorship, because a county fair had required all his attention from noon to night the previous day; but on the fateful morning, after early breakfast, from which Martin was absent, he sought Peachy, hidden in the cool recesses of the dairy, and announced, from the open door :

"Honey, maybe you don't hold it cruel to starve dumb folks, but I do. I don't say it wasn't smart, but I do say it was bitter hard on the fowls, and hard on the beetles too. There's nothin' that's more a lesson to me than pertater-bugs— busy as yallerjackets all the time, eatin', breedin', workin', trudgin' all the way from Colorado to here, and nobody wantin' 'em there or here or anywhere. There's such a thing as bein' entirely too enterprisin'. All the way from Colorado to here to be eat up by ducks and geese and hens and keats and turkeys! There won't be a bug in that field by noon."

"Peachy!" It was Martin's voice at the doorway. A great pan of milk slipped from Peachy's hands, and a white wave splashed across the floor to Martin's feet.

"My soul, honey!" said Mr. Esip, and Peachy sat down on the milk-bench and burst into mingled tears and laughter. "What's a pan o' milk?" said her father, wondering. "'Cept for the trouble o' wipin' it up. It's nasty to clean up, milk is. I guess you've been in this dark hole too long, honey; I'll tend to this moppin'. Take her to the pertater-patch, Mr. Pope, and show her what's goin' on. It's a murderous sight, but it's mighty interestin'. I don't know how you ever thought o' such a thing."

Peachy stood between the two flowering plum-trees and looked into the enclosure. There, scrambling from prostrate vine to vine, cackling, crowing, gobbling, quacking, hissing, but eating beetles all the time as if life depended on hurry, was every beaked creature on the farm, a great flock, including the jacketed geese. The noise was deafening.

"They've had nothing to eat, nothing at all, for twenty-four hours," said Martin, complacently. "You see, I remembered that there were more fowls on this farm than anything else, including potato vines. It was a simple question in arithmetic and hunger."

Peachy stood staring for a moment, then she suddenly began to laugh; she laughed until the tears ran down her face, and she had to lean against the trunk of the plum-tree for support. Martin regarded her anxiously.

"It's nothing," gasped Peachy, wiping her eyes, "only it's so absurd. Don't you know how to be anything else?"

"I must have worked you too hard yesterday," said Martin, tenderly. He spread his coat under one of the plum-trees and insisted that Peachy should rest upon it, while he lay at her feet, resting also. Joey, his eyes popped with amazement, stood in the plum-tree doorway. Thus they watched the murder of the beetles.

Mr. Esip was right; before the clock struck twelve those beetles were no more; or, rather, so few remained in the patch that it would have been hypercritical to mention their existence. At Martin's word, Joey drove the replete fowls from the enclosure and away to the barn-yard, while Martin himself rolled up the muslin. It was a long white bundle when he brought it back to Peachy, now standing under the plum-tree, and laid it at her feet.

"Here is the shroud of the beetles," he said,

significantly, as he bent one knee on the muslin and bowed his head, waiting.

"Can't you be sensible for once?" said Peachy. There was something wistful in her tone, though she was laughing.

"No, I can't. This is the way I am made; and if you like me at all, you ought to like what I am."

"Well, I don't," said Peachy.

Martin looked up quickly. For a brief moment his face was as serious as could have been asked. Then he saw Peachy's irrepressible blushes and dimples against the white blossoms above her. Martin's gaze was fixed upward admiringly.

"By George! if women knew how becoming a flowering plum-tree is, there'd be one growing in every drawing-room."

But Peachy turned her head away. "Couldn't you just—just for one moment be like other people?"

"Suppose I was—"

"Why, then"—a hesitating sigh, half serious, half comical—"why, then—I might— If only," she cried out — "if only I were sure about Lydia!"

"I know just how you feel," said Martin, with sympathy. "I was just that way myself."

There were no more blushes and smiles under the plum-tree.

"I think," said Peachy, haughtily, "that this

had better end. I don't really care for you, Mr. Pope, and won't pretend I do. I wish you'd stop kneeling there. Perhaps Lydia—"

"There she is now !" said Martin.

Yes, there she was, sitting in a carriage that was slowly passing the farm-house. By her side was an old friend of Martin's. They both beckoned to him. The carriage stopped, and Martin sprang up and ran out into the road. Peachy watched them from the garden, saw them talking earnestly, and then Martin suddenly began shaking the hand of one and the other, then the other and the one, over and over. At last they drove off, and Martin came slowly back to the garden.

"They're engaged," he said, shortly. "Lydia's engaged to my best friend. She told me herself. She said you looked like one of those plum blossoms dropped from the tree. Lydia never was mean. I always said that for her. Now she's engaged."

"What did you say to her?" asked Peachy. Her voice was forced, but Martin seemed not to notice it. His gloom deepened.

"I told her you were a heartless girl. Haven't you let me do everything to win you—from herding geese to killing potato - bugs? And now you say calmly you don't care anything for me. I believe you have been laughing at me all the time."

"Did you tell Lydia that too?"

"Yes, I did," said Martin, savagely. "I told her you had ruined my life—and you have ; that you didn't care a pin for me, and you never had, and you never would. I told her all that too."

"You did? Oh, Martin, I love you !"

Peachy was stretching out her hands to him with a dazzling smile and fascinating abandon.

"I do love you," she repeated.

Martin turned with a smile as radiant and a laughing triumph in his eyes.

"There !" he cried. "I knew that would settle it ! Of course we love each other." And they did—in their way.

" I don't know why any of us ever expected anything different," said Lydia. "Nothing of a usual nature ever happens to them. Why shouldn't their baby be a freak child ?"

" Lydia," I said, gravely, " under all the circumstances that's not a wise way for you to talk of the Popes. If you had said that to any one but me, it might have been thought you had some private animus."

"I wasn't saying it to any one but you, and if you mean any one might think I wanted Martin Pope myself, why I certainly did, and would have had him, too, if Peachy's geese hadn't saved Rome. The way they altered events was a salvation for us all, wasn't it ?" and Lydia turned on me one of those glances that are still her own, and hers only.

" Don't look at me like that," I said ; "you melt me like butter. You can't call the Pope baby a freak. It isn't one. It's only phenomenally tiny."

" Didn't you tell me Martin had been bothered out of his life by enterprising showmen ?"

" Yes ; he has had some startling offers for the child—humiliatingly startling."

Lydia began to laugh provokingly.

" And then you tell me it's not a freak baby."

" I tell you it's not a freak," I retorted, warmly. " It's only very undersized, and it's not nice of you to laugh at the poor thing's misfortune. Probably they are thinking a half loaf is better than no bread."

Lydia was silent for a moment, while I began to repent of my harshness, for we ourselves had no offspring of any size. " I might put up with half a loaf," she said, at last, as if considering the matter, " but a quarter loaf, and particularly a quarter-loaf baby, I never could stand. Why, I really never remember hearing of a freak baby in one's own class of life ; did you, dear ?"

" No, dear," I said, meekly, " I never did until Martin's freak baby came." Then we looked at each other and laughed. The train was drawing us into a station of the town where the Popes were then living. It was this circumstance that had turned our thoughts to them and their affairs.

" I suppose you are right," said Lydia, generous when her point was gained. " It's only a preternaturally small child, and not a freak at all. Why, do look ! Isn't that Mr. Pope now ? The one with the little champagne-basket in his arms. It *is* Mr. Pope."

I looked where she directed. Yes, there was but one Martin Pope, and that was he. As I saw him I burst out laughing shamelessly.

"My dear Lydia, as sure as you live, he's got the baby in that basket." Lydia pressed her nose flat against the glass in her eagerness.

"Why it can't be ! yes, he is carrying it as if he had something alive in it. Oh, nonsense, it's his cat or a dog."

"Look behind him," said I. "Does that go with a cat or a dog ?" Close on Martin's heels, and with eyes fixed on the little basket walked an evident nurse-maid, cap, apron, anxious air, and all. Lydia flung herself back in her seat and choked with laughter.

"Oh, if it were anybody but Martin Pope it would have a chance to be pitiful. But it's so —it's so distractingly appropriate. How can I help laughing ?" cried Lydia.

I certainly could not show her how to help it. Indeed there had been something too exquisitely ridiculous, though what we could not exactly state, even to ourselves, in that passing glimpse of Martin paternally hugging a champagne-basket, and followed by a nurse. It was not until the train had steamed out of the station that we recovered nerve.

"Well," said Lydia, "I see now what a far-seeing genius a showman is. I should have said I dreaded nothing more than having Mr. Pope come into this car with his—I don't know what to call it exactly—and now I am consumed with an unholy and unquenchable curiosity to see inside that basket."

Absurd as Martin had looked in that passing glimpse, the old-time friendship had stirred warmly in my heart at sight of him.

"Lydia," I said, irritably, "I do wish you would stop talking in that way. I tell you. Martin's child is only undersized. He wrote me that it might take a start and grow any day."

Lydia stared at me. "Well, if you aren't unreasonable. As if you didn't laugh too."

"I knew where to stop. When you insist on laughing at everything and everybody, it makes you extremely difficult to deal—"

"Then why don't you shuffle me?" interrupted Lydia, with imperturbable good-humor.

"I prefer to cut you at present," I retorted, and then I whirled my chair around with judicious haste before she could possibly reply.

The sharp movement swung me a little too far; so much so that before I could stop myself my foot had struck smartly against the knee-cap of a man who was hurriedly entering the compartment carrying a little glass of white liquid in his hand. The blow felled him instantly. The glass and the liquid landed in Lydia's lap, where the man himself would have followed but that Lydia, with her wonted promptness, caught his arm and held him up.

Before I could pick up the débris of my own scattered wits or come to my wife's rescue, I heard her high, cool voice.

"Walk right in, Mr. Pope," she said, pleasantly. "Walk right in. Milk? Yes, I supposed so. It doesn't make the least difference. My dear, aren't you going to apologize to Mr. Pope?"

Apologize! Martin and I were on each other's neck, and not altogether metaphorically either.

"You'd like to see the baby, wouldn't you?" said Martin, beamingly. He was still affectionately holding my hand, and I feared he would surely feel my apprehensive start. I looked quickly at Lydia, and saw an honestly frightened look on her usually composed features. I felt much the same way myself.

"I was getting some water to weaken her milk when I met your foot," said Martin. "She's in the end compartment with her nurse. Don't you want to go back with me now and see her—both of you?"

Lydia gripped the arms of her chair convulsively, looking up to me with imploring eyes, but I braced her with a glance.

"Yes, indeed we do," I said, cheerfully: "of course we do. Come, Lydia," and I dragged my wife to her feet and drove her before me and after Martin, heartily wishing that there was some strong man back of me again to per-

form for me a like office.   Martin led us to the
door of the compartment, chatting all the way.

"Just excuse me a moment," he said, over
his shoulder; "I'll see if she looks nice," and he
slipped within the door, closing it after him.

"Now run," said Lydia, turning and pushing
me back with both hands. "I can't go in
there—I can't, and I won't."

"You must," I said, sternly, but my own
heart was beating with an absurd force.

"If you make me look at it, it's ten to one
I'll laugh right out.   We *can't* risk it."

I set my teeth.   "In we go," I said, "and if
we laugh we laugh."

Lydia collapsed in my hands.

"Then hold my hand tight," she said.   "I'm
just as crazy as ever to see it, but I'd give all
I possess to be able to run away."

I grasped her hand in mine, and the door
opened for us.   My own position was not easy.
Martin was an old and dear friend, and the
next moment might separate us forever.

"Did he tell you anything about baby's
size?" asked Martin of Lydia as we entered.

"I told Lydia that the baby was small," I
said, weakly.

"Small!" said Martin, scornfully; "do you
call that *small?*"   He turned and lifted a light
veil that covered the little champagne-basket,
and there lay something that brought Lydia
with a rush to her knees beside it.

"Oh !" she cried.   "Oh !"

"That's what I knew you'd say," said Martin.   "Now don't wake it. The last person that saw it I sent into the nursery alone, and she came out and said the baby wasn't there— there was only a French doll in the crib."

"Doll !" said Lydia, scornfully ; "there never was a doll in the world like this."

I peered gingerly over her shoulder and saw something that neither small nor doll adequately described.   It was a baby so tiny that one hardly dared breathe lest it might be blown away, and yet it was so perfect and plump and rosy, a microscopic vision, that I held my breath for quite another reason.

"Oh !" cried Lydia again, "*do* you think it will have to grow ?"

"Not for some time, I hope," said Martin, delightedly, "though she may take a start and grow any day. I don't want to be selfish about it, though personally she fascinates me just as she is. But she wouldn't like it herself, you know, as she grows older. It wouldn't do at all to keep on carrying her in a closed basket, and that's what has to be or she'd draw a mob ; and besides there are other dangers." His whisper grew solemn. "Do you know, that little thing is worth thousands as she lies there.   We are in constant terror of her being stolen. She's never left a moment alone, day or night, and I have to take a whole compartment for her when we travel. The smaller they come the more they cost—like Blue Points."

"Get me out of this quickly," breathed a smothered voice in my ear. I looked down, and on seeing my wife's face, acted hastily. A chair that was not secured to the floor was near me, and I kicked it over. The wee-est and the most fairylike of screams immediately pierced the air. Martin rushed to the champagne-basket, and Lydia and I fled.

When we were once more installed in our own chairs outside, I looked over at my wife.

"Well," I said, " what were you going to do in there, please—laugh, or cry, or faint? I couldn't tell which."

"Neither could I," said Lydia, from the depths of her handkerchief. " It was the most serio-comic thing I ever went through. Why, he loves it dearly. And yet I know he's going to exhibit it sooner or later. I know it. He couldn't be Martin Pope and not do it."

" Exhibit it !" I repeated, amazed and indignant. " How could Martin do such a thing?"

"He couldn't," whimpered Lydia, " and that's why I am so sure it 'll be done. He never yet did anything he could. It makes me feel dreadfully to think of that lovely little baby in a show."

" Don't be silly," I said, severely ; and then, resorting to Martin's formula, " Evidently the child is soon to take a start and grow."

"You only have Mr. Pope's word for that," said Lydia, emerging from the cambric. "Mark my words, that child will live to be exhibited."

"Have it your own way," I answered; and, as usual, Lydia's way it went, though not quite as even she had expected it to go.

There was something wrong with the Popes. Lydia recognized that there was, and so did I; but neither of us could imagine what it might be. They had moved to the metropolis where we lived shortly after our meeting in the cars, but though they had spent the whole winter not many squares away from our house, the families saw little of each other. Women can make distance as absence and absence as distance in questions of family intimacy. Martin and I met, as it were, by stealth now and then; but there could be little real intercourse. Then one day late in the winter Mrs. Pope herself suddenly appeared in my office. I am not using the word suddenly in any rhetorical sense; it was a fact that I looked up from my writing to find her sitting by my desk.

"Mr. Griffin," she said, abruptly, "did you ever have an obsession? Do you know what they are?"

"Not as well as you must," I answered. "When I want occult or psychic information I know to which sex to go for it in these days. To what cult do you belong, may I ask? My wife belongs to five." But Peachy was not to be dashed.

" I only found out about obsessions the other day," she said, gravely. . " I have one. That's what I wanted to consult you about."

I looked anxiously at Peachy's flushed and pretty features, but could not find there or in her innocent eyes anything to justify alarm.

" There are all kinds of obsessions," she went on, "and one is a kind that makes you want all the time, and want dreadfully, to do something that you know you ought not to do at all, and wouldn't do for the world if you could help yourself ; but you can't. My obsession is wanting to exhibit the baby."

It was not unnatural that I should have started in my chair and exclaimed aloud before I could control or check myself, but as she heard me two great tears rose in Peachy's eyes and rolled down her face.

" My dear Mrs. Pope," I said, taking her hand in mine, " Martin is the dearest friend I have in the world. Now what can I do for his wife ?" By which words it will be seen that an ardent appreciation of feminine emotion does make me lose my head in a crisis.

" You are very kind. I knew you would be when I came to you," said Peachy, wiping her eyes. "You see, the temptation is terrible. We do need money so horribly."

I breathed easily again. It was nothing

abnormal after all, but a complaint more or less common to all flesh. How they had contrived to attain such a position with Martin's known means of supply was what I could not comprehend, though he spent money like water. Peachy explained it all to me. It seemed that Martin was most peculiarly placed. He had no income. His moneys dropped in to him not yearly, but in large lump sums at irregular intervals, wholly contingent on his good behavior. The bulk of his property was to be handed over to him on his thirtieth year, which was not far off, if before that date Martin had not contrived to disgrace the family name. In the latter case he was to receive nothing. The full power of disbursement and dispossession lay in the hands of an eccentric old uncle of Martin's, and the will was made by Martin's father. After this hearing it did not seem to me difficult to account for Martin's peculiarities. In the past I had always tried to lay them at the door of his artistic genius, but that had not adequately supported them. This explanation did.

"You see now," said Peachy, "how important it is for us that Martin should be able to meet a note for five thousand dollars that will fall due to-morrow. If we don't meet it, Uncle Pope may call that a disgrace. One of the hard things about Father Pope's will has been that Martin never knows what Uncle Pope may call a disgrace. He wasn't sure he wouldn't be angry at his marrying me ; and then, when the baby came and was so little, we were afraid he might call that disgraceful. Martin says he knows he'll call it perfectly disgraceful and extravagant for us to have a note falling due for five thousand dollars to-morrow and nothing ready to meet it. Do you think he will ?"

"Well," I said, "I'm afraid he might view it so."

"We can scrape about one thousand dollars together," sighed Peachy, "and that's all."

"Of course, under the circumstances," I said, " you can't call on your uncle for an advance, as you don't want him to know your need, but I should think it would be easy enough to arrange for an advance of four thousand dollars from any one on such expectations as Martin has. It's pretty late in the day, but I think I can negotiate a loan for him by noon to-morrow."

"Why, no, you can't," said Peachy, practically, "because we haven't any security to offer."

"Well, I can only try," I said, at last. "I wish I had the money myself, Mrs. Pope."

"Oh, I knew you hadn't a cent, or I wouldn't have come to you," said Peachy, with delightful frankness. "I'm afraid you think we have been awfully extravagant ; but, you see Martin miscalculated. He thought we had plenty to last until he was thirty, but it all seemed to go suddenly. You know how it is with money. And then the baby's an awful expense. We have to guard her so carefully. She is watched all day, and we keep a night nurse sitting up with her with the door locked on the inside. I suppose it's foolish, but we still keep getting such offers for the poor little thing it makes us awfully nervous."

"I don't call it foolish at all," I replied. "I should go still further and keep the nursery door bolted on the *outside*, and the key in my own pocket. A nurse might be unfaithful. But you haven't told me about your own exhibiting obsession, Mrs. Pope." Peachy looked a little embarrassed.

"Well, I really haven't one, you know. I just said that to open the conversation. I didn't know how to open a business talk, and so I tried to think how my husband would probably begin, and that's about the way I thought he would. You won't tell *any one* I came to you, will you? I got desperate after Martin left me to-day, so I came to you myself."

"Of course I'll do all I can, but don't feel too hopeful," I answered. "Expect me at your house rather late. I shall be kept very late at the office to-night."

But I did not keep my promise of going to

the Popes that night, because, just as I was preparing to seek them with the distressing news that I had nothing and could get nothing for them, my office door burst open and Peachy hurried in, crying like a hurt child.

"Here it is," she sobbed, trembling, and drawing forth from under her wide cloak a tiny basket. In its depths I recognized the infinitesimal hope of the Pope family, sound asleep as usual. And then I saw a strange sight. I had in my varied experience seen maternal emotion lavished on a fair - sized child, but in this case I was to see what was more like going through with the motions than anything else. The baby was far too small to receive Peachy's wild caresses, and the basket got the most of them.

"Oh," sobbed Mrs. Pope, "she's been *exhibited* every night for weeks and weeks — ever since we've been in this city! My baby, my little, little baby. Oh, that wicked woman! If you hadn't suggested it I'd never have thought of it. You saved my baby." And down she went on her knees and kissed my hand.

"My dear Mrs. Pope," I said, "do get up and tell me what has happened." But Peachy was sitting on the floor by the basket examining that sleeping little Quarter Loaf all over to its very finger-nails, and would not answer until she had assured herself that in every particular it was exactly as it should be—except for size.

" It's all right," she sighed, at last. " I've let the woman go, but I hope you won't think it weak of me. She was dreadfully frightened, and she was only that wretched man's tool. He confessed that himself. He was dreadfully frightened too. I'm afraid I made a terrible scene."

By slow degrees I came to understand what had happened. My words of the morning had roused Peachy's fears, and on that night, after the baby and night nurse were seemingly locked in together, she had gone to the nursery door and demanded entrance, obtained it with difficulty, and the baby was gone from the cradle. I could imagine that Mrs. Pope might be quite formidable, when roused, in the way that a brooding bird is formidable if its young are attacked. Apparently she had flown at the nurse with such fury that the woman confessed all on the spot. She had been hiring the baby to a showman for an hour or so each night, smuggling it out of the house to one of his myrmidons and back again unnoticed.

" I made her get in a carriage with me," said Mrs. Pope, " and drive right to the show, and I rushed in and grabbed up my baby and ran in here with it. It's right around the corner from here, a miserable poor little show ! Oh, my little abused baby !" And she fell to kissing the basket again.

Now I have not lived as a legal adviser in my native town some forty odd years and read three newspapers daily for nothing, so what Mrs. Pope said opened a window in my mind and let in light upon some old newspaper information stored there.

" Round the corner, did you say, Mrs. Pope ?" I asked. "Was the show called the ' Eureka,' and did it have life-size portraits of all kinds of freaks outside the door ?"

Peachy shuddered her assent, drawing her baby closer, but I had no time to mince words just then.

"My dear lady," I said, "the man that owns that show owns dozens like it in as many towns. That's his horrid business and it yields him enormous profits, on which he lives in this city. His offence against you is a serious one, and it's not his first offence of the kind either. It would go hard with him if he were hauled up. Did you promise his showman anything ?"

" I ? Good gracious, no. They were promising me everything, and I just ran away from them all as I told you."

" Where's Martin ?"

" Out trying to collect that wretched four thousand ; he'll never get it."

" No," I said, " he won't, but he may have it

gotten for him." I disengaged Mrs. Pope from the baby and led her to my desk. "Now sign this," I said, and a moment later I had her name tremulously written beneath these words: "Mr. Griffin is fully empowered to act for me in this matter."

Now what I did with this slip of paper I shall never tell. It's not a transaction that I am proud of, and as a struggling lawyer it is not an episode that I care to publish. It was a fair case both of love and war—love for Martin and war for the showman. Suffice it to say that I drove away furiously in Mrs. Pope's carriage, bidding her wait for me in my office; and when I at last came back to her I had in my hand another bit of paper, oblong in shape, which I did not show to Mrs. Pope. I locked it away carefully in my desk, and for it substituted a check torn from my own checkbook, and made out for the sum of four thousand dollars. With this I turned to Martin's wife.

"I have been more successful in raising that sum we were talking of to-day than I thought I could be," I said, "and here it is, Mrs. Pope; you can tell Martin that those who sent it to him didn't want their names to appear. They feel themselves under obligations to him, and are glad of the chance to settle them. He can pay the money back when he is thirty years old if he then wants to, but there's no need whatever to do so." I held out the check, which Mrs. Pope took from me in an absent-minded way. She was hanging over the baby with an eager interest on her face.

"Have you an inch measure here?" she ask-ed, with such suppressed excitement in her tone that I knew something important was about to happen.

I produced the measure, and with evidently practised fingers Peachy lifted that mite of a baby and laid it flat on my desk, face down. Then she measured its back from end to end. I bent over the measure as eagerly as she.

"Has it taken that start?" I asked; and as she saw the figure reached by the back of the baby's little heel, Peachy dropped the measure and looked up at me, with her big eyes swim-ming in tears.

"Oh, Mr. Griffin!" she cried.

What had come to pass may be gathered from a little scene that took place one day not many years later, when my wife and I met Peachy and her first-born walking together on the street.

"Lydia, my dear," I said, "look; yon's the Quarter Loaf"; and Lydia walked straight up to the pair and held out her hand to the daugh-ter with her most radiant smile.

"Why, my dear," she said, *looking up*, and Lydia is not short, "allow me to congratulate you. Mrs. Pope, the next time I see your daughter I only hope she won't have grown as much again as she has since the first time I saw her." And this wish was a kindly one, so meant and so accepted.

THE END